TRIAL *by* FIRE

TRIAL *by* FIRE

D. W. Buffa

G. P. PUTNAM'S SONS
NEW YORK

G. P. PUTNAM'S SONS
Publishers Since 1838
Published by the Penguin Group
Penguin Group (USA) Inc., 375 Hudson Street, New York, New York 10014, USA • Penguin
Group (Canada), 10 Alcorn Avenue, Toronto, Ontario M4V 3B2, Canada (a division of
Pearson Penguin Canada Inc.) • Penguin Books Ltd, 80 Strand, London WC2R 0RL, England
• Penguin Ireland, 25 St Stephen's Green, Dublin 2, Ireland (a division of Penguin Books Ltd)
• Penguin Group (Australia), 250 Camberwell Road, Camberwell, Victoria 3124, Australia (a
division of Pearson Australia Group Pty Ltd) • Penguin Books India Pvt Ltd, 11 Community
Centre, Panchsheel Park, New Delhi–110 017, India • Penguin Group (NZ), Cnr Airborne
and Rosedale Roads, Albany, Auckland 1310, New Zealand (a division of Pearson
New Zealand Ltd) • Penguin Books (South Africa) (Pty) Ltd, 24 Sturdee
Avenue, Rosebank, Johannesburg 2196, South Africa
Penguin Books Ltd, Registered Offices:
80 Strand, London WC2R 0RL, England

Library of Congress Cataloging-in-Publication Data

Buffa, Dudley W., date.
Trial by fire / D. W. Buffa.
p.   cm.
ISBN 0-399-15281-4
1. Antonelli, Joseph (Fictitious character)—Fiction.   2. San Francisco (Calif.)—Fiction.
3. Attorney and client—Fiction.   4. Trials (Murder)—Fiction.   5. Law teachers—Fiction.
I. Title.
PS3552.U3739T75   2005   2004060015
813'.54—dc22

Printed in the United States of America
1   3   5   7   9   10   8   6   4   2

This book is printed on acid-free paper. ∞

Book design by Stephanie Huntwork

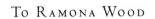

TO RAMONA WOOD

"... but Antonelli I was myself."
NIETZSCHE

Chapter One

ALBERT CRAVEN, the last of the original partners who, nearly a half century earlier, had founded the firm, walked into my office to announce that I had once again been the source of endless trouble and another sleepless night. I put down the morning paper and gave him a dubious glance.

"I sometimes envy you, dealing with murderers and thieves and decent people like that," said Craven as he sank into the overstuffed chair the other side of my desk. Though a few unknown years the other side of seventy, there was not a visible line anywhere on his round pinkish face.

"Yes, that's exactly right. I had not thought of it before, but that really is the essential difference in what we do." A smile spread like mischief across his bow-shaped mouth. "You deal with people accused of doing something wrong; I deal with people who spend all their time accusing someone else. Seldom anything very specific, you understand; always a more generalized complaint. And of course I'm supposed to make it right. After all, I'm their lawyer, and—as they never fail to remind me—they've employed the firm for a great many years."

Craven rocked back and forth, trying hard not to laugh at the predictable stupidities of the world.

"There is no more pitiable sight than a rich man—or a rich woman, by the way," he added with a quick, decisive nod, "who doesn't get his or her own way. Which brings me to the reason I had to see you: Harry Godwin isn't happy, he isn't happy at all."

"Who is Harry Godwin?" I asked.

Craven threw up his hands. "My God, Antonelli—you don't know anything, do you?"

He gave me an incredulous look. "Who is Harry Godwin? The biggest client we have."

"The biggest client you have."

"The biggest client the firm has," replied Craven with a wave of his hand. He settled back into a more comfortable position. "And you're part of the firm, after all."

That was the issue, never resolved, and never really discussed. He had invited me to stay after I had finished the case that had first brought me to San Francisco. Instead of the small room I had occupied as a temporary visitor, he had given me an office that for sheer opulence rivaled his own, and his own had to have been one of the largest and most expensively decorated in the city. I took the criminal cases I wanted and kept the money I made. When I first raised the question concerning my share of the expenses, he dismissed it with the remark: "I own the building."

I reminded him that he did not own my secretary or any of the other people in the office who were now doing most of the work I used to do myself. "That doesn't matter; doesn't matter in the least," he had replied with what I can only describe as cheerful impatience. He tried to explain away his generosity by reminding me that the firm had more money than it knew what to do with. What he had not told me was that a lot of the money came from Harry Godwin.

"Our client, Harry Godwin, happens to own the television network that wanted you as a guest on one of its shows, an invitation that for some reason you decided to turn down. Harry wants to know why. He called me from Sydney this morning—two-thirty this morning, to be precise. Harry forgets the time difference, that Australia is a day ahead. And because Harry never sleeps himself, he thinks no one else should either. Anyway, he called. He's not happy. He wants you on the show."

Now I remembered who Harry Godwin was. He did not just own one of the fastest-growing independent cable networks; he owned radio stations, newspapers, magazines, publishing houses, and he owned them everywhere. He was not yet in the movie business: an attempt to take over one of the major studios in Hollywood had recently failed, but there were rumors that negotiations to buy another had already begun. There were always rumors swirling around Harry Godwin.

I looked at Albert Craven as if he must be out of his mind. "I don't want to be on television."

Laughing to himself, Craven shook his head. "Everyone wants to be on television."

I gave him a jaundiced look. "That's what the network said when they asked me. I said I didn't want to, and their argument was that everyone else wanted to. Strange argument, when the only answer that matters is what other people think."

Craven got up and went to the window. He looked down the narrow city street to the bay, rolling steel gray in the gloomy drizzle of a winter afternoon.

"This dreadful weather can't last. Gray skies get me a little depressed."

He turned around and with his back to the window, twisted his head to the side. With a puckish grin, he gave me a searching look.

"Would begging work?"

Under his hopeful gaze, I began to relent. "I didn't know it was Harry Godwin's station." Craven kept looking at me, waiting for me to say yes. "Their idea of a discussion of the death penalty is to have live coverage of an execution," I protested. Craven kept looking at me in that same helpless way.

"You're not really asking me to . . . ? Why would Harry Godwin even know that I'd been asked to be on one of the network's shows?" I began to shift uneasily in my chair. "This isn't some prime-time broadcast. And even if he knew," I went on, growing obstinate as I felt myself being backed into a corner, "why in the world would he call you from Sydney to complain about it because I refused? He must have better things to do than that."

A shuttered expression, a private, often-pondered thought, moved slowly across Craven's smooth pink lips. He came away from the window and again sat down in the chair. He was in many respects one of the most extraordinary men I had known. After a lifetime of loneliness, occasionally interrupted by brief and mistaken marriages, he had acquired the habit of taking a greater interest in the lives of other people than he did in his own. In the relative solitude of his own existence, he would think about the people he knew, examine them from every angle, every different perspective, until he discovered the special characteristic, the single eccentricity that set them apart.

There was something incorrigible about his fervent insistence on the infinite possibilities of human behavior. Someone might be dull and incoherent, unable to string together a sentence, much less carry on a conversation; he might be among the most relentlessly stupid people you had ever met; but Albert Craven could make you think that this same person was in fact one of the most interesting people alive. When one of his close and socially prominent friends was arrested on a dozen different violations of the securities laws, Craven, instead of joining everyone in the hypocrisy of moral indignation, expressed a certain admiration for the intelligence behind the intricate malevolence of the scheme. With irresistible exuberance, he now insisted that Harry Godwin was one of the most intriguing characters he had ever known.

"Harry Godwin is a self-made man. It's the Horatio Alger story, except there isn't any happy ending. You know: become rich, marry a beautiful girl, settle down and live to what presumably will become a ripe old age."

Craven's laughing eyes darted toward the gray marble fireplace that, as far as I knew, had never been used, and then back across the thick carpeted room. They lingered for a brief moment at the window and the dreary scene outside, and then, abruptly, came back to me.

"I always wondered about that word—'ripe.'" His soft hands settled on the paunch that even the tailored suits he wore could never quite hide. "Always made me think of a pear beginning to rot."

His hands gripped the arms of the chair as he leaned forward. The expression on his face became wistful and more serious.

"That never happens with self-made men: certainly not with men like Harry Godwin, someone who starts with nothing—literally nothing in his case. Harry Godwin was an orphan, abandoned by his mother at birth, raised in an East End orphanage in London—one of those places out of Dickens where they treated the children as the devil's own, their only chance for redemption to have every evil impulse beaten out of them the first time it showed. Beatings, bad food and little of it, cold water once a week to bathe—that was Harry Godwin's life for the first six years. That's when he left: six years old and he just walked away. Lived in the streets, an urchin. Oliver Twist. God knows how he stayed alive; God knows how any of them did.

"He did not become a thief—or if he did, he wasn't one for very long. He became a newsboy, working for pennies a day, starting each morning hours before dawn. He told me once he never slept in a bed until he had left England for good. He slept in alleyways and doorways, wherever there was a bit of warmth and he thought it might be safe. After a time that must have seemed like aeons to someone that age, but was not really more than a few months, he got himself a job as a kind of printer's helper. They probably liked him, a young boy with that kind of pluck, the ink-covered workmen in the printer's plant; treated him like the stray he was, gave him things to do, taught him the way things worked. It would not have taken very long to figure out that Harry Godwin was no ordinary boy. He told me once that as soon as he saw the printing presses, all that rapid moving machinery, all that clacking noise, he knew he had to learn how all of it worked, what each part of it did. That was his job, and that's where he lived: right there in the plant—slept on a wooden pallet with sheets of newsprint as a blanket."

Albert Craven's small guileless eyes stared at a point in the middle distance, his head thrown back at an angle of intense contemplation. It was the look of someone who has lived long enough to have gained some understanding of the allotted cruelties of fate.

"I was raised in the comfortable surroundings of a respectable and rather wealthy home," said Craven. "I never wanted for anything. I sometimes wonder what would have happened to me if I had: if I had gone hungry, never had a bed of my own, had to worry every night whether I would still be alive in the morning—if I had had a childhood like the one Harry Godwin had. I wonder what I would be like now." He gave me a sudden, inquiring glance. "Do you ever wonder what would have happened to you?—I mean, if things in the beginning had been different, much different, than they were."

Craven waved off his own question. He did not need an answer. It was the kind of question that when you reach a certain age, answers itself; or rather reminds you that most of the questions that go to the heart of who we are do not have answers at all.

"Harry might still be in London, an aging printer working for someone else. Who knows what would have happened? But the war came and the British began to move all the children out of London—out of harm's way—when the Germans began their endless nighttime raids, bombing everything they could. Harry of course had no family, and he was not about to go to some rural institution where he might be stuck with other orphans his age. He was twelve years old, but he was used to working with men and living on his own. Somehow he talked himself onto a ship on which a number of British families were sending their children to Australia to live with relatives for the duration of the war. Harry did not have any relatives in Australia or anywhere else; but he managed to make someone believe he did. Whatever he told them, it worked: He left England, sailed to Australia and did not go back until he had the beginnings of what would become his media empire and was ready to make his first European acquisition. He bought the paper that had given him his first job. And do you know what he did? He fired everyone in management, and then he broke the union."

With a long, searching look he let me know that while he could not withhold a certain reluctant respect for what Harry Godwin had achieved, it was overshadowed—tainted—by the methods Godwin had employed.

"There has never been an ounce of sentimentality in anything Harry Godwin ever did."

Pausing, Craven stole a glimpse at his smooth pink fingers as he spread them apart, getting them ready, as it were, should he decide to list the ways Harry Godwin had violated the unwritten rules of conduct by which decent, cared-for people were expected to behave.

"He fired everyone because he wanted everyone who worked there to owe their jobs—their livelihood—to him. But there was another reason, a more important one: It was the only way he knew to make sure each one of them did their jobs exactly the way he wanted it to be done. Not the way they had done it before; not the way they had been trained to do it for generations; but his way."

With a brief motion of his small, round head, Craven bent forward, wagging his index finger back and forth. His voice sank to a bare whisper, as if what he was about to share was a secret meant to be kept between us.

"It's what I told you before. He always had to know everything, every detail—nothing was too small. There isn't any ending for Harry Godwin; there isn't some far-off, distant but still reachable goal. There never is for people of his sort. For him—for people like him—it isn't what you have that counts: It's always the getting more.

"You might as well ask what a shark is trying to achieve: Why this endless search for something to kill; why this constant lust for blood. That is what makes Harry Godwin so damnably interesting: There isn't anything he wants—he just wants more. He must be the fourth or fifth richest man in the world. Do you think anything would change if he became the richest? As long as there is a single newspaper, magazine, television station or even one radio broadcast he doesn't control, he thinks he's in a war; a war that, if he isn't careful, if he doesn't keep his eye on even the smallest detail, he might lose."

Craven put his hands on his knees and stared down at the carpet, thinking about what he was going to say next. He raised his eyes, a kind, thoughtful smile on his lips. Then he got to his feet and stood next to the chair.

"Whatever you think of him, Harry Godwin is a remarkable man. See if you don't think so after you've met him. But in the meantime, do an old man a favor: Do the television show. Whatever they want to talk about, you'll certainly be an improvement over what is usually said on those things." He was halfway to the door when he added: "And if they want to talk about the death penalty, tell them the truth—what you told me once: that you oppose the death penalty, but only because you prefer torture instead." Craven's slight shoulders shook with laughter. "What was it you said? 'Why should the punishment for the worst imaginable crimes be nothing more than a painless sleep.' Say something like that, Harry Godwin will want to give you your own show."

Chapter Two

I GAVE MY NAME to the receptionist and told her I was there for the Bryan Allen show. She picked up the telephone and with soft indifference announced my arrival. I took a chair, thumbed through one of those magazines in which words—short, simple and ungrammatical, explain the pictures, and then tossed it back on the table. I was in what could generously be called a murderous mood.

I had been thinking about it since the day Albert Craven asked me to appear on the show Harry Godwin thought so important: how I would respond, the answers I could give to all the questions that might be asked, hearing in my head the endless dialogue, the constant back-and-forth; the answer, the question, the answer after that. It was as bad as getting ready for trial, anticipating—or trying to anticipate, because you never really could—all the things that might happen, all the things that might get said. It was worse than preparing for trial. I knew what I was doing in a courtroom: I had been doing it for more than half my life, trying cases in which someone was accused of a crime. No matter how much I might worry about it in advance, once I sat down at the counsel table, once those twelve citizens were called into the jury box, once the trial started, I was in charge. I asked the questions; I decided how they should be asked. I could keep a witness on the stand for hours—days, if I needed to—taking him one question at a time, first in one direction, then another, using the answers to paint the picture I wanted the jury to see. But television? A show on which someone would ask questions of me? Everything was turned around: I was going to be the witness, a witness put on the stand not only without preparation, but without any idea what he was going to be asked. All I knew was that we were going to discuss something about the state of the criminal law, and that I would not be the only guest. I had not even had the wit to ask who the others might be.

"Julian Sinclair. I'm here for the Bryan Allen show. Unless you'd rather have dinner."

I looked up. A young man I guessed to be in his early thirties was leaning nonchalantly against the wall next to the sliding glass window, his hands shoved into his pants pockets, one foot crossed over the other. He was staring at the young receptionist, and she was staring back. Smiling to myself, I turned away and watched out the window at the rain-splattered sidewalk, remembering with a certain vague nostalgia that youthful feeling, that sense of confidence and excitement, when just by chance you suddenly found yourself face-to-face with a pretty girl and heard yourself say something that later made you wonder how you had ever found the courage.

"You're Joseph Antonelli. I'm Julian Sinclair. I've always wanted to meet you."

Seen straight on, he was even better looking than when I had caught that first fleeting glimpse of him from the side. He was my height, or perhaps a half inch shorter: the tousled head of hair, a light brown color that in a certain light seemed almost blond, made it hard to tell. His eyes were strikingly intelligent, but more than that, candid and full of life. It would have been impossible to imagine him telling you a lie unless he first looked away, shielding them, the way you cover the ears of a child from something he should not hear.

We shook hands and he told me that he taught criminal law at Berkeley. "The only reason I agreed to do this," he remarked, gesturing toward the framed photographs of the various network celebrities that covered the lobby walls, "was because they told me you were going to be on."

"The only reason I said I'd do it is because I got trapped."

The door next to the receptionist opened and we were summoned inside.

"The others are already here," said the show's producer as he led us down a long corridor. He moved with an awkward gait, his shoulders pushing back and forth in a strange synchronous balance with the sliding flat-footed motion of his slightly bow-shaped legs.

"They're ready for you in makeup. Won't take more than a few minutes. Then we'll be on the set. Bryan's certain it's going to be a great show." He added this last remark in a tone of reassurance, meant to dispel our fears that we might not measure up, that we might make fools of ourselves on national television in front of a few million strangers.

The woman doing makeup dashed a bit of powder on Julian Sinclair's nose, teasing him with how little she had to do. She became rather more serious as she set to work on me.

"Do you get nervous before one of these things?" Sinclair asked me as we stood just inside the studio door, watching the others on the set.

"Nervous? Not exactly. Cautious."

He gave me a quick, sidelong glance. There was a question in his eyes, or rather the beginning of an interest, the start of a discussion that might go in a dozen different directions. That was when I began to understand how quick he was, that in that single instant he had seen all the nuanced complexity that might be involved. He dropped the thought, set it aside, held it in abeyance until there might be time to take it up as part of a longer conversation. His eyes shot forward to the circular table where a technician was adjusting the small microphones in the lapels of the other two guests.

"Looks different when you watch it on television, doesn't it? You wouldn't know it wasn't anything more than a raised platform surrounded by cameras and cables, in the middle of a room the size of a warehouse or an airplane hangar, everything completely dark except for that single circle of light in the middle. It's like falling down a mineshaft and finding, way at the end of a cave in the back, a handful of miners playing poker under a half dozen well-lit lamps."

Sinclair's eyes were shining with some fugitive thought. His head spun around; his eyebrows shot straight up.

"What do you think would happen if you brought those people in here, had them sit there at that table for an hour, each of them eager to say something millions of people will remember, and then, at the end, when one of them asks for a tape of the show, tell them: 'No, we weren't on television: We just wanted to talk.'"

The producer was coming toward us in that gaggle-style walk.

"Not much chance of that happening this evening, though," remarked Sinclair with a rakish grin. "Do you know those two?" he asked as we started toward the set.

"I know one of them," I replied, shaking my head. How stupid I had been not to ask who else was going to be on. Not even Albert Craven could have talked me into coming on a show with the abrasive and vindictive Paula Constable.

I sat at the table directly opposite Julian Sinclair. A thin brunette with doe-like eyes and a rather wide mouth sat on my left. Staring straight ahead, she pulled her shoulders back and lifted her chin. With a look of intense concentration, she began a series of breathing exercises, like an athlete getting ready for the next event. At the end of the table, the host, the famous and controversial Bryan Allen, shuffled through a small stack of note cards with an air of indifference, as if it was more a part of a remembered ritual than anything he needed for his own preparation.

The technician finished attaching the tiny microphone to my suit coat lapel. I made sure my tie was in place and that the jacket had not bunched up at the back of my neck. Paula Constable waited for me with a glittering smile of perfect insincerity. She was always dressed in red, with lavish red lipstick and hard black eyelashes to match her shiny black hair. The two colors, red and black, heightened the sharp definition of a face in which the skin was stretched taut from prominent cheekbones to a small pointed chin.

Her eyes, black and impenetrable, stayed on me for only an instant. The smile turned cold, distant. She ran her painted index finger down what appeared to be a typed list of things she wanted to say, the phrases that could make her sound as quick and decisive as she wanted everyone to think she was. I remembered what a lawyer who had faced her in court had once told me: You never had to worry that she might stab you in the back—she took too much pleasure in seeing the look on your face when you realized you were about to die.

Julian must have noticed the changed expression on my face. Slouching back, one arm thrown casually over the chair, he had a broad grin on his mouth. I had the strange sensation that with the power of a clairvoyant he must have heard the same fugitive remark that had just slipped uninvited through my mind.

"Ten seconds," said the producer from somewhere in the surrounding darkness. A red light moved slowly behind Julian. One of the cameras was getting into position for the opening close-up of Bryan Allen. Sliding the short stack of index cards off the table, Allen put them in his pocket. He leaned forward, his elbows on the arms of the chair. He licked his lips, then pressed them together, took a deep breath and held it.

"Three seconds, two . . ."

"Good evening, and welcome to 'The Bryan Allen Show.' I'm Bryan Allen."

It was the first time I had heard his voice. He had not said a word to any of us.

"The country has been riveted by the story of the murder of Angela Morgan. Angela Morgan—the young woman, married less than a year—murdered, according to the police, who after a three-month investigation arrested him this week, by her husband, Steve. Angela Morgan, her body cut up into pieces—found in a storage locker; put there—again according to the police—by her husband, Steve Morgan. Here with me tonight, to discuss the latest developments in this case that has the whole country waiting, are four people who know as much about this case as anyone and a good deal more than most. Let's begin with Daphne McMillan. Daphne is an assistant district attorney here in San Francisco, where the murder was committed.

"Daphne, you've followed this case since the beginning. You've been a frequent guest on the show. You couldn't have been surprised when they arrested Angela's husband this week. You've been saying all along that you thought they would."

She did not look at Allen. She found the red light, the light that let you know which camera was on.

"It was the way he acted, the things he did," she explained in a voice that made her seem even younger than she was. There was no range, no expression; it was flat, thin, drawn in on itself, the voice of a girl too good-looking to have had to worry much about making what she said sound interesting.

"Three weeks after Angela disappeared, he sold the car she drove. That isn't the kind of thing a husband does who is worried about his missing wife. He knew she wasn't coming back. He knew it because he killed her."

Knowing that the camera would often come to him while one of his guests was still speaking, Allen followed each word with a solemn gaze, nodding in agreement with Daphne McMillan's shrewd observation. He was about to follow up with another question, when, suddenly, Julian Sinclair laughed. Allen, who could change his expression in an instant, looked at him in astonishment.

"Are you going to try to say that Steve Morgan didn't do it, didn't kill his wife in cold blood?" Allen's eyes went immediately to the camera. "Julian Sinclair is a distinguished law professor at the University of California. So we have a prosecuting attorney—someone who is out there, in the trenches, with real experience of what criminals are really like—who thinks Steve Morgan did it. Apparently, Professor Sinclair—you don't practice law, do you, professor?—doesn't. Tell us, if you would, Julian, what did Daphne say that you found so funny you had to laugh? Some people—Angela Morgan's parents, for example—may not think murder is something that ought to be laughed at."

Julian bolted forward, planted both elbows on the table and rested his chin atop his folded hands. "It was the kindest thing I could think to do."

In a gesture Allen had used countless times before, a gesture that combined confusion with contempt, he furrowed his brow, shrugged his shoulders and turned up the palms of his hands.

"The kindest thing you could think to do?"

"Yes. Faced with an argument of overwhelming stupidity—it was the kindest thing I could think to do. How does Daphne McMillan—how does anyone—know how someone—some particular individual, not some statistical average—worries or grieves. He sold her car; he bought a truck. Must be guilty. Might as well hang him now. No point bothering with a trial."

"So you don't think he did it? But if he didn't do it, who did? And how do you explain the fact that he's married less than a year and he was already having an affair? Isn't that right?" asked Allen, turning to Paula Constable. "He was having an affair with your client Tracy Weathers, wasn't he?"

Allen looked over my head at the camera looming in the darkness behind me.

"Paula Constable is the famous trial attorney—brought in some of the largest verdicts ever on behalf of women deprived of their civil rights. She's representing Tracy Weathers, who will be called as a witness for the prosecution."

Constable looked at the same camera. "That's right, Bryan. Tracy has been declared a material witness. Unfortunately, she did have an affair, though a brief one, with Steve Morgan. She didn't know he was married."

There was an ominous pause. Constable's eyes drew close together and her chin jutted out. It was the expression of an attitude, the long-coming defiance of someone too often used and abandoned, lied to and then let go as if she had never existed.

"He told her that he had been married, but that his wife had died. She felt sorry for him. He took advantage of that."

Julian Sinclair laughed again. "What exactly is she going to testify to? She can't testify to that—that he lied to her, that he told her he was single when he was not. It isn't relevant; it has nothing to do with the case. It has no evidentiary value whatsoever. Not only that, it's hearsay, something he supposedly said to her. You can't try a case like that; you can't convict someone of a crime against one person because he lied to someone else—if he did tell the lie in question," he added with a quick, doubting smile at Paula Constable. "You can't convict some-one just because you don't think he should have sold the car his wife drove three weeks after she went missing. This isn't evidence—it isn't even suspicion—it's gossip, and that's all it is."

His voice did not quite stop. It seemed to idle like an engine, as he caught up with himself, decided which of several possible directions he wanted to go, and then sped off. Julian Sinclair had lost all aware-ness of himself. We were watching him, each of us nervously waiting for the next time it was our turn to be on camera, watched by an au-dience of millions, worried whether we might make some stupid mis-take, and he was completely in the moment, oblivious of everything but the argument he was determined to make. His eyes were intense, alive, struck by the humor, or the seriousness, of what he said. Every-thing about him was passionate and instantaneous, no time for reflec-tion, for the second thought that allows and invites irony or doubt.

"It seems to me that a lawyer has an obligation to explain the law: to explain what happens when someone is accused of something as se-rious as this; to explain that the presumption of innocence is not something that you can just ignore; that you have to wait for the trial to decide whether someone is guilty of what they have been accused of doing; that to do otherwise—to start telling everyone that some-one must be guilty because . . . because what? . . . because everyone else says he is?—is no different than taking a rope in your hand and leading a lynch mob."

"I resent that!" exclaimed Paula Constable. "If you knew what I knew. . . . If you knew what my client knows. . . . If you knew what Steve Morgan told Tracy . . . !"

"Joseph Antonelli, what do you think of all this?" Allen stared past Julian Sinclair into the eye of the camera. "After a series of high-profile cases, Joseph Antonelli is perhaps the best-known criminal defense at-torney in America."

Allen had made his reputation, and acquired his enormous following, by saying what most of those who watched him wished they could say themselves. If lawyers generally were distrusted, defense lawyers were despised.

"They say you never lost a case you should have won, Joe," he began. I bridled at the way he assumed an informality that suggested we were friends. "But you'd have to agree that if you had this case, you should lose. What the professor says is all well and good for a law school class, but you've been around courtrooms a long time. You know when someone is guilty. Most of the people you've gotten off were guilty, weren't they? If you were representing Angela Morgan's husband, wouldn't you be more concerned with making some kind of deal to keep him off death row?"

In his early fifties, with reddish brown hair that had turned gray around his ears, Allen had sharp blue eyes that looked right through you as he concentrated on what he was going to do next. There was an artificial, puppet-like quality to his interrogation. He did not want to know what you thought: he wanted to goad you into a response that would show everyone just how far removed from the normal, decent opinions of ordinary people you really were. I started to answer the question—one of the questions—he had asked, but he waved me off.

"Now, let me ask you something I've always wanted to know, something most of my viewers want to know: Why does someone like you—smart, well educated, able, I'd imagine, to do pretty much anything you want—why does someone like you become a criminal lawyer? What's in it for you? Why get these guilty guys off—the money?"

It was automatic, reflexive, the immediate response I had given for years, the answer that was no answer at all, unless you took the time to think it through.

"When a jury brings back a verdict of not guilty, that is what it means: not guilty. And that means, Mr. Allen, that all the people that I have, in your phrase, 'gotten off' were not guilty."

Allen shrugged his shoulders and turned up his hands. "Please! You're trying to tell me that all these people you've gotten off were innocent? Like Steve Morgan is innocent?"

"You miss the point," Julian Sinclair said, flashing a quick, eager smile. "That isn't what a trial is about."

"It isn't to decide whether someone is innocent?" asked Paula Constable, as she turned a taunting eye on him.

Julian measured her for a moment, trying, as it seemed, to decide whether she really meant what she said or, as was rather more likely, had only said it for effect.

"You've tried criminal cases?"

Bristling at the implication that there might be something she did not know, she replied, "I've tried every kind of case. Have you tried any?"

The smile on Julian's face broadened. "I'll rely on your experience. What is the choice given a jury on the verdict form in a criminal case?"

It caught her off guard. Whether under the pressure of the moment her mind went blank and she could not remember, or whether she did not want to be put in the position of answering his questions, she grew angry and threw the question back at him.

"What difference does it make what the verdict form says?"

"The verdict form has two boxes: 'guilty' and 'not guilty,'" Daphne interjected quickly. "But juries make mistakes, especially when the defense attorney distorts the plain meaning of the evidence."

"And the prosecuting attorney isn't good enough to show the jury what those distortions are," Julian replied instantly.

He looked diagonally across the table. There was a subtle change in his expression. Paula Constable was a middle-aged woman, aggressive to the point of belligerence, the kind of advocate who when you won would still claim that you had lost. Daphne McMillan might be every bit as determined, every bit as assertive, but she was in her twenties and as lovely as any young woman you were likely to see. Julian Sinclair was smiling at her with his eyes.

"But leaving that aside," he went on, "the jury has to find the defendant either guilty or not guilty—correct?" She forgot the camera. Her eyes stayed on his. "And that's the point, isn't it: guilty or not guilty? Not whether someone is innocent, but whether they're not guilty. There is a reason for that, isn't there?" he asked in a way that seemed to suggest that however things might appear on the surface, they agreed on the things that were most important.

A hint of a smile started onto her mouth. She caught herself, remembered where she was and how she wanted to be seen; but she tried too hard and overshot the mark. When she spoke, her voice was harsh, brittle, confused and a little hot.

"Not guilty, innocent—either way it means the jury decided the defendant did not do it, even, sometimes, when he did."

Julian looked at her the way someone does when they know you are only saying it because you're afraid of what other people might think if you told the truth, what you really meant, what you would say if it was just the two of you and no one else was around.

"What are you trying to say, professor? You think it makes a difference what the verdict form says?" asked Allen with a low, derisive chuckle.

"All the difference in the world," I insisted. Allen turned to me, waiting. "The jury isn't asked—don't you know this?—to decide what really happened. The jury is asked to decide only one question: Has the prosecution proven beyond that famous reasonable doubt that the defendant did it? You see the difference?" I asked, leaning toward him. "It isn't: Do you think the defendant did it? It's: Did the prosecution prove he did? Mr. Sinclair's point went right to the heart of it. Do you know what really happens in a criminal trial, Mr. Allen? Do you have any idea? The state is put on trial. Twelve citizens are asked to decide whether the state, with all its power, has done more than just accuse someone of a crime. Anyone can do that, make that kind of accusation, whether they have the evidence to prove that accusation or not."

It was throwing pebbles at an onrushing train: He just kept coming, relentless, unstoppable, his eyes as blank, as impenetrable, as the lens on the television camera.

"That's a lawyer's answer, isn't it? The kind of thing you say to confuse things, to get people all mixed up. You and I both know that a trial is about the defendant—whether he did it. The question is whether Angela Morgan was murdered by her husband. So why don't you tell us what you think—either one of you—instead of hiding behind all this legal doubletalk. Do you think he did it or not?"

"Decide right now?" asked Julian with a smile that in its seeming innocence mocked Allen's heavy-handed style. "Decide as if we're the jury, and we have to render the verdict: guilty or not guilty?"

"Exactly, professor; exactly."

"That's easy: not guilty."

"Easy? What do you think, Daphne—easy to decide Steve Morgan is innocent, that he didn't murder his wife?"

She made an effort not to look at Julian. "Easier, I would think, to conclude that he did," and she began methodically to list the reasons why he had.

"And don't forget," added Paula Constable, the moment Daphne paused, "the things he said to my client, the promises he made, the—"

"Isn't there some limit to how far you want to go to convict someone before the trial has even started? They used to lynch people in this country. Some of them were guilty. Did that make it right? What about when he was innocent, when someone else did it, when someone else got away with it because the lynch mob couldn't wait for the trial. What are you going to do when it happens here? When one of these people you're so certain must be guilty, is really innocent—but they get convicted anyway because after all the talk, after all this postured certainty, you can't find a jury that has not already been told what the verdict has to be?" I looked at Daphne McMillan, then I looked at Paula Constable, and then I looked again at Bryan Allen. "Would you want to be accused of a murder, a murder you did not commit, and have everyone convinced you must be the killer because everyone on television says you did?"

Chapter Three

THE PRODUCER STOPPED ME in the hallway. "You were terrific," he remarked with a hurried glance over his shoulder. Julian Sinclair was talking in a quiet voice with Daphne McMillan just outside the door to the
studio. "Bryan would like you back next week." He read the skepticism
in my eyes. "You were terrific," he repeated in the belief that any doubt
I might have about doing this again must be the result of a lack
of confidence. "You were even better than we thought you'd be. Most
people end up getting intimidated. They come in, think they've got
something to say, but as soon as they have to say it on camera—soon
as they have to go toe-to-toe with him—they freeze. Not you, though;
you were terrific, just terrific!"

Again he glanced over his shoulder. Still talking, Julian and
Daphne began to move in our direction. Paula Constable, who had
lingered behind to exchange a few private words with Bryan Allen,
pushed open the door.

"Think about it," he said when I did not respond. "We'd love to
have you on a regular basis. And not just us. Harry Godwin called just
a few minutes before the end. He said to tell you it was one of the best
performances he had seen."

The producer shook his head, asked me in a whispered, confidential voice to think it over and give him a call. "Tomorrow, if you could." He greeted the others with a cheerful wave. "Great show, everyone. You were terrific, all of you; just terrific!" he exclaimed as he opened the studio door and vanished into the darkness inside.

"Want to buy me a drink?" asked Paula Constable with a bold smile. Her voice sounded husky, tired. She cleared her throat, put her hand over her mouth and coughed twice. "I need that drink more than I thought," she said, shaking her head in partial embarrassment.

It must have been that momentary breach of her brash demeanor, that sudden flash of vulnerability that made me agree. Too late, I began to look for a way out, a way to avoid having to spend an hour alone with a woman I had to make an effort not to hate.

"Would you like to come along?" I asked. Julian Sinclair and Daphne McMillan looked at me, then looked at each other. There was an awkward silence. Daphne glanced nervously at her watch.

"I'm afraid I can't," she said. "I still have work tonight."

"And I have an eight o'clock class," explained Julian as he took me aside for a private word. "I wonder if we might talk sometime soon?"

"Anytime you like." I scribbled my home number on the back of my card and said he could call me either there or at the office.

Paula Constable knew a bar just blocks away, the other side of Market. A lot of network news people congregated there every night, according to her eager report.

"There's something going on between those two," she said after she had taken a long sip from her martini. She picked the olive out of the glass by the toothpick and began to twist it back and forth in a slow, circular motion, bumping it gently against the rim. She looked older now, older than she had under the artificial studio lights, but her eyes were still sharp, incisive, relentless.

"Did you see the way they made a point of not leaving together? Well, good for them!" She laughed as she lifted the glass and took another long, slow sip of gin and vermouth. She put down the glass, dropped the olive back into it with a tiny splash and seemed to study the reflection of the smile that with a hint of evil glee stalked across her mouth. "What's the point of being married, if you can't have an affair on the side? A girl needs a little excitement, doesn't she?" Her heavy black lashes sprang open and she gave me a garish grin. "Listen, you didn't take anything I said back there personally, did you?"

She was sitting directly across from me, bending toward me, playing with the green olive in her martini the way a high school girl played with the straw in her cherry Coke, except of course that the high school girl was thirty years younger and did not have to worry about the light. There was something sad about the way Paula Constable dressed herself in short tight skirts and pointed high-heel shoes, painted herself in blazing bright colors, and became a kind of neon advertisement of herself.

"I guess I envy her a little—to be that young, that gorgeous, married to one of the richest men in town; to have a career, always be in demand—she must be on three television shows a week now. They all want her. She may sound a little stupid; she may not know anything more about the law than your average first-year law school student, but with that face, that body . . . They did not want her because she's F. Lee Bailey. For that, they have you. So, did you enjoy it?"

Sprawled back against the hard leather booth, I tugged at my tie, loosening it far enough to get the top button open, and took a deep breath.

"Not very much," I replied, reaching for the scotch and soda on the table in front of me.

"You looked like you were having the time of your life," she said over her glass. "But you always look like that. I've watched you in court. You always know what you're doing." Her eyes stayed on me as she raised the glass to her mouth; stayed on me, but still kept moving, boring in, trying to get closer, searching for whatever secrets I might be trying to hide. "At least that's how you always seem: confident, sure of yourself, in control; as if you know everything that's going to happen." She put down the glass. Her long sharp nails, painted to a glossy red finish, closed around the base until they touched. "As if you already knew how it was going to end; and of course, the only way it can end—and the reason you look so confident—is that you're going to win."

Lowering her gaze, she ran the tip of her middle finger along the lipstick traces at the edge of the round V-shaped glass. The lines in her forehead, not so much hidden by makeup as reduced to inconsequence by the dominance of her hard, shining eyes and the constant, flashing movement of her mouth, deepened and spread.

"I never had that, that ability—whatever it is—to make everyone think I know something they don't, to make everyone think I'm the one person in the courtroom—or anywhere else, for that matter—they can trust."

A short, rueful laugh escaped her lips. Her eyes flashed with self-mockery. She bent forward, laid the edge of her chin on the heel of her hand and pressed her lips together into a bitter smile.

"So I do this! Strut around like I don't have a doubt in the world, dress like I'm some bubble gum chewing teenager, try to think of something more outrageous to say than what anyone else has said yet, and all so that people keep talking about me. Hate me, love me—it doesn't matter, just so that my name is out there, out there in TV land, because that's the only way anyone knows anyone anymore. That's how I get clients: because they know I'm on TV. Because I'm on TV, I'm important. I walk into court now, everyone knows me—even the judges."

Moving her hand away from her chin, she rubbed her fingers against her temple. A bittersweet smile crossed her mouth. The brittle belligerence in her eyes vanished as if it had never been more than an actor's mask. Her voice was quiet, subdued, with a strange, eerie sensibility, a kind of commentary on the false self-importance with which it had been employed.

"I went to Harvard, just like you. You didn't know that, did you? Do you know what I wanted to be? A judge, not a trial court judge, an appellate court judge—not the Supreme Court, but maybe the federal court of appeals, a place where you decided interesting questions of the law, constitutional questions, the really important questions. I finished in the top ten percent of my class, but I didn't get to clerk for a federal judge somewhere; I was not asked to join one of those prestigious New York firms where you had the chance to argue cases in front of the Supreme Court, where you could develop a reputation, a serious reputation, as a constitutional lawyer. They weren't hiring many women in those days. Oh, I could have joined a firm, somewhere—worked in the trust section, become remarkably good at doing the same dull thing over and over; probably made a fair amount of money at the end, and become a gray-haired old lady, one of the first women to become senior partner in a firm."

A smile, warm and friendly, all the bitterness left behind, gave her face a cheerful aspect I had never seen before.

"I would have dressed in blues and grays, and no doubt been utterly scandalized at women—at least women who wanted to be taken seriously—who dressed in red." She tossed her head in faint, half-hearted derision. "Maybe that wouldn't have been so bad, after all."

I sipped on the scotch and soda. Paula pushed her martini glass to the side and bent forward over her elbows.

"I fought for everything I got; made demands, showed them they couldn't just ignore me, treat me like some dim-witted female who didn't know her place. I studied harder, learned the law inside and out, spent twice as much time preparing for each case I got than the other side, and made damn certain everyone knew it."

The memory of it delighted her, made her want to tell more. A conspiratorial grin cut across her mouth. She leaned closer.

"I miss that; I miss the fight. No, that's not it: I miss the challenge, the sense I was doing something important, that I could help change things, make it so that women would not be treated any different than men, make it so that if you finished at the top of your class at Harvard, the only thought anyone would have was that you had earned your chance to be considered for a clerkship on the Supreme Court or to be hired by a Wall Street firm."

She looked at me with the hard-earned, world-weary wisdom that comes at the end, when you can see how different things are than what you had thought they would be and you wonder why you had not been able to see it before.

"I won—we won—the war is over. The law schools are filled with women—more of them than men. It's only a matter of time before the same thing happens in the courts and in all the major firms. So here I am, an aging warrior, making a fool of herself on television because I don't want to be left behind. Does anyone remember—no, does anyone care—about the battles I fought? You saw the answer tonight: Daphne McMillan. You think she would have fought those battles, or even understood what they were about? Become a lawyer then? Her? She would have become a legal secretary, slept with her boss, a senior partner twice her age who in a fit of midlife exuberance and stupidity would have divorced his wife of thirty years, married her and then probably died in bed of over-exhaustion! But now, with nothing standing in her way, she becomes a lawyer, dresses like a fashion model, bats her eyelashes at the camera and in that insipid little voice of hers mouths every politically safe thing she can think to say."

Paula sat back. A smile full of nostalgia and regret shadowed her small, tight mouth. "Daphne McMillan isn't exactly the 'new woman' some of us had in mind."

She looked around the room. Certain no one was close enough to overhear, she bent forward and whispered, "But then neither is that street-smart little broad I'm supposed to be representing. I swear to God, people will do anything to get on television!"

She immediately caught the irony of it. "I know, I know—but not like this. This kid barely finished high school, works as a waitress at some diner. She wants to be on television; she wants other people to talk about her. She denies it, but it's true. She says she just wants to be left alone, so she calls me and asks if I can help her do that. You call someone like me—famous, high-priced, a celebrity lawyer you saw on television—not because you face any criminal charges, but because you used to sleep with a guy on trial for murder. A guy who told you he was single but won't give you his phone number or tell you where he lives. Do you sense there may be something wrong here? And then it turns out that not only is he married, but that his wife turns up first missing, then dead. You're surprised—stunned!—that this horde of reporters suddenly wants to talk to you. You decide you better find someone to help you with all this. You don't have any money, but your future prospects may not be all that bleak. They make movies, television movies, about things like this, don't they? And might not your story—how you were taken advantage of by this man that everyone now knows murdered his wife in one of the most grisly murders anyone has ever seen—be a story worth telling?"

I started to laugh. "Did she really? Is that what she said when she came to you?"

"You know I can't talk about anything a client has said. But I can tell you this: She's a tough little cookie, shrewd as they come. That makeover? The new look that everyone thinks was my idea?" Constable clicked her teeth, then pushed her lips into a scornful circle. "Tracy knows what she wants, and she thinks she knows how to get it. I'll never see a dime of it if she does, but that doesn't matter. The publicity is worth millions. I've got people lined up from here to New York, desperate to have me take their case." Her eyes were suddenly full of a secret she could not wait to tell. "One of the national newsmagazines—I can't tell you which one—is doing a story on 'Television Lawyers.' It'll be out week after next." She bit her lip, which instead of suppressing only heightened the pleasure that lit up her eyes. "Guess who's going to be on the cover?"

I must not have reacted the way she hoped; or perhaps she thought she had said too much. The disappointment in her eyes was unmistakable. I had not intended to hurt her. I tried to make it right.

"That's terrific," I said, hoping that it did not sound quite as artificial as it had when that television producer used the same word. "Really, it's just terrific."

"Not bad," she admitted, beaming. She patted my hand, then drew back. "It'll mean more television," she said as she began to calculate the benefits. "Might even lead to my own show. We'll see. Now, there's something I want to ask you: Are you going to take the case?"

I had just picked up my glass, rattled the ice, and started to drink. I paused, gave her a look that told her I had no idea what she was talking about and finished what was left of the scotch and soda.

"The Angela Morgan case. Are you going to represent the husband? Are you going to take over the defense? The lawyer he's got can't handle a case like this: He's a celebrity lawyer—he spends all his time on television."

I threw up my hands. "Who doesn't?"

She gave me a blank look. "Doesn't what?"

"Spend all their time on television."

She reached across the table and clutched my sleeve. "Listen to me," she said in a manner that, more than serious, was almost severe. "I do it because I have to, but I'm a lawyer, a trial lawyer, and a damn good one. You came on tonight—I don't know why you did, but I'm glad you did, because you're the best there is. Morgan knows his lawyer isn't up to it. There's a rumor that he's about to fire him and get someone else. The rumor is that he's going to ask you."

"He hasn't."

"He will, and when he does—take it," she said emphatically. "It's a case you can win." With a cool, appraising glance, she added, "You may be the only one who can."

"You seemed pretty sure he was guilty. What was it you said? 'If you knew what I knew; if you knew what Tracy told me.'"

"That was television," she said, dismissing it out of hand.

"What did Tracy tell you?"

She dismissed this with the same contempt. What she said on television, what her client said in private—perhaps what her client said anywhere—was irrelevant. What had happened to Angela Morgan—whether she was murdered by her husband or by someone else—was irrelevant. What was relevant was the case, the case that had caught the country's attention, the case that would make you famous, one of the handful of lawyers whose name everyone knew.

"Sometimes these things start out with everyone thinking it's the trial of the century," I reminded her; "and then something happens—another murder, another crime—and everyone gets so swept up in it they forget all about the other one."

"They wouldn't if you were in it. You don't take that many cases anymore, and when you do, everyone knows it's important."

I understood now what she was after. I wondered why I had not caught on before. She wanted a guarantee of her own celebrity, a way to keep the story alive right down to the last day of the trial.

"Is that why you wanted to have a drink? To talk me into this?"

"Look, I can help," she said with a new intensity. "I know some people who know the family. All I have to do is mention that you'd be interested and . . ."

I grinned from ear to ear. "It's been a long time since anyone offered to help me find work. But, thanks anyway. I'll just limp along as best I can."

"I didn't mean—"

"I'm not taking the case—even if someone asks."

"But why?"

"Because I don't take that many cases anymore, and I only take ones that seem different to me, unusual, something I haven't seen before. Morgan doesn't seem particularly interesting, and what happened to his wife, unfortunately, isn't that unusual, either. And because, to be quite frank, I really don't want any part of this media circus. I saw enough of it tonight."

I paused, not quite certain whether I ought to say out loud the thought that had been troubling me since I left the studio.

"You were terrific," she said with a puzzled expression.

"The only one of the four of us who acted the way I think he must act all the time was Julian Sinclair. He didn't care what anyone thought; he said what he meant and he meant what he said. If you agreed with it—fine; but if you didn't . . . well, that was all right, too. I liked him; I liked him a lot."

Paula had taken a lipstick out of her purse. Peering into a small compact mirror, she added another layer to her shiny red mouth.

"You liked him because he reminded you of yourself at that age," she said, checking one last time before snapping the compact shut.

"He's just like you, a younger version. Smart, sure of himself, with those dashing good looks that women can't resist."

She started to slide out from the booth. "There's someone I have to see," she explained without apology. She stood at the corner of the table, looking down at me. "He's interesting: you're right about that; but part of that is because he's still young enough that you can read into his future some of the things maybe you wish you had done with your past." Paula put her hand on my shoulder. "You're more generous than I am. I looked at that young twit, Daphne McMillan, and all I saw in her future was more of the same self-absorption I saw tonight. One thing I can tell you for sure: if they both live to be a hundred, they'll never have lives as interesting as ours. Thanks for the drink."

I turned and watched her go. Before she had taken three steps, she was calling out to some producer she knew in the crowd gathered around the bar, "If you want me to save your ratings, Charlie, better do it soon. They're starting to book me three months in advance!"

Chapter Four

LATE THE NEXT MORNING, Albert Craven dropped by my office to tell me that he had watched the show and that he thought I had not done too badly. Then, as if he had almost forgotten, he mentioned that Harry Godwin had called.

"He said he thought you were terrific and—"

"'Terrific.' Is that the word he used?"

Albert raised his wispy eyebrows into a puzzled half circle. "Yes, why?"

"It's what the producer said; it's what that idiot Bryan Allen said. Do you think there's something a little wrong with a medium that can make a superlative sound like faint praise?"

Albert pretended to give a start. "Don't be angry with me. I'm just telling you what Harry said. And for what it's worth, Harry doesn't often give praise, faint or otherwise, to anyone." Lowering his gaze to the blue Persian rug, Albert slid one hard polished shoe in front of the other, the tentative posture of someone with a question he does not want to ask.

"Tell him I said no."

Albert looked up. A knowing smile danced at the corners of his small round mouth. "I did better than that. I told him it was like pulling teeth to get you to say yes the first time. Harry understands what a favor means. All he said was that he hoped you would change your mind and that the invitation was always open." The smile on his face broadened into a kind of triumph. "Didn't think I could do it, did you? Didn't think I could stand up to Harry Godwin, the firm's biggest client? You should have heard me. I was . . ."

"Terrific. Yes, I know."

Albert laughed and started to go.

"What did you really think last night?"

"Of you?" he asked, turning slowly on his heel. "What I said before: not bad."

"Thanks," I said as I started to study the appellate court opinion I had been reading. "That's what I thought."

"Julian Sinclair, on the other hand, really was terrific."

I slammed the book shut and sat straight up. "That's what I thought, too. What do you know about him?"

"Brilliant mind; finished top of his class. Never left Berkeley. Did all his work there: undergraduate degree, law school—now teaches there. Could have gone anywhere. Tested off the charts when he started high school, from what I've been told; then close to perfect on the Scholastic Aptitude Test his senior year."

Craven drew in his cheeks, pursed his lips, bounced his head from side to side. He looked down at his shoes and frowned.

"I know this because I'm on one of the committees at the law school that looks over the people they're thinking about hiring. It's unusual to hire someone who graduated that recently from your own law school. Julian Sinclair is probably the closest thing to a genius the law school has got." A quick, impish grin shot across his lips. "I didn't say he was a genius, mind you; let's just say he's one of the most gifted young men I've come across in a long time. It sort of disproves everything you thought you knew about genetics. Or maybe it doesn't," remarked Craven, a slightly baffled look in his pale blue eyes. "It's the reason he never left Berkeley—at least I think it is. How else do you explain something like this?"

I had learned a long time ago not to expect to understand immediately everything Albert Craven said. The pieces never quite fit together until the end. Of course, it all made sense to him; and he was certain it would all make sense to you as well, if only you were patient and let him lead you through the various complications without which you could never really understand what he wanted you to know. "Every story has a beginning, a middle and an end," he had once explained to me with patient humor when I protested that the more he talked, the more lost I became. "But you have to know something about the middle before you can appreciate the beginning." The truth was that whenever he started talking he invariably remembered something he should have said before. There were no simple stories.

"How do you explain someone who knew at a very young age that he could go anywhere—be anything—knew that every university in the country would not only have admitted him but given him a full scholarship if he would come? He grew up in Oakland. He could have gone to Harvard, Princeton, Yale—anywhere; and he went three miles down the road to Berkeley. Yes, well, I went there, too, and no one needs to tell me that it's a great university. But Julian Sinclair graduated at the top of his class from college, had a near perfect score on the Law School Admission Test, but instead of Harvard or Yale or Chicago, he stayed right where he was. Seven years going to school in Berkeley, and then, a year or two after he graduates from law school, again at the top of his class, what does he do? He applies for an opening on the faculty."

Craven rose up on the balls of his feet, placed both hands on the small of his back and stretched his neck. "He could have gone anywhere, done anything, but he stayed at home."

The heels of his shoes hit the carpet. With a dramatic flourish he threw his right arm out in front. "His mother! That's why he did it, why he never left—his mother. Rather, the woman who raised him; not his real mother at all—though the only mother he knew. He was a foundling, in the literal sense of the word: found by the woman, though whether he had been left on her doorstep, or abandoned somewhere—under a bench in some public park—I don't know. I don't imagine anyone does."

Albert Craven moved the few short steps to the chair and sat down. He pulled each shirt cuff down below the sleeves of his coat, threw his hands over the ends of the arms of the chair and crossed his legs.

"That's what I meant," he said with a polished, abbreviated smile. "It either disproves everything you thought you knew about genetics—or it doesn't."

I rolled my eyes in a conscious attempt to make him feel some obligation to get to the point. It seemed to amuse him. His lips quivered slightly; his head turned just a little to the side. He gave me a droll look.

"You must have thought the same thing yourself."

I gave him the same look back. "Often," I said in as dry a voice as I could.

"I thought as much." He stared at me a moment longer, an irrepressible smile of generosity and goodwill crumbling the mask of stoic indifference. With surprising agility, he sprang to his feet and walked briskly to the window. Clasping his hands behind his back, he surveyed the scene on the busy street below.

"He was born with that astonishing intelligence. He had to have been. But where did it come from? From his parents—whoever they were; but what kind of people would abandon a baby—not give him up for adoption, take some step toward making sure he'd be all right. What's the first thing you think of?" he asked as he spun back around.

"Some young unfortunate, some homeless waif, who gave herself away for drugs or money, finds herself pregnant, can't take care of herself—what's she going to do with a child?" Craven twisted his head at a downward angle and squinted his left eye. "But that girl's baby—Julian Sinclair? It seems impossible. And the father—with a girl like the one we're imagining? That seems more impossible still."

Leaning against the casement, one foot crossed over the other, he seemed to follow some fugitive thought of his own, one of those distant possibilities all the more attractive for being so different from what we ordinarily expect.

"It would make sense of course if his mother had been the beautiful daughter of some rich and powerful man, fallen in love with a young man of a different class, forced to give up the child because of what might happen to the boy she loved if she did not. It's an old story—the child of nobility, abandoned as the only way to save it from the murderous ambition of an illegitimate king, raised by shepherds, grows up to become the savior of his people."

Albert Craven shrugged. "I don't know who his parents were; but I know something about the woman who raised him. It's a miracle he survived at all. She must have had a decent heart: she took him in, after all; raised him—or tried to raise him—as her own. She was an alcoholic, probably was never sober two straight days in her life. Whether she also used drugs, I don't know; but what would have been the chance that she did not? She lived with one man after another, never for more than a few months at a time; most of them repeat offenders, drunks and addicts and small-time thieves, the ones who never seem to learn anything except new ways to get caught. Every man she lived with left her, and everyone who left made sure he beat her up first."

Craven raised his eyebrows, a troubled, pensive look in his eyes. "And with all that we have, not a psychotic killer, or another mindless addict, but Julian Sinclair. He stayed here; he did not leave. He stayed because he had to; because without him, that woman he calls his mother would have died. He stayed to take care of her, to give her a decent place to live; to keep her away, as far as he could, from the kind of people who would do her harm. He is, I think, without exception the most extraordinary young man, and I haven't any idea how he can be explained. There is simply no category into which you can possibly make him fit."

I was sitting back, my hand wrapped around my knee, watching Albert Craven struggle to understand the mystery that none of us could solve.

"It's the gift, Albert; that's all it is."

"The gift?"

"The gift of existence; the fact that you can never tell what anyone is going to be." I sat up and looked past Albert Craven to the window and to the city outside, the city that was too beautiful to ever let you get close enough to know it. "Would it really be less mysterious—an intelligence like that—if you knew everything about Julian Sinclair, or thought you did; if he had been raised by his parents, and his parents were well-educated middle-class people? How many of the children of the great American middle class have grown up to be as interesting as Julian Sinclair?"

Suddenly, I remembered what Albert Craven had told me before, not about Julian Sinclair, but about Harry Godwin.

"Maybe there is a certain advantage in having to raise yourself. It's what Harry Godwin had to do. Isn't that what you said? The only difference is that Godwin only had to worry about himself; Julian had to worry about someone else. Do you think that's the difference in the way they turned out?"

"I hadn't thought of it," admitted Albert. "Perhaps it is. He certainly doesn't have Harry's hard edge, nothing like that same single-minded devotion to his own ambition. To tell you the truth, I'm not sure I could tell you what Julian Sinclair's ambition might be. It isn't money, that much is clear. But what it is, what he really wants . . . ? Whatever it is, it isn't something most people want, or perhaps can even comprehend. What does Julian Sinclair want? Probably to learn eight languages fluently, discover a lost civilization somewhere, write a book that only ten people will ever read and only half that number understand. Harry Godwin is a type; Julian Sinclair is . . . I don't know what he is—but he isn't that."

With a last glance out the window, Albert headed for the door. "Maybe we should ask if he'd like to join the firm," he remarked after he had opened it.

He seemed to consider his own suggestion, view it in an objective light, the way he often analyzed a problem he had been given to solve. The great mistake was seeing it only the way you wanted it to come out, instead of taking into account the interest of the other side.

"He'd probably be bored to death, wouldn't he?"

I wondered if he would. There was a chance that he might instead have become bored with teaching the same thing over and over again to the kind of students who, if they had not changed since I was in school, took criminal law only because they had to and never gave a thought, most of them, to anything except how to make the law a profitable career. It was a question worth pursuing. Julian Sinclair had said he wanted to talk to me, and now I had a reason to talk to him. I waited a week for him to call, and when I did not hear, I called him.

"I didn't think I should call you right away," he remarked. It seemed an odd thing to say, and I was not sure how to respond. "I know how busy you must be," he explained in a modest, respectful tone. "I didn't want you to think I was not conscious of the demands that must be made on your time. I thought I would wait a couple of weeks and call then. How good of you to call instead," he added with a youthful exuberance.

I confess it made me feel a little like a walking reputation. It was a forceful, if unintended, reminder that he was a generation younger and that the future, whatever that future might be, belonged to him.

We agreed to have lunch. He offered to come into the city, but I suggested we meet in Berkeley instead. I had just finished a trial and I wanted an excuse not to start on the next thing I was supposed to do. I thought I would have lunch with Julian Sinclair and then wander around the campus, and perhaps get a sense of how much, if at all, college life had changed. But the main reason was that I wanted to see how much, if at all, law school had changed. When I slipped into the empty back row of the lecture hall and listened to Julian Sinclair prove to two hundred future lawyers that they did not know what they believed on the most important points of the criminal law, I thought I had stepped back in time.

"Miss Fairbanks," he said, addressing an intense-looking student three rows up in the middle. "Your point, if I understand it, isn't that capital punishment is cruel and unusual and should therefore be struck down on constitutional grounds; but that it is immoral. Is that correct?"

I remembered the first time I had been called upon my first year at Harvard. I said something senseless and incoherent, but the fact that I had been able to say anything had seemed a kind of triumph. Miss Fairbanks did not seem nervous; she certainly did not seem unwilling to stand her ground.

"Correct. It is immoral," she insisted. "How can you justify having the state do the very thing it says an individual cannot?"

Sinclair's eyes lit up. "That's what quite a few people say, isn't it? But it can't be right, can it?"

He was looking straight at her, telling her she was wrong, but also telling her that she was smarter than the other people who made the same mistake because she could figure out what that mistake was.

"You don't believe in slavery, do you? But despite that, you agree—don't you?—that the state has the right—and not just the right, but the duty—to enslave."

"No, I don't agree with that," said an astonished Miss Fairbanks. "I don't see how anyone—"

"You're against the death penalty. You favor as the alternative—what? Life in prison? Well, what is life in prison, what is incarceration, if it isn't slavery? So, if slavery, like the taking of a human life, is never defensible, how can you justify allowing the state to do what, as you quite properly point out, we would never allow an individual to do?"

"Mr. Hutchinson," he called out, turning quickly to the far side of the room. "Help us out. What other argument can be made against the death penalty?"

Hutchinson looked up from his laptop computer as if he had been caught in the act.

"Mr. Hutchinson is engaged in what I believe is called 'multitasking.' It used to be called 'schizophrenia,' but that was before the inmates took over the asylum and the inability to keep your mind focused on anything for longer than a few seconds became a virtue to brag about, instead of a disease that might with help and understanding be cured."

A smile shot across Sinclair's mouth. "That's all right, Mr. Hutchinson, go back to what you were doing." Sinclair started to turn away, but just as the unfortunate Hutchinson began to relax, he asked abruptly: "And just what penalty do you think the court would have imposed in the case you were assigned today, the famous English case, Regina v. Dudley and Stephens?"

Hutchinson's mouth dropped open, but nothing came out. His eyes were wide open, frozen with fear. I watched Julian Sinclair watching him. It was one of the worst things law school did, teaching the lesson that it did not matter what you said as long as you said something—anything—to keep the exchange alive. Before they had learned the first thing about the law, they were expected to talk as if they knew it all. If you were called upon, you replied, and pity the fool who had the honesty to say he did not know. No wonder we turned out lawyers who could not think and judges who could not write.

I kept watching Sinclair, trying to measure what that somber look in his eyes meant as he moved as close to the paralyzed young Mr. Hutchinson as he could.

"That was exactly my reaction the first time I read the case. Exactly that," he said in tones of amazement, as if in Hutchinson he had found a kindred soul. "It's incredible, isn't it? A shipwreck, four survivors, far off the main shipping lanes, no chance they're going to be found. No food, almost no water; the young boy dying. Two of the three men decide to help things along, because if they don't—if they wait—it will be too late and they'll all be dead. So they kill him, that young boy, and they eat his flesh and they drink his blood, and then, four days later, they're found, they're saved. They're put on trial: murder, and worse than murder, cannibalism. And what defense do they have?" he asked, looking Hutchinson straight in the eye as if Hutchinson surely knew. "Necessity. That there was no choice, that what they had to do they did, and that only by doing that awful thing were they able to avoid the greater evil, the death of all of them."

He smiled at Hutchinson with a kind of gratitude, as if Hutchinson had been doing the talking, instead of sitting there, speechless, embarrassed and ready to quit.

"That's where we'll start on Monday, ladies and gentlemen," announced Sinclair, waving his hand briefly in the air. "The law of necessity." They were rising from their seats when he added, "And you might think about this as well: If you were convicted of murder, what would you rather do—receive a lethal injection or spend the next fifty or sixty years kept in a cage, an animal in the zoo? Have a nice weekend."

It was a law school question, one of those questions that scholars and students struggle with, as if by thinking about it they could know what that grim alternative really meant. Those who were actually faced with the possibility that instead of life in prison they might be sentenced to death, seldom saw the issue as one that could be argued on either side. They always, or almost always, chose life.

"Difficult to dream of escape if you're dead," replied Julian Sinclair when I mentioned this to him at lunch. An incorrigible grin stretched across his straight, clean mouth. But then, afraid that he might have sounded less serious than he should, he shoved his nearly empty plate to the side and crossed his forearms on the table. "After a while, though; after you've been there, in prison, for twenty years or so; after you've given up all hope of ever getting out, then don't you think . . . ?"

"No," I replied, dabbing the corner of my mouth with a napkin. "The lifers I've known, the ones that have been there for years— prison becomes their home, their world. I asked that question—the one you asked in class—to someone I knew, someone I had represented when I was just starting out. He was in prison for murder when I first met him; he had been there thirty years. I asked him whether he ever wished that he had been given the death penalty instead of spending all those years locked up. He told me that it was his life, what he was used to. And he said this with only a hint of resignation. He meant it: it was his life; maybe not the life he would have chosen, but maybe not as bad as the lives led by some of the people he knew outside."

We were having lunch at the faculty club, an old redwood structure with a heavy shake roof and faded hardwood floors that sloped off center and creaked under your step. A wooden plank bridge with hand railings made from saplings, the axe marks plainly visible at the ends, crossed the creek that twisted through the redwood trees that surrounded the building and shaded the light. It was the Berkeley of the 1920s, when there were still more horses than cars, and the campus was a retreat from the world. George Santayana taught here then. I wondered if anyone remembered.

Julian had listened with intense interest, his chin in the hollow of his hand. "I wonder . . . ," he started to say. He shook his head and sat back, a grim, thoughtful smile on his face. "It really isn't much of a choice anyway, is it? What I mean is that, even if you were sentenced to death, that isn't really what you get. There are six hundred men on death row across the bay in San Quentin. Twenty percent of them—and I'm willing to bet that figure is low—have lost their minds. If they weren't crazy when they got there, living like that, alone in a cell, cut off from everything, let out just an hour or two a week—how could anyone stay sane? Some of them live like that for years—twenty, twenty-five years, some of them. So that the difference between a death sentence and life without parole isn't as clear-cut as most people think." A slight shudder passed through him. "Just the thought of it . . . No, I could not do it; I couldn't live locked up like that. Never."

It was the honest assumption, the candid assessment, of someone who knew that he would never have to find out.

"It makes you wonder though, doesn't it? About how Bryan Allen and the others like him are so eager to convict someone, call for their execution, or at least that they be locked up forever, without chance of parole, before there has even been a trial. What did you think of that business?"

Before I could answer, he bolted forward. "What do you think he'd be saying if he were the one being charged with murder?" Julian's eyes glimmered with eager malice. "It's what you said before, isn't it? The way we believe with such certitude when we're only observers, when it isn't us. What would he do—how would he feel—about what Paula Constable has been telling everyone on television: that the defendant must be guilty because he had been having an affair! It's an electronic lynch mob. Death by public opinion." His mood suddenly brightened. "You'd figure out a way to use that, though, wouldn't you? Use the fact that everyone thought the defendant was guilty, the fact that all these publicity-hungry lawyers had gone on television to say he was guilty. Isn't that the secret: turn what seems the biggest weakness into the biggest strength?"

I turned the question back on him to see how far his interest ran. "You ever think about becoming a trial lawyer yourself? There's a difference, you know, between talking about the theory of the law, talking about what an appellate court decided a trial court should have done, and getting inside the thing itself, pulling it together, using all the law you've ever learned to build the case from the start. I'm asking this for a reason. I think you know Albert Craven. He thinks you'd make a great addition to the firm. So do I."

"Criminal law?" He asked this in a way that suggested he thought of it as a limitation.

"The law: criminal, civil, all of it, or as much of it as you want to explore. And trial work, as you want it, and as you feel comfortable with it. Or," I added with a searching glance, "as you feel driven to do it. That's what will happen. There will be a case that you'll get into, a case you can't let go of—a case that won't let go of you—and you'll take it to trial because trial is the only place to get it done right."

I sipped on my coffee, watching the way he took it all in. There was none of that false modesty that, covering vanity, wants praise. He would not insult either one of us by questioning whether it was something he could do.

"I've thought about doing it, practicing law instead of teaching it. I tried it once: six months, right out of law school, in a prosecutor's office;

but I was doing the same thing over and over again. They start you out doing simple misdemeanor cases—that's how I met Daphne. . . ."

He gave me a strange look, as if he were afraid that he had given something away; and, more than that, annoyed with himself for saying something that he felt he had to conceal.

"Daphne McMillan. We met in the DA's office. That's why I made that remark, called what she said 'stupid.' She knew I was only trying to make a point."

"You didn't like the work."

He seemed grateful for the reminder, the chance to get back to what he had wanted to say.

"No, it was tedious, boring, and worse than that, hopeless. All we were doing was convicting the same people for the same things, except for the new ones who got their first convictions and started a lengthening record of their own." He raised his eyebrows and threw back his head. "It wasn't Clarence Darrow kind of work."

"So you left; but Daphne stayed? It wasn't McMillan then, was it?"

Julian threw one leg over the other and sat sideways on the chair. "No, it wasn't McMillan," he remarked with a furrowed brow as he watched his foot swing back and forth. "It was Della Rosa, Daphne Della Rosa—beautiful name; beautiful girl. And yes, Daphne stayed. She has always had a very clear idea of what she wanted." He paused, a private smile on his mouth. He looked up. "Perhaps because she's always been able to get it."

He glanced at his watch and seemed startled at the time. "I didn't realize . . . It's almost three. I have a fencing lesson, every Friday at three-thirty. Would you like to walk over with me? It isn't very far, and we can talk on the way."

Outside, as we moved from under the dark verdant trees into the mild February light, he told me he was very much interested in what I had said and that he would like to explore it further. He wondered if we might get together after he had had a chance to think about it a little more. We agreed to meet again the next week. This time he would come to the city and Albert Craven would join us for lunch.

"I took up fencing the end of last year," he explained as we stood chatting just outside the gym. "It's taught me more about balance and keeping concentration than anything else I know. Have you ever tried it? Want to learn?" he asked with such boyish enthusiasm that for half a moment I almost thought I should.

Chapter Five

THE MORE I THOUGHT about it, the more it made sense. Everything about him—the lithe, graceful way he moved, the quick, easy smile, the crystal clarity of his eyes, the Cartesian certainty of his mind— had the air of someone most alive when living close to the edge. Fencing, even if it did not draw blood, reminded you that it could: that a moment's mistake, a reaction just a fraction of a second too slow, a rapier thrust that missed its mark and left you for half a heartbeat exposed, would have, unprotected, cost you your life. I could not imagine Julian Sinclair ever playing chess.

He came to the city that next Friday as we had agreed. Albert Craven had made reservations at his private club, a place you could have passed a thousand times and not noticed it was there. It was down an alleyway a few blocks south of Market. There was no sign, nothing to indicate what was behind the solid wooden door. Albert handed the car keys to an attendant who materialized out of nowhere, stood directly in front of the plain, windowless door and pushed a buzzer.

"Afternoon, Mr. Craven," said an olive-skinned man who might have been Lebanese. He glanced quickly up and down the alley like someone running an illegal operation.

It was not really a club at all, in the usual sense of a place where members could come and relax: it was a restaurant; a small one, with, if I counted right, ten tables arranged on the lower level and four more on a level two steps up at the back. There was nothing grand or opulent about it; nothing that someone, told they were going to have lunch in perhaps the most exclusive club in San Francisco, would have expected. The tablecloths were plain white linen, while the chairs were the armless kind you find in cheap spaghetti joints where the candlelight comes in Chianti bottles covered with wax. As we settled into our places at one of the tables in the back, Julian looked around, a whimsical expression in his clear, brown eyes.

"What can we get for you today, Mr. Craven?" asked the same man who had let us in. He was wearing a dark suit and a dark tie. His voice was low, confidential, discreet.

Albert wanted his guest to go first. Julian unbuttoned his sports jacket and looked at our host. "Perhaps I could see a menu?"

"I'm afraid we don't have menus here."

There was a faint glimmer of recognition in Julian's eyes as he began to understand why this nondescript place, as dark, as dingy as some roadside café, should be as private and exclusive as he knew it was.

"What do you have, then?" he asked, raising an eyebrow as he smiled to himself.

The response was casual, indifferent, given with the kind of benign neglect that, as Julian seemed to expect, went right to the heart of what it meant to be rich.

"Anything you like. Anything at all."

We talked about a great many things that afternoon at lunch—the law, what Julian wanted to do, what he would do if he joined the firm, what he would be giving up if he abandoned the teaching career he had started only a few short years before—and it was only gradually that I began to realize that he never had to think about anything he said. There was never a pause, never the slightest hesitation. Ask a question and the answer came, clear, immediate, as fully formulated as if, like someone cheating on an exam, he had gotten the questions early and written out the answers in advance. I had seen the same thing the night we did the television show together and had marveled at how on the spur of the moment he could come up with a concise, tightly reasoned argument that left the others sounding like ignorant, sputtering fools. He had done it again, though with more kindness and tact, in his law school class. It was not glibness: he never tried to talk his way around a point. It was more disconcerting than that. For all his charm and good manners, for all of what I have no doubt was his sincere wish to be of help however he could, there was nothing anyone could say that he had not heard before; nothing anyone could think of that he had not thought of already.

He liked people—he was not some misanthrope who hated the world—but I had the feeling he never liked them quite as much as he thought, and hoped, he would. Because I was older and had a certain reputation as a lawyer who knew what he was doing in court, Julian thought I was someone from whom he could learn. But as I listened to him talking in such confidential tones with Albert Craven, a man more than twice his age, I had the sense that it would not be long before he was finishing my sentences in his mind and wondering if I would never say anything new.

After we had said goodbye to Julian and gone back to the office, Albert Craven told me that while he did not disagree with what I thought, he saw it in a rather different light. He was sitting on the edge of the upholstered dove gray chair behind the dark and hideous Victorian desk that had been the unwelcome gift of one of his wives. The tips of his slender fingers flattened against each other as he pressed them tight together just in front of his chin.

"It was my first reaction to my own suggestion. Remember? That he'd be bored. What I discovered at lunch today was that he doesn't know it yet, and because he doesn't know it, he's excited about the prospect of doing something new. He's tired of teaching—you could tell from the fact that he never once said a word about how much he might miss it—but he'd be tired of whatever he was doing once he learned it all and knew that it was not enough. Remember what he said about the money? Nothing, not a word. He wants to do this because he's ambitious, more ambitious than perhaps anyone you or I have ever met."

A smile darted over Craven's face. He pushed against the left arm of the chair, shifting positions until he was staring out the window to the side.

"Imagine someone like Napoleon born two hundred years too late. That's Julian Sinclair: a mind that never rests; a relentless desire to conquer the world, to do something great. What is he supposed to do? Where is the room for that in this democratic age of ours where everyone is equal and nothing is more important than anything else? Julian Sinclair teaches law at a first-rate law school, and what does he do with all that pent-up energy? He learns to fence. If you want to write the life of Julian Sinclair, find another Cervantes, because what we have here is another Don Quixote."

Albert rolled his head until his eyes met mine. "Even if the attitude toward love isn't quite so high-minded and ethereal. Quixote, if I re-member correctly, thought Dulcinea, a woman of the lowest order, a noble woman, chaste and devout." Lifting his eyebrows, Albert sighed. "Julian Sinclair, on the other hand, seems to spend a fair amount of time in bed with a married woman of what today passes for the upper class—not noble, perhaps, but quite rich."

"Daphne McMillan?"

"You've heard. Yes, that's the rumor. It's none of my business, of course. No one's, really; but it is a little dangerous." He gave me a worldly look. "Not because she's married, but because of whom she's married to. His friends call him eccentric, but if you ask me, I think Robert McMillan isn't quite sane."

"Maybe it isn't true," I ventured as I stood up to go. It was nearly quarter to six and there were things I still had to do. "They worked in the district attorney's office together for a while. They're friends."

Albert Craven gave me a skeptical look. "You've seen them together. Is that really what you think? But whether he is involved with her or not, we still have a decision to make. Do we want him or not?"

We both knew the answer to that. "It'll be a way to keep ourselves from getting bored: finding ways to make him think that it takes years to become as good—as great, Albert—as you and I really are."

"And how long do you think we can keep him from guessing that he already knew more than we do the moment he stepped in the door?"

But the truth was that Albert rather liked the prospect of creating the decent illusion that there were things the young and inexperienced Julian Sinclair still needed to learn and that some of them were within our power to teach.

I began to look forward to Monday morning when, I promised myself, I would call Julian first thing. He had probably started thinking about what his new life in the law would be like while he was still on the Bay Bridge, on his way back to Berkeley. He had that kind of imagination, each scene in the future already vivid in his mind. By the time he got home he would have given a dozen summations to a dozen different juries, all of them waiting breathless for the chance to do what he told them they had to do if they wanted to do justice, which of course they did.

When I woke up Saturday morning I decided not to wait, but to call him right away so he could start thinking about how he wanted to make the move. He could not stop teaching in the middle of the year; but he could join the firm and put in what time he could, and in that way make the transition less abrupt. I called information, but his number was not listed.

I wonder now if that would have changed things; whether, if I had been able to reach him, we might have decided to talk some more in person, perhaps meet somewhere for dinner. I suspect the same thing would have happened, that even if I had called him Saturday rather than waiting for Monday and the beginning of the week, Julian Sinclair's disillusionment with the world and everything in it would still have started late that night and not, as Albert Craven and I had hoped, sometime years in the future instead.

I had gotten used to late night telephone calls from people in trouble, but a call at six o'clock on a Sunday morning was something new. I knew who it was before he had finished speaking my name; I knew he was in trouble—serious trouble—the moment I heard his voice. It seemed to surprise him, as if hearing it, he was not sure it was his voice at all.

"Could you come over? Something terrible has happened."

He sounded traumatized. That is what scared me, that trance-like quality in his voice, as if he was not sure what was going on.

"Are you hurt?" I asked, trying to sound calm and reassuring. "Do you want me to call an ambulance?"

Then I realized that perhaps he already had. "Have you called 911? What is it you think I can do?"

He ignored everything I said. Pausing every few words, as if he had to stop to remember, he gave me directions to his house. He lived high up in the Berkeley hills. One wrong turn and I would be hopelessly lost.

"Give me the phone number there," I said in a burst of impatience. I hung up the telephone and started to get dressed.

The city was still asleep. A layer of gray, impenetrable fog had begun to pull back toward the ocean. The towers of the Golden Gate

Bridge burned a brilliant reddish orange under the rushing sun. The empty streets had the grimy, patient look of a padlocked bazaar. I made it from the top of Nob Hill to the Bay Bridge in five minutes; ten minutes later I was on the other side. Berkeley was just a few miles ahead. I tried not to think about what I was going to find.

I knew what had happened, or at least I thought I did. It was not a matter of some strange precognition, the knowledge of something you could not yet know because it had not yet happened, but it was more than intuition. Julian had called me at six o'clock on a Sunday morning. That was something you did only when you had news that could not wait. Then there was the stark, deathlike tone of his voice. Someone was dead, and whatever the cause of that death, it seemed almost certain that it had either been an accident, or, worse, far worse, than that, it had been murder. The phrase he had used, "Something terrible has happened," might have suggested the former; but then why had he called me at that hour and not the police? Julian was in trouble and he was smart enough to know it.

I wound my way through the Berkeley hills until I was nearly at the top. The street number was marked on the mailbox post at the front of a long steep driveway that led through a tangled mass of ivy to Julian Sinclair's hillside home. The house was one of those 1960s contemporaries, long and low, all wood and glass, with a stunning view of the bay. I looked out to the Golden Gate and, beyond it, to the distant horizon where the water met the light. I looked at the city, bright and clean and magnificent, the fog vanished like last night's dream.

A dark green Jaguar convertible, this year's model or last, with a shiny hood and mud splattered wheels, was parked in front of the carport on the side closest to the house. I bent down and looked through the driver's-side window. A silk scarf had been tossed carelessly over the gearshift knob, a lipstick left in the ashtray. There was a cell phone on the passenger seat. I had never seen her drive it, but I knew whose car it was. I kicked at the ground with my shoe and muttered under my breath a brief lament.

I did not hear the door open; I did not hear a sound. I did not hear anything until Julian called my name. His voice surprised me: there was nothing deathlike left in it. He sounded the way he always had during our brief acquaintance, except for this morning's early call. He seemed quite normal, quite himself, as if nothing had happened, as if nothing was wrong. Had I misunderstood? Taken what might have been nothing more than a call asking for help with some manageable difficulty and turned it into murder or worse?

"Thank you for coming," he said with a formal glance that would have gone unnoticed by a stranger, someone he had never met, but seemed forced and artificial to me. As I moved closer, I saw that his eyes were tense, anxious, filled with nervous exhaustion. It was taking all the strength he had not to collapse. He held the door open, but he did not step aside.

"What's happened?" I asked, trying to sound calm. I glanced past him to the living room inside.

He must have felt it, the shock and disbelief that made my stomach start to sicken and my hands begin to shake. He pulled the door shut behind him and stared at me, his eyes turned wild. He clenched his teeth until his head began to shudder. I grabbed him by both arms and forced him away from the door.

"Stay here! Don't go anywhere! Just wait!"

I grasped the doorknob and for a moment that was all I did. That one quick glance had shown me all I needed, or wanted, to see. My hand still on the door, I asked Julian the question that I had to know.

"Did you . . . ?"

The answer took care of that question and the next one I would have asked.

"That's what the police will think. That's the reason I called you instead."

He had recovered something of his self-control. "Everything is the way it was when I woke up. I started to call 911, but then I realized—unless there is some forensic evidence, everything points to me."

My hand fell away from the handle as he gently pushed in front of me and opened the door.

I had seen a great many places where a murder had been committed. In an odd way, it was often prosaic, the way a room looked after the police had already been there and the body had been removed, the only trace of violence perhaps a bit of dried blood where the body had been. I had never seen anything like this. There was blood everywhere, spattered on the living room walls, dragged downward on the mirror that ran from the floor to the ceiling directly opposite the open flagstone fireplace with the dining room on the other side. The outline of two hands, pressed flat against the mirror—two hands that then slid downward in a jagged trail, traced the dying fall of the woman lying with her dress ripped open on the rug. Thickened in clumps along the profile of her hands, the blood was still wet. Daphne McMillan was curled up on the floor, what was left of her dress soaked in blood, her abdomen sliced open from multiple wounds from a knife. She was looking up at me, a puzzled expression frozen in her vacant eyes. I could almost hear her small, pretty voice asking, "Why me?" Whatever had passed through her mind, whatever pleading thought of a last-minute reprieve, even a temporary pause in this horrible, gruesome attack, had died silent on her lips. Her throat had been cut deep and straight across.

"Call the police! Do it now!" I instructed Julian. "Call 911. Tell them there has been a murder. Tell them to come at once. Then tell me what happened, everything you know."

Chapter Six

No one believed him. The police did not believe him when they arrested him and took him away. The district attorney did not believe him when she went before the grand jury and came out with an indictment for murder. No one on television believed him when all the public wanted to hear were the reasons why Julian Sinclair was guilty and what should be done with him after a trial. Bryan Allen had the advantage of being able to talk from experience, not only about the victim, the beautiful and talented Daphne McMillan, but also about the killer, the brilliant and deranged Julian Sinclair. He could also talk about the lawyer, Joseph Antonelli, who had built his reputation on helping the guilty go free and who was trying to do the same thing again.

Allen knew them all. They had been on his show, not just individually, but all together, at the same time, taking up the question of a murder that, ironically, was something like this: a young married woman killed in cold blood. Every show of his was now devoted in whole or in part to the gruesome murder of Daphne McMillan and the murderous treachery of Julian Sinclair. When he was not talking about it on his own show, he was talking about it on the show of someone else.

It was stunning how quickly things built to a frenzy, and how speculation fed on itself. Yesterday's rumor became today's unquestioned assumption, the well-established fact that no one interested in justice for the victim and her family could possibly doubt. Julian Sinclair, a young man in his early thirties with what an earlier generation would have called "matinee idol" good looks, had dated a number of women and, with perhaps one exception, a girl he had gone with in college, had not been serious about any of them. The enviable and interesting life of a bachelor, who could spend time with whoever wanted to spend time with him, was described as that of a womanizer who had only one thing on his mind. Without concern for consistency, the fact that Sinclair had been known to go for months without seeing anyone at all, seldom leaving campus, staying close to home, oblivious of everything except whatever scholarly pursuit had so captured his interest, proved that there was something unusual, abnormal, even perverse, about the way he lived.

A womanizer who preferred to be alone, a solitary thinker often seen about town—call him what you will—there was no one willing to call him not guilty and that, at least on the face of it, was a potential problem with getting a fair trial. The murder had happened in the Berkeley hills; the case would go to trial in the Alameda County Courthouse in Oakland, just a few miles away. I filed a motion for a change of venue, asking that the trial be held somewhere else.

The judge seemed sympathetic, to a point. With heavy, gnarled hands, and a broad, pockmarked face, the Honorable Conrad H. Jarvis had gone to law school after a short and much injured career in professional football. After five operations on his knees, he had called it quits while he could still walk. Without any apparent regret, and with none of the nostalgia that made so many of the others who played the game old men in their thirties looking back on the exploits of their youth, Jarvis began a second career with the same drive and enthusiasm he had brought to the first. Ten years in private practice, and now ten more on the bench, he had won the respect of everyone he dealt with, not only because he was fair-minded, but because everyone knew what he had done before. With the money he had made, he could have spent his days fishing or telling stories with his friends, but instead he had decided to do something he thought important. You liked him before you knew him, and you liked him even more once you did.

"Where do you suggest we move it, Mr. Antonelli?" he asked in the deep, gravelly voice that more than any voice I had ever heard could fill a room. "Granting the validity of what you say: that there has been a tremendous amount of pretrial publicity; granting further that all of it has been—how shall I say?—neither temperate nor fair; your own motion—the sworn affidavit that supports it—calls the publicity national in scope."

Leaning back in a slow, stiff motion, Jarvis clasped his knee in both his hands. He looked at me with rust-colored eyes, waiting.

"China, Your Honor," I said with a straight face.

The corners of his wide, heavy mouth bent downward. He began to nod in a thoughtful fashion.

"China. Yes, well, I see your point. There probably has not been too much notice taken of the case over there. But I wonder, Mr. Antonelli, if you have considered that language might be an issue? Perhaps you could think of something a little closer to home?"

Crossing my arms over my chest, I studied a spot on the floor. "England," I said, glancing up. "There will still be problems with the language, but perhaps not so great."

"Why not Paris, so we can all learn French?"

Madelaine Foster—Maddy to those who knew her—shrugged her broad shoulders as she lumbered to her feet. Her thick gray hair, pulled back in a knot, fell loose around her neck. She looked at me the way a teacher might look at a schoolboy she liked who had tried the same thing twice before.

"Is Mr. Antonelli perhaps trying to make a few headlines of his own, suggesting that he can't get a fair trial for his client, that we might as well go to China for all the chance of that?"

"I could not have said it better myself, Your Honor. Ms. Foster has made my point. However, the motion itself requests that the trial be moved to Los Angeles. That would at least take it out of the reach of the local media that have covered this case the most."

Jarvis stared down at his hands, a troubled, pensive expression reflected in the furrowed lines that spread across his ruddy forehead and cut deep into the skin. He raised his left hand, the hand closest to the bench, and spread his thick fingers.

"If this were only local media—if it was only local interest—I would be inclined to grant the motion, to send this trial as far from here as I could."

He paused, cast a warning glance across the courtroom crowded with reporters for whom any proceeding, whatever happened, was news.

"And it's precisely because of the kind of coverage this case has attracted that the court on its own motion is barring all television cameras and all photographers from not just the trial, but from the courthouse altogether."

He turned back to me. "As for the defense motion for a change of venue, that motion will be denied. However, I wish to make it plain that the defense will be given every reasonable opportunity during voir dire to explore the degree, if any, to which any prospective juror has formed an opinion as a result of the coverage in this case."

It was not a victory and it was not a defeat. The trial would not be moved to another location, but the judge was aware of the bias that existed and was willing to take what steps he could to keep it from having an influence at the trial. But there was nothing he or anyone else could do to prevent it, when the only way not to have been influenced was not to have picked up a paper or turned on a television in the months that had passed since Daphne McMillan's death. I knew it, and so did Maddy Foster, but all she would say to reporters when they asked if Julian Sinclair could get a fair trial was that the prosecution would do its job and so, she was certain, would the defense. That was not the kind of answer that would make it into the evening news; it certainly was not the kind of thing the jackals on television wanted to talk about.

"China!" exclaimed Bryan Allen as he opened that night's show. "Antonelli—Julian Sinclair's hired gun—has the guts to stand there—in a court of law, an American court of law!—and claim that his client can't get a fair trial in his own country! Isn't that pathetic? Well, I suppose not, if you think a fair trial means getting someone off for murder when all the evidence says it has to be him."

Allen peered directly into the camera, his jaw clenched tight, his eyes narrow, cold, determined. One second, two; he held his gaze steady, serious, relentless, letting all those millions know that he was just like them: outraged, sickened, by the blatant disregard for decency and truth shown by the kind of lawyer who will do anything to win. It was the face on the screen you could trust, the one that would tell you who was doing what and how they should be stopped. It was the look of contempt and disgust that said louder than words ever could that people like this were what was wrong with the country and that the sooner something was done about them, the better.

"What did you think of what Antonelli did? Was it a shrewd attempt to deflect attention from all the evidence against his client, or is that just what defense lawyers do: make that kind of smart-ass remark. Because that's what it was, wasn't it? You don't make that kind of remark—trivialize the process that way—not if you have a case, do you?"

Allen had turned to one of his guests. Now he turned back to the camera.

"Paula Constable has been a frequent guest of ours. She was here the night Daphne McMillan was on. The same night Julian Sinclair and his lawyer were here."

His eyes were back on her. "You know this guy Antonelli. Is this the kind of cheap trick he pulls?"

Before she could answer, he added, "We asked him to be on, to give his side of things. He won't even return our calls. I guess that tells you what kind of case he's got. Go ahead, Paula, what were you going to say?"

She must have owned a hundred red jackets, each one different, and yet all the same: bright and tight-fitting, with short straight collars that made her hand-painted face look rigid and alert, full of energy and all pulled together. With a quick, red-lipstick smile, her black lashes flew open and her black greedy eyes started their frenzied, meticulous dance.

"Joseph Antonelli—I've know him for years—is one of the best trial lawyers I've ever seen. No one with Antonelli as his lawyer is in any position to complain about not getting a fair trial. I don't know why he made that remark about the only way to get one was to take the case to China. My guess—because he never does anything without a reason—is that he was trying to win the sympathy of the court. And he may have done it. He's already got the judge talking about giving him unusual latitude on voir dire."

"'Unusual latitude!'" I shouted at the television screen.

Alone at home in my study, I followed that outburst with a sullen and emphatic expletive. I sank into the cushioned soft corner of the sofa and listened to myself laugh. China? I should have said Tibet. The law professor and the prosecutor, the brilliant young scholar and the gorgeous young blonde, the good-looking bachelor and the wife of one of San Francisco's wealthiest and most socially prominent men—the murder had become a dozen different stories told all at once, and told with the breathless candor that on television made anything mentioned seem like news.

I had made myself sick watching the shocked faces and the phony high-pitched voices as each of my brethren in the law, sworn to uphold the honor and integrity of their profession, discussed the twisted motives that had driven a man they had never met to murder, and derided not just the tactics, but the character and conduct of the lawyer for the defense. Smug and complacent, a former attorney general of the United States had gone so far as to wonder whether sanctions, including perhaps disbarment proceedings, ought not be filed against a lawyer who had visited a crime scene without first calling the police. When a defense lawyer suggested that it was not at all clear that Antonelli had known a crime had been committed, he was asked to explain for what other reason Julian Sinclair might have called. There was of course no logic to this, but television is more visual than verbal: the gaping inconsistency of the words was lost in the scowling condescension with which they were spoken.

It went on, day after day, night after night, a constant, unremitting barrage of voices; a strident electronic chorus, repeating over and over again that Julian Sinclair was guilty of murder and that the penalty should be death. Television had made the whole nation a mob. The trial, though public, would be conducted off camera, as they now liked to say; but by then it would be too late.

"Would you mind calling Sydney?" I asked Albert Craven two days later. "Tell Harry Godwin I'll agree to do what he asked. I'll go on television; I'll talk about the case. But with a condition: It has to be one-on-one. No other guests; just me."

Albert placed his soft hands on top of his desk and laced his fingers together. The drapes on the windows had been pulled partway across, allowing only a narrow strip of thin late afternoon light to fall through the gauze curtain to the thick rug on the floor.

"Harry will of course be delighted, but are you sure this is such a good idea? What about one of the other networks? Perhaps one of the Sunday shows, something more traditional, where at least they try to ask serious questions. If you do this . . . Well, you've been on that show; you've seen what they're doing now, the things they've said about Julian, and about you. . . . What is it you really think you can say? It won't be a conversation; it won't be a discussion; it will be a bare-knuckle brawl."

Albert Craven searched my eyes, wondering if I had thought it through.

"Are you sure you want to join this circus, even if only for one performance? Isn't there some danger that you give it by your presence more legitimacy than it might otherwise have? What does Julian think, or have you had the chance to ask him yet?"

"Julian agrees that we have to do something, that we can't let this go on, day after day, unanswered. The trial doesn't start for a month, but if you can find anyone who doesn't think he's guilty, I'd be glad to know it."

With a sigh, Craven acknowledged the tragic truth of it. "I was sorry to hear what happened at the law school. I made my objections known, of course; but in fairness I suppose there was not much they could do. Though it's a damn bad lesson, and one I hope they one day have reason to regret."

His eyes darkened into an intense, implacable stare. "A law school, a class on criminal law, and half the female students walk out in protest because the same teacher they had all thought so great is accused of a murder he insists he did not commit," he said with withering contempt. "Presumption of innocence, reasonable doubt, the basic requirement that you have to prove with hard evidence what you accuse—not important, apparently, when it is up against the necessity to demonstrate your opposition to violence against women. Well, all I can say is, good for the ones who stayed, the ones with guts enough to do a little thinking on their own."

One of the windows had been pushed open to let in some air. The sheer white gauze curtain billowed out between the heavy drapes, then, like a breath expired, fell back again. Somewhere in the distance, the tin metal sound of a bell measured the slow steep cable car ascent.

"It probably wasn't a good idea to try to finish the term," I offered, hoping to improve Albert's mood. "It was a minor miracle he got out on bail. He wouldn't take a leave of absence. They offered. I think he knew what it was going to be like; he's too smart not to have known. That's why he did it."

Albert Craven nodded wisely. "Because not to do it would have seemed to him an act of cowardice."

"And that's probably the same reason I'm going to do this: go on television and try to set a few things straight."

One telephone call and the only question was how soon I could do it. Harry Godwin made the arrangements while Albert Craven was still on the line, calling out to some assistant that the lawyer in the Daphne McMillan murder had finally said yes. Three nights later I was again on national television, this time alone. Bryan Allen was waiting for me, a smirk on his face, while a pair of hands behind me adjusted the microphone. After a brief, formal introduction, Allen led with a question that was nothing less than depraved.

"I understand that you're the defense lawyer and that you've got a job to do, and I understand all about the defendant's right to a fair trial; but tell us this, counselor, how is anyone supposed to trust lawyers when your client, an accused murderer, was over there in Berkeley, still teaching in the law school until a group of students said enough is enough and told the administration that if Julian Sinclair did not go, they would—they'd quit? What kind of man is this? All the evidence says he killed her, and he thinks he should still teach? Ironic, isn't it—that he was teaching criminal law?"

I squared my shoulders and faced him head-on.

"Julian Sinclair has been accused of a crime. 'Accused' is the operative word. You may have tried him on television—nearly every night for the last three months—but he has not yet been tried by a jury in a court of law. 'Accused,' Mr. Allen, not convicted. The law presumes him innocent, and so should everyone else, especially those students— the ones whose lynch mob justice you are so eager to applaud—who are supposed to take the law seriously, and who ought to know that Julian Sinclair isn't guilty of anything."

Allen's reply was immediate, emphatic, belligerent, sure to appeal to the most basic prejudice of everyone who watched.

"Would you want your daughter being taught by someone accused of murdering a woman, slashing her to death in the living room of his home?"

My response was just as quick, but, as I was fully aware, without the same dramatic, heavy-handed effect.

"I'd be honored if any child of mine was taught by Julian Sinclair."

"You don't have children, do you, counselor? You've never married. Isn't that true? Let me tell you, as a father of two girls and a boy, you aren't quite so worried about the rights of criminals when the children they harm may be your own. But enough about that. Tell us, if you would—because I can tell you that there are a lot of us who don't understand—if Sinclair is innocent like you say, why didn't he call the police? Why did he call you? That's what happened, isn't it? He called you, a famous defense lawyer, first."

He was asking the questions, and I was there to answer, but there was a way to turn that around.

"Why did he call me? Or why did he call the police? He did both."

Allen gave me the look he had given me before, the look he used so often it had become his trademark, the look of incredulity that seemed to laugh in your face.

"He called the police, but he called you first. The question, Mr. Antonelli, is why would someone innocent do that—wait to call the police until he had called you; wait until you had arrived and had a chance to look around, see how things would look to the police?"

"Are you sure those were the reasons he called me? Are you sure that's what I did when I first arrived? Or is this just another one of those things you find so easy to assume?"

Allen stared back at me, and then, as if my silence proved his point, remarked with a jagged, knowing grin, "Well, if you don't want to answer . . ."

"Oh, but I do. You want to know why Julian Sinclair called me right away? He called me because he was in shock. He called me because he was about to join our firm, and because the first thing anyone would do in those circumstances is to call someone he knew he could trust. You think he called me because he thought he needed a lawyer?" I asked, challenging him to say yes. "He's a lawyer himself, one of the most gifted I've ever known."

"That may very well be, but—"

"You're still missing something," I interjected. "The question you did not ask."

Allen threw back his shoulders. A scowl rippled over his mouth. "Really? Well, counselor, go ahead—enlighten us. What question is that?"

"Why did he call anyone? If he had murdered Daphne McMillan, the way you seem so eager to assume, why would he call me? Why would he call the police? If you killed someone—killed her in your own home—wouldn't your first thought be how to get rid of the body, how to get rid of all the evidence of what you had done? Wouldn't you move the body, take it anywhere rather than leave it right there, on your living room floor?"

"Everyone says you're just about the best there is, but—forgive me if I put it like this—isn't that just a little like throwing sand? How was he going to get the body out of there? How was he going to clean up all that blood? I mean, there are all sorts of reasons why he might have done what he did—called you, the defense lawyer he knew, instead of trying to hide the evidence of the crime. Admit it, counselor, there was just too much to do! He killed her, and given the way he killed her, he must have been in a rage! Then, when it was over, when he realized that he had left all this evidence, that he couldn't possibly get rid of it all, he called—not the police—you."

"Don't you think if that had happened, he might at least have gotten rid of the knife?"

Allen nodded eagerly. "The knife, the murder weapon—the knife belonged to him! He admitted that."

"Of course the knife belonged to him. It was taken from his kitchen. But again, you missed the most important question."

Allen spread open his hands and waited.

"Why weren't there any prints on the knife? Why had it been wiped clean?"

He looked at me like I was a fool. "Come on, counselor! That's the first thing a murderer would do."

"When it's a kitchen knife, a knife you use almost every day? When it's a knife on which the police would expect to find your prints?"

It was a mistake. I had gone too far. I had not given Allen enough credit. He was smarter than I had thought. He immediately took advantage, or tried to take advantage, of the opening he had been given.

"It's pretty clear, isn't it? He wiped his own prints off the knife to make it seem like someone else had wiped off theirs."

"He had the presence of mind to think that far ahead, but getting rid of the murder weapon was something he could not think clearly enough to do? And there is still that other question, the question that destroys the whole idea that he killed her but then did not have time to move the body and get rid of the evidence. According to the coroner, Daphne McMillan was murdered between midnight and two in the morning. If he killed her, Mr. Allen, what do you think he was doing for the six hours between the time of the murder and the time he called me?"

Allen threw up his hands. "Who knows what goes through the mind of a murderer? It's the middle of the night. Maybe he started looking for a place to do what you said—get rid of the body, bury her somewhere. Maybe he got in his car and just took off, his only thought that he has to get away. Killers do that, don't they? Take off running because it's the first thing that comes into their head. And then, after he's driven around for a while, he starts to calm down. He goes back, then decides what to do. Call a lawyer, tell him he knows it looks bad, but he didn't do it, and he knows he needs a defense."

I had the strange, disquieting sensation that I was listening to the collective consciousness of the great American public mind, convincing itself all over again of what it already knew: that Julian Sinclair was guilty and that every attempt to prove that he did not murder Daphne McMillan only proved he did. There was a reason for everything once you stopped believing in his innocence and agreed with everyone else about what he had done. I looked at Allen, wondering if beneath that crude and arrogant exterior there was anything beyond the ruthless ambitions of a confidence man, a charlatan who, without quite knowing how he had done it, found himself the temporary favorite of all those millions who depended for nearly everything they knew on what they saw on TV.

"And just why, Mr. Allen, would Julian Sinclair have murdered

Daphne McMillan, a woman he had known for a number of years, a woman he considered a very good friend?"

Allen's thick eyebrows shot straight up. "Very good friend, Mr. Antonelli? They were having an affair," he said in a harsh, scornful voice. "Why did he murder her? Because she wanted to end it; she wanted to make her marriage work. She had told her husband, admitted her mistake, said she was going to break it off, and said she wanted to try again. Your client did not want to let her go. The motive? The jealousy of someone who could not stand the thought that someone could say no to him."

I looked Allen square in the eye. "Daphne McMillan never told her husband she was having an affair with Julian Sinclair. How do I know that? Because she was not having an affair with Julian Sinclair. What was she doing there that night, in the Berkeley hills, at Julian Sinclair's home? I'll only tell you this much: it had everything to do with sex, but not with him."

Chapter Seven

CONRAD JARVIS, a pair of small rectangular wire-rimmed glasses perched at the end of his nose, turned away from the twelve citizens whose names had been called at random into the jury box.

"Mr. Antonelli, you may inquire."

It was the middle of summer and the trial of Julian Sinclair had finally begun. I looked at the faces in the jury box, my gaze moving slowly from one to the other, down the first row, then the back, stunned by the sullen certainty in their eyes.

"I won't insult your intelligence, Mr. Bristol," I began with the first juror, "by asking if you have formed any opinion about this case. Everyone in America has an opinion about this case—isn't that true?"

Tall and overweight, with slow-going eyes, Bristol shifted uneasily in the wooden chair. He began to fidget with his hands, not quite sure what to say.

"Everyone knows the defendant, Julian Sinclair, is guilty. Surely you must think the same thing?"

His face reddened; his eyes went blank.

"I'm not trying to embarrass you, Mr. Bristol. I promise I'm not. But this is very serious business. Can you, despite what you now think, listen to the evidence, follow the judge's instruction on the law and . . . change your mind? Can you, in other words, despite everything you have heard on television and other places, be fair and impartial? Can you base your verdict on the evidence—the evidence presented in this courtroom—and on that evidence alone?"

He said he could, and I have no doubt he was honest in his answer; but the bias was still there, dangerous and ineradicable, shaping, forming, everything he thought. Months before the trial had started, the burden of proof had shifted from the prosecution to the defense. They did not have to prove the defendant did it: I had to prove he did not. Julian Sinclair was halfway to his execution the moment those twelve jurors first filed into the box.

With each juror I tried to draw the same thing out, the way they had come to the same conclusion: that the defendant was guilty, and that in this rush to judgment not only had we jeopardized the whole notion of a fair trial, but that if you convict the wrong man, you let someone else get away with murder.

"Then you would have a double injustice, wouldn't you?" I asked the fifth juror, or perhaps it was the sixth.

We were in the second day of voir dire. The hostility, at first naked and intense, had largely vanished.

"A double injustice, Mrs. Williams," I said as I leaned toward her. "An innocent man is convicted for something he did not do; and the victim, Daphne McMillan, does not get the justice she deserves."

Madelaine Foster, prosecuting the case, never once objected, never tried to argue the defense was taking voir dire too far. She did not engage in any of those cheap theatrics—bolting out of her chair, shouting her indignation; throwing up her hands in outrage at the obvious and calculated violation of the rules—by which too many prosecutors tried to tarnish the defense attorney with the crimes of the accused. With only her calm demeanor, she was the embodiment of that kind of rock-solid confidence that nothing can shake. It was intangible but real, as real as anything I had ever seen in a court of law: this sense she had about her that made you think that anything she said had to be the truth, because the last thing she would ever think of was telling anyone a lie.

"I think what Mr. Antonelli wants is the same thing we all want," she said in that quiet, understated voice of hers; "a jury that is fair and impartial. If you have for any reason, whether because of what you may have seen on television or what you may have read in the newspapers, come to any conclusion about the guilt or innocence of the defendant, then, I can assure you, I don't want you on this jury any more than he does. Now, let me ask you, just to be sure: Is there any reason why you cannot be fair and impartial, why you cannot base your verdict solely on the evidence that is produced during the trial?"

In each case the answer was the same. And each time it was given, Maddy Foster smiled her firm, grandmotherly smile and passed the juror for cause. It was no wonder that in her long years as a prosecutor she had almost always won, or that one of the few cases she had lost had made her something of a legend at the bar. Halfway through the testimony of a police officer—testimony that was crucial to the prosecution's case—she discovered an inconsistency with something the officer had told her during their preparation for trial. It was something no one else—certainly not the defense—would have known, but it proved to her that he had lied and that his testimony was perjured. She subjected him to what was in effect a withering cross-examination, confronting him with the inconsistencies, the lies, showing that he had fabricated evidence. She ended it with an open apology to the court and a motion, granted on the spot, that all charges against the defendant be dismissed.

Maddy Foster's rugged blunt honesty was the perfect shield for every bias the jury had. How could Julian Sinclair be innocent, when she was there to tell them that he was not?

Perhaps it was because Julian Sinclair was a brilliant legal scholar and could, even as a defendant, serve as a reminder of what the law could be; perhaps it was nothing more than a desperate search for an antidote to the poison that the television coverage had poured into every juror's mind—I tried in my opening statement to impress upon them their obligation by showing how much the whole idea of a trial had changed.

"We like to think that trial by jury is the only fair and reasonable means of getting to the truth, of deciding whether someone charged with a crime is guilty or not. Years ago, in England, before the Normans came, when the Anglo-Saxons made the law, the law was in certain respects rather more interesting than it is now."

I was a few feet in front of the railing of the jury box, smiling to myself at what I was about to tell them, watching them watch me.

"They had a trial, but not like this, a peaceful jury of your peers. They called it, in their tough-minded way, trial by ordeal, and the ordeal was, to our more sensitive ears, harsh and difficult and strange. There were four kinds, and let me confess at the outset my ignorance as to how, or by whom, one was chosen. What was common to them all, however, was the belief that, faced with an accusation of an act against the law—or as they used to say, against the peace—a case too difficult for the feeble judgment of men, the only alternative was to leave it in the hands of God.

"The first ordeal was by hot iron." At this phrase, a few of the jurors winced. "It was quite simple. The accused carried a piece of red-hot iron in his hand for nine steps. His hand was then sealed up with a bandage. Three days later the seal was broken, the bandage taken off. If the hand had festered—if it had blistered in any way—he was guilty; if not, he was innocent and free to go. The second ordeal was the same as the first, but instead of hot iron, hot water was used. The arm was plunged into the water to a depth that, oddly enough, depended on the seriousness of the crime: the wrist if relatively minor; the elbow, or the whole arm, if he had been accused of something really awful.

"The third ordeal will strike you as simply ludicrous and completely unfair. It involved not hot water, but cold. The accused was thrown into it and everything depended on what happened next. If he sank—if he drowned—he was innocent; if he floated, he was guilty and must die."

They were shocked, but more than that, amused, at the ignorance and the barbarism of what the Anglo-Saxons had done. Beneath the surface of their expression was a sense of assurance and contentment at how far more civilized we had become.

"If no one walked away from watching that ordeal with any feelings of outrage and disgust, you must remember that they believed in something absolute: God and a life after this one spent in either heaven or hell. Believing that, what better justice than taking home to heaven someone falsely accused of a crime here below?

"That same belief in the active, rigorous judgment of God is just as evident in the fourth ordeal, a trial that without that belief, a trial that if we attempted to do it today, would make it almost impossible to convict anyone of anything. It was called the 'ordeal of the morsel.'"

My hand on the railing, I repeated the phrase, doing nothing to hide my astonished wonder at the power of belief.

"The accused was given a piece of bread or cheese, a single ounce in weight, and he was told to eat it. If he swallowed it, he was innocent; if he choked on it, he was not." I paused and glanced down at the floor. "There was one other thing," I said as I raised my eyes to the jury's waiting gaze. "Before he was given it, the morsel was, in the words of the older treatises on the law, 'solemnly abjured to stick in his throat if guilty.' It makes sense, doesn't it?" I asked as I began to advance toward the other end of the jury box, sliding my hand along the railing as I moved. "If you know you're guilty; if you believe—and I mean believe absolutely, without reservation, without the slightest doubt—that God knows everything you do and holds you, at the risk of your immortal soul, answerable to Himself, then you could not get that morsel down; conscience-stricken, in fear of something more valuable—much more valuable—than your life, you would not be able to help yourself: you'd choke!"

I stopped at the end of the jury box and only slowly and with a show of reluctance, turned around.

"Of course in these more enlightened times we might laugh at what those people—the distant ancestors of our law—believed about what ought to be done with someone accused of committing a crime. It seems to rest on nothing more than superstition, but then, every belief seems a superstition when it is no longer our own."

I had always thought it a mistake to read any part of either an opening statement or a closing argument in a jury trial, or even, for that matter, to refer to a note. How could you convince anyone that you believed what you were saying if you had to look at something written to remind you what you wanted to say? But this time I wanted all the authority I could summon, an ancient source to underscore the single point I was determined to make, the point I had to make if Julian Sinclair was to have any chance at all. From the counsel table, I picked up a faded brown tattered-cover book, opened it to the page I had marked with a slip of paper and read to the jury an abbreviated account of the surprising first reaction to the abolition of trial by ordeal.

"'Doubtless there was a very strong feeling that to try a man by jury, when he had not submitted to be so tried, was thoroughly unjust.'"

With a whimsical glint in my eye, I held the book up, examining the spine as if to remind myself who the author was of this extraordinary claim.

"F. W. Maitland, *The Constitutional History of England,*" I read aloud, my expression solemn and subdued. "One of the greatest legal scholars Britain ever had. The book is made up of the lectures he gave at Cambridge, back in 1887. Now, what is the reason for this 'strong feeling' that forcing someone to trial by jury was 'unjust'?" I turned the page and read some more.

" 'The accused ought to be allowed to demonstrate his innocence by supernatural means, by some such process as the ordeal or the judicial combat; God may be for him, though his neighbors be against him.'

"The 'judicial combat,' I should explain, was something the Normans devised. And if it sounds a little more impartial than those four strange 'ordeals,' it was based on the very same belief. If you were accused of a crime, you had the right to fight to the death with someone chosen by the other side. It was sometimes called an 'appeal to heaven,' because the winner would be decided by God's intervention."

I closed the book and dropped it on the table, and took three steps toward the jury box before I raised my eyes.

"What is Julian Sinclair to do? Appeal to heaven, because all his neighbors have decided him guilty? Choose one of those strange savage ordeals to prove that all those smug faces saying on television that he's guilty have it all wrong? When he testifies in his own defense—and I promise you that though he does not have to, he will—he will swear under oath that he had nothing to do with the death of Daphne McMillan and that he does not know who did. There was a time, hundreds of years ago, when that sworn denial would have been enough; when, as Maitland put it somewhere in those lectures from which I just read, men believed without question in God and eternity, and for that reason 'will not foreswear themselves though they will freely lie.' Lie to each other, lie to themselves, but never, under any circumstances, at the peril of their immortal soul, lie upon an oath."

I took a breath and retreated half a step. "So by all means listen to all the testimony, view carefully all the evidence; but when you sit there watching the defendant, Julian Sinclair, testify, ask yourself if you really believe that this is someone who, even to save his own skin, would, under oath, even think about telling something that was not the truth."

The strange thing was that I believed it, believed that if Julian had done it, actually murdered Daphne McMillan, he would admit it rather than give false testimony in a court of law or, for that matter, anywhere else. A lie was beneath him, the mere thought of it to be treated with contempt. He had too much certainty about his own identity, too much pride in what he had become, to pretend to something he was not. He was not overtly religious, and I cannot honestly say he believed in God. Perhaps he did, though not, I think, in the conventional sense of a supreme being that demanded obedience and listened to prayers. If he believed at all, it was in that unmoved first mover of whom Aristotle and others wrote—a divine perfection that drew toward it those who found some part of that same possibility in themselves. Whatever Julian believed, he believed in honor. How much he believed in it, I would only gradually come to understand.

Julian believed in honor, and I believed in him. It was clear that night, as I sat watching TV in my study, that there were not too many people who believed in either one. Julian was of course still guilty, and after my opening statement, I was seen as something of a fool. With a knowing smirk, Bryan Allen leaned into the camera and in the twisted simplicity of a few caustic words, dismissed what had taken nearly two hours.

"Hot water, cold water—trial by ordeal! The defendant did not do it. Why not? Because he's willing to swear that he did not. Don't you love it—what these lawyers can do!"

Not every lawyer, of course. Some were real credits to the profession. On a channel devoted to nothing but cases in court, a blond, blue-eyed reporter with a dazed, cross-eyed look, could not get over the difference in styles.

"Madelaine Foster—they call her Maddy—stayed right on message, talked only about the facts. Antonelli's histrionics didn't faze her a bit. She's what every lawyer should be: quiet, calm, efficient. Of course, to be fair, unlike Antonelli, she has all the facts on her side."

I switched the channel and found myself watching different faces saying the same thing. My televised appearance on the Allen show, if it had made even that much difference, had only given everyone a chance to catch their breath. My opening statement, like a self-fulfilling prophecy, only taught the lesson that the defense was desperate and that, as they had never really doubted, Julian was guilty.

I could not remember any trial in which I had been as discouraged as this; worried, not just about my client, but what this frenzied rush to judgment, this unconscionable insistence on knowing at the beginning just how things were supposed to end, meant for the country and what I had always believed was its basic sense of fairness. Angry and embarrassed, unwilling to admit that I had only turned the television on to see what they were saying about me, I turned it off, vowing not to watch again.

For an hour or so, I tried to concentrate on the list of witnesses that, starting in the morning, the prosecution would use to make its case. It was little more than an exercise to test my memory, to see how quickly, at the first sight of a name, all the disparate pieces of information that had been assembled, all the things I knew, fell into place. Days, weeks of preparation had gone into getting ready for what might be a cross-examination that lasted only a few minutes at most. Three years of law school and a lifetime of practice, it was the common discipline of anyone who tried cases, but most of those who did it could not cross-examine a tree. The trick was to take the witness, one question at a time; take each thing he said and use it to tell a different story than the one he had. That meant being ready for every answer he might have, anything he might say, and then, on the instant—because you did not get a second chance—your eyes still on him, never leaving his, fire the next question before his voice became an echo in the room. And the only way you could do it was to spend your time doing nothing else. Read, study, think what you can do with each statement the witness will have to make—do it for days and weeks and months. And go a little crazy the closer you get to trial; do it so long, do it so hard, that at the end, you do it in your sleep; so that when you hear yourself asking that first question of the first witness you take on cross, you smile a little to yourself because you have heard yourself ask it so many times before.

I was wide awake and still working at quarter till midnight when Julian called.

"I thought you might still be up."

There was not a sign of strain or tension in his voice. It was as calm, as even-tempered as the first time we had talked, that day when we were both waiting to go on the Bryan Allen show. He had a strange request.

"I was wondering if I might borrow the Maitland book? I've never read it, and I think I should."

That was not the reason, the real reason, he had called.

"I thought what you did today was extraordinary. I don't know of any other lawyer who would have tried it." He paused, an uncomfortable silence that told me he had the same feeling I had, that with this jury, or perhaps any jury, the fight was all uphill.

"The jury followed every word," he began tentatively. "They believed everything you said—about the law and what it meant."

He hesitated, a certain reluctance to go forward; afraid, I think, that he was stepping onto ground where he had no right to go. He understood, better than nearly anyone I had represented, that the lawyer was all alone, that the best thing a client could do to help in his own defense was to answer honestly any question he was asked and try to resist the temptation to ask too many of his own, and never, under any circumstances, begin to offer suggestions about what the lawyer should do.

"They believe you know what you're doing; but they are not ready to believe me, swear it on an oath or not."

I knew that, and he knew that I did. We had spent so much time together in the last several months going through everything that had happened, everything he knew, that we could grasp each other's meaning from the first few words spoken, and sometimes even less than that.

"Daphne's husband," I said in the manner of someone noting an obvious fact.

"That's why she was there that night; why she had come to see me. She was scared to death of him, of what he might do—of what she knew he was capable of doing."

Robert McMillan, rich, respectable, a member of every important charitable organization in San Francisco, a leading light of the city's civic elite; and yet behind the affable exterior of a generous man was something dark and forbidden, twisted, possessive, perverse, deadly and insane. Daphne McMillan had been the victim of it, beaten—abused, locked in dark closets for hours, sometimes days, at a time—and all because of some chance remark that meant nothing, but that quite inexplicably sent him into a rage. Sometimes it was a look, a gesture, innocent in itself, but that in his diseased imagination took on the aspect of an obscenity directed at him. Sometimes it was just a single word about another man, and she was suddenly what he had always known she was: a whore, a harlot, a woman who was going straight to hell.

McMillan was a madman and, I was absolutely certain, a murderer as well. I had no doubt at all that he had killed his wife, but there was not a thing I could do to prove it. The world saw the grieving husband of a murder victim, a man who broke down in tears during the only television interview he gave. Even knowing what I did, I felt a certain sympathy for the suffering in the close-up face that flickered on the screen, until I remembered what he had done and that what I was watching was staged and not one word of it was true.

"I'll have to break him on the stand," I remarked. "Hope he shows something of who he really is. Daphne told you about him, but . . ."

Julian finished the thought. "She was too scared to tell anyone else. No one else would have believed her. He was like Jekyll and Hyde. She told me that—that she sometimes thought he did not remember what he had done; that he could go into a towering rage, do all sorts of unspeakable things, then, next day, it was as if it had never happened. She said his mind was like two different rooms with a door between them. Whichever room he was in was the only room he knew. The other one did not exist."

We said goodbye and I was left to wonder what I was going to do with a witness I was sure was a murderer, but who was so far deranged that he might actually believe it when he denied all knowledge of the crime.

Chapter Eight

CAREFUL AND METHODICAL, Maddy Foster went about the practiced business of proving each element of the crime. There was a death, a murder—we knew that; we knew why we were here—but she still had to prove it.

"Tell us, Dr. Connor," she asked the county coroner, "in your professional opinion, what was the cause of death?"

"Multiple stab wounds, any one of which would have killed her."

There was no change of expression on Maddy Foster's face; no parade of emotions marching with self-righteous fury across her aging, indefatigable eyes. She asked one question, then another; each one driving with a kind of relentless solemnity to her point.

"Multiple; yes, I understand. Be more precise, Dr. Connor. How many?"

Connor, balding and bespectacled, a small lump of a man, shifted his tight-closed mouth back and forth.

"Seventeen . . . at least; perhaps a couple more."

"Any one of which would have killed her?"

Under her serious, questioning gaze, Connor qualified and took back a little of his answer. "Certainly any of the first several. I'd have to say she was dead the moment he finished slashing her throat."

She showed him the butcher knife, marked as an exhibit, and asked him if it fit the nature of the wounds found on the body of Daphne McMillan. Not only was the knife consistent with the depth and width of the injuries inflicted, but the victim's DNA matched the blood found on the blade.

The prosecution had Connor on the stand for nearly two hours; I was finished with him in less than five minutes.

"Dr. Connor, I take it from your testimony—or rather your silence on this point—that there is nothing you can tell us about the order in which the stab wounds were inflicted?"

"No, but I'd guess that—"

"I'm afraid you're not allowed to guess anything, Dr. Connor. But you can answer this: It's possible—is it not?—that the first wound inflicted, which according to your testimony was enough to cause her death, was the one across her throat. Or was that your guess?"

"Yes, I mean—"

"Now, if I remember correctly what you said, that cut was so deep that it sliced the larynx. And that means that she would not have been able to cry out, to scream for help, does it not? No one would have heard her, if, for example, they were sound asleep in a bedroom down the hall?"

Three witnesses and two days later, Foster finally called the detective in charge of the investigation. Earl Duncan sat on the witness stand rubbing the edge of his small black mustache with the back of his index finger. His reply to each question was immediate, automatic, rattled off with the casual efficiency of repetition. Nothing surprised him, nothing could; he knew the crime scene inside out, he had been over every inch of the house. He described the blood spatter on the wall with clinical precision. He had seen blood on the walls, blood on the floor, blood all over the victim: on her hands, on her slashed-to-ribbons clothes, in her hair, her nails, everywhere. He talked about it in a flat, fastidious voice that made it sound even more gruesome because, listening to him, you found yourself thinking that it was somehow normal, routine, the way things must look every day on his job. And once you realized that, you drew back, shocked at how easy it was to be drawn into that world of violence and murder so far removed from you and your everyday life.

"All the blood belonged to the victim?" asked Foster when he was through.

"Yes."

"There was no blood from anyone else?" she asked, giving the impression that it was important he be sure.

"No."

"In other words, no evidence that she had been able to inflict any injury on her attacker?"

"That's correct."

"Anything under her nails?"

"No."

"What about marks on her hands or arms? Cut marks—anything to indicate that she had tried to resist?"

"No. As I said before, it's clear she was overpowered—probably taken by surprise. The first knife wound—I'd say it had to have been the throat—the wound was across the throat, right to left." He hesitated, then shook his head in chagrin. "I'm sorry. It's actually the other way: left to right. The knife was drawn across her throat from the side of the left ear to the right, from behind."

Foster looked at the jury. "So the killer must have been right-handed?"

"I would have to assume that he was."

Foster, dressed in a gray skirt and jacket, walked to a table in front of the clerk. She picked up the same knife she had earlier shown to the coroner.

"This knife has been identified as the murder weapon. Did you find it?"

"Yes, I did."

"Would you please tell the jury where you found it and when?"

Duncan's small suspicious eyes moved in a level arc from Foster to the jury box on his left. He held the knife by the handle, the evidence tag dangling from a string.

"It was on the floor, approximately two feet from the victim's body."

"And to whom does the knife belong?"

"To the defendant," he said, turning just far enough to nod toward Julian Sinclair sitting at the counsel table next to me.

"And how were you able to establish that fact?"

"First, there was a knife missing from the knife block in the kitchen, the largest one, and this one is a perfect match. Second, the defendant admitted it was his."

Maddy Foster lowered her eyes as she moved close to the jury box. Grasping the varnished wooden railing, she raised her eyes, but only to the heavy sharp knuckles of her hand. She seemed fixed on it, as if the intensity of her gaze was somehow necessary to the concentration of her mind.

"Did he also admit he was there, in the house, when she—the victim, Daphne McMillan—was murdered?"

"Yes, he did."

Her head came up; her hand let go of the railing. Broad-shouldered, heavyset, she moved with a kind of firm authority as she headed away from the witness, away from the jury, toward the counsel table the other side of mine. Not two steps from her chair, she stopped. She pulled her shoulders back and slowly turned around.

"One other thing. The only blood you found belonged to the victim." She paused until the last words echoed softly, dying back, and then, with hushed, grim-faced anger asked, "And was any of the dead woman's blood found on him?"

Duncan grabbed the arms of the witness chair and held them tight. "Her blood was on both his hands. He had tried to wash it off, but it was there and it was hers."

Earl Duncan had done everything he was supposed to do and done it right on cue. He never started an answer before she was finished with the question; he always made sure to look at the jury during at least part of his reply. But as soon as the prosecution had finished with him, his attitude changed. He looked at me with contempt, and to show how well prepared he was, started telling me what I was going to ask.

"You want to know why, if he admitted the knife was his, his prints weren't on it? You want to know why he would have wiped it clean; why he would do that instead of just getting rid of the knife? Well, the reason, counselor—"

"Your Honor, would you please inform the witness that he doesn't get to answer his own questions; he has to answer mine."

Twisting around so that Duncan was forced to look him in the eye, Conrad Jarvis settled the matter with a single, ominous word. "Don't." He held him for a moment longer, warning him with his eyes that he meant it and that he would not warn him twice.

Duncan nodded meekly and buried his resentment; and then sat back and watched me with dark, relentless eyes.

"You testified that the defendant admitted that the kitchen knife, the murder weapon, belonged to him?"

"Yes."

"You asked him, and that was his answer?"

"Yes."

"This conversation took place at his home, where you were summoned after a telephone call reporting a murder?"

"Yes."

"Just so we are clear on this point, the call to the police was made by Julian Sinclair—is that correct?"

"That's my understanding," he said with a shrug of indifference meant to be irritating.

I did not move from my spot at the side of the counsel table, directly in front of him and not more than ten feet away. The jury box was three feet to my right.

"Your 'understanding'? Do you have any reason to think that call was made by someone else?"

"No."

"When you arrived, Julian Sinclair was waiting for you outside—correct?"

"Yeah," replied Duncan, shifting position like someone so bored he had to give himself something to do.

"And I was there with him, wasn't I?"

"You were there." The lines in his forehead cut deeper; a look of wasted time wrinkled his mouth.

"How many homicide investigations have you been involved in during your career, Detective Duncan?" I asked, my voice rising. "One, two . . . ?"

He did not like that, he did not like it at all. He uncrossed his legs, planted both feet on the floor and, with his elbows on the arms of the chair, bent forward at the waist.

"This is the eighty-third." His voice was calm, firm, confident. "I have three more that are in progress, which makes eighty-six."

"Then you're well aware that no one can be compelled against his will to talk to the police. You're certainly aware, as we all are, of those famous Miranda warnings that a police officer has to give someone once they're in custody before—"

"He wasn't in custody. He wasn't arrested until some time later, after he talked to me at the scene of the murder, at his house. You were there, you know—"

"I know that he answered every question you asked, Detective Duncan. Isn't that true?" I asked, staring back into his narrow, hostile eyes. "Now, indulge me—the defendant answered your questions; it's your turn to answer mine. Or do I need to ask the judge a second time to tell you what to do? Good. Now, tell me this: You agree that he had the right not to talk to you—whether or not he was under arrest?"

"Yes."

"He teaches law—at Berkeley, Boalt Hall?"

"Yes."

"Teaches not only criminal law, but criminal procedure?"

"That's my understanding."

"He probably knows as much as any lawyer—perhaps even as much as any police officer—the right he has under the Constitution not to talk to the police. Would you agree?"

"Yes."

"And, as you've already testified, I was there, standing right next to him. Now, whatever you may think of me personally, or whatever you may think of defense lawyers as a class, would I sound too arrogant if I suggested that I was also reasonably well informed about a defendant's right to remain silent, not to answer any questions at all?"

"Sure, I suppose."

"So that we all understand this: It's your testimony that despite the fact that the defendant knew he did not have to talk to you; despite the fact that another lawyer was standing right next to him and could have advised him not to talk to you—the defendant did talk to you. Not only that, he answered every question you asked. Is that correct?"

"He answered the questions I asked. That doesn't mean the answers were honest, or that I believed him."

"Yes, well, we'll come back to what you believe and why you

believe it, in a moment," I said as I moved around the corner and began to pace up and down in front of the counsel table.

"The blood on his hands—the blood you said he tried to wash off." I stopped, looked up. "He told you he had done that, didn't he?"

Before he could answer, I fired another question and another one after that.

"He told you that he had woken up, found the body lying there in the living room, blood all around—didn't he? Told you that his first, his only, thought was to see if by some miracle she might still be alive? That he felt for a pulse, that when there wasn't one, he was overcome with grief, grabbed her, held her close? That only later, when he started coming back to his senses, he let her down where she lay, and got himself cleaned up? He told you that—all of it—isn't that true?"

"That's what he said."

"Then the answer is yes. Now, Detective Duncan, the question you wanted to take up at the beginning, before I had had a chance to ask you any of my own—he admitted the knife was his; not only that, he showed you, in my presence, the precise location where it was kept in the kitchen, correct?"

"Yes, he did."

I had moved to the far end of the jury box, farthest from the witness.

"The knife, the murder weapon—no fingerprints were found on it, correct?"

"Yes, that's right. It was wiped clean."

"You say that—wiped clean—because if the murderer of Daphne McMillan had, for example, worn gloves, there would still be the fingerprints of anyone who had used that knife before, isn't that right?"

"Yes, that's right."

My hand slid along the railing as I took a step forward.

"It wouldn't have been difficult to get rid of that knife, would it? Lose it somewhere in the Berkeley hills, or drop it somewhere in the bay?"

"No, it wouldn't be difficult."

"But the knife, I believe you testified, was found two feet from the body. Curious, isn't it? You've investigated—what?—eighty-six homicides. Wouldn't you say that was a bit unusual—murder someone like that, slash her to ribbons in what must have been a rage, in your own home? Then, not only leave the body there, but leave the knife? Leave the knife, but wipe off the fingerprints, the fingerprints that everyone would expect to be there, because, after all, the knife was his, wasn't it? Then do what? Why go back to bed, sleep from midnight—which is the approximate time that, according to the coroner, Daphne McMillan was murdered—until six in the morning and then, instead of trying to hide the evidence of your crime, call the police and answer all their questions. Tell us, Detective Duncan, in all your years as a homicide detective, among all the eighty-six murders you have investigated, have you ever come across anything so extraordinary as this?"

Maddy Foster had risen from her chair. Instead of shouting an outraged objection, she waited, silent and patient, until Judge Jarvis raised his hand to stop me and then looked at her.

"The defense, quite properly, enjoys considerable latitude during a murder trial in what it can do on cross. We don't object to that. However, I wonder whether Mr. Antonelli may not have strayed a bit too far?"

Her voice was calm, dispassionate, the voice of reason that never thinks of its own advantage. It made me look overzealous, and by comparison made her look fair. Jarvis did not say a word: he looked at me in a way that left no doubt that he agreed that, in the heat of the moment, I had forgotten that I was there to ask questions and not to give speeches.

Unbuttoning my suit coat, I plunged my hands deep into my pants pockets, squared my shoulders and lowered my head. I stared hard at Duncan until the smirk at the corner of his thin-lipped mouth disappeared.

"Julian Sinclair told you why she had come there that night, did he not? Told you that Daphne McMillan was scared to death of her husband, that she was leaving him, that she was not going back?"

Earl Duncan cocked his head. His eyes were cold, hard, cynical—the look of a man who thought that no one ever told the truth before you first caught them in a lie.

"That's what he said."

"He told you she arrived a little after nine in the evening, frantic, scared; that they talked until sometime around eleven-thirty, when he went to bed."

"That's what he said."

"That she was going to spend the night in the guest room, but that she said she wanted to stay up for a while?"

"They were having an affair," Duncan lashed out, his eyes angry, intense. "Why would she be sleeping in the guest room? Why would he be sleeping alone?" he demanded as he shot a disgusted look at Julian Sinclair sitting undisturbed in the second chair at the counsel table.

"They were having an affair! And the evidence for that is what, Detective Duncan? The statement of her husband, the man she had decided to leave? When you went to talk to him—you did talk to Robert McMillan, didn't you?—did you ask him about the stories of abuse, about the things he did to her?"

Duncan had inched his way forward until he was sitting at the very edge of the witness chair. His temples were throbbing, the blue veins on the back of his hands as he gripped the chair coursing thick and fast.

"Have you ever had to tell a man his wife has been slaughtered? Have you ever had to ask someone to come down to the morgue to identify a body after something like that? But yes, I asked him. I asked him why his wife would have been there, at the defendant's home, up in the Berkeley hills, late at night like that. He told me they had had some difficulties in the marriage; that they had tried a separation; that she had started seeing Sinclair; but that they had decided to try again, to make the marriage work. She had gone there that evening to tell Sinclair that it was over; that she was not going to see him anymore. She was going back to her husband; she was breaking off the affair."

There was a vicious look of vindication in his eyes, absolute certainty that he had destroyed any chance I may have had to blame the murder on someone else.

"So he knew she was there, at Julian Sinclair's house in the Berkeley hills. But that means that he knew where he could find her, doesn't it? I mean," I added with a little vindication of my own, "if he was lying and Julian Sinclair had all along been telling you the truth."

Robert McMillan was the prosecution's last witness. Maddy Foster made sure that the jury understood that, just like them, he had his failures and his weaknesses.

"There was a considerable difference in your age, wasn't there, Mr. McMillan? Your wife was in her twenties, you were in your fifties, when you married. Did this cause difficulty in the marriage?"

Robert Mandeville McMillan prided himself on his appearance. An avid tennis player, a scratch golfer, he was remarkably fit. He had a straight nose and a firm chin, high cheekbones that gave a faintly arrogant aspect to his face, and the most domineering pair of eyes I think I have ever seen. They were bluish-gray in color, with the texture of something almost metallic that, instead of drawing light inward, reflected it away; drove it, if you were looking at him, back on you. Whether it was that, or the angle at which he held his oval-shaped head, he managed to convey the impression that he was looking down at you. He was distant, unapproachable; but so polished and well mannered, so fastidious in his language, so polite, that it took some time before you were convinced that your first instinct had been right and that below the surface of all that well-bred charm there was something truly evil. Of all the witnesses I have ever faced in court, Robert McMillan was the most difficult. I knew he had killed his wife, and we both knew I could not prove it.

Prove it? I could not get anyone to so much as think it possible. Robert McMillan a murderer? It was too absurd. No one who watched him on the witness stand; who listened to his trembling voice recount all his own emotions when he was told that his wife—his beautiful young wife—was dead; who saw the tears start in his eyes and the grim determined look with which he drove them back and held himself in check, would ever believe that he was capable of that.

"Did it cause some difficulties in the marriage?" repeated Maddy Foster in a quiet, sympathetic voice when he continued to gaze out at the crowd with a confused, troubled expression, as if he was not quite certain why he was there or what good he could do, now that it was too late and his wife was gone.

"Yes, I'm sorry," he said, blinking his eyes. "Yes, there were difficulties. I'm not sure all of them were because of that, but I'm sure some of them were. She was young; she needed to do things with friends her own age. She liked to go dancing, out to places with loud music and big crowds; things, I'm afraid, I didn't have that much interest in doing. And I made the mistake of thinking that she'd be content with doing them just once in a while. Of course, what she thought was once in a while, I thought rather too often." He forced a thin, apologetic smile. "Things like that."

"Beyond a difference in taste with respect to forms of entertainment, was there any difference in terms of the respective needs for intimate relations?"

For the first time, that carefully guarded façade seemed to crumble. His eyes, gray and impenetrable, flared with something close to anger. His voice, however, remained as calm, as wistful, as lonely, as ever.

"If you're referring to our sex life, it was always satisfactory."

There was no change of expression on Maddy Foster's face, but I had a feeling that it was not the answer that she had expected. Had he told her that the problems in the marriage had included something to do with sex? He could not possibly have told her the kinds of things that Daphne had told Julian, and that Julian had told me.

"But at some point she had an affair?"

"Yes, with Julian Sinclair. Apparently, it went on for a number of months. I didn't know anything about it, until she told me. We were separated for a while. That's when it started. She wanted me to know, she said, because she wanted us to start over with a clean slate, and that meant that there were not going to be any secrets. She told me that she was going to break off the affair, and that she was going to do it right away, that very night."

"When—exactly when—did she tell you this?"

"That day—at lunch. I had a business trip. I was in Los Angeles overnight." With a grim, anguished expression, he added, "We had made plans. We were going to spend the next week at our place in Santa Barbara."

That explained, or appeared to explain, why he had not known until he was called by the police that his wife had not come home that night. Or did it?

"Your wife told you that day, at lunch, about her affair. Did I understand that correctly?" I asked as I rose slowly from my chair.

McMillan lifted his chin. "Yes."

"The same time—the same conversation—in which she told you she wanted to make the marriage work?"

I tried to make it sound routine, just a few questions to clarify any possible ambiguity. I fumbled with the button on my coat, finally got it through, raised my head and gave him a hard, searching glance.

"She told you all that—this affair she wanted to end so she could start her life all over with you—and the first thing you do is fly off to L.A., where you're going to stay overnight? Is that a fair measure of the intimate nature of your married life?"

Maddy Foster saw it before it was even there; she had seen it once before. She was on her feet, the sweet voice of reason vanished, gone.

"Objection!" she exclaimed in tones of wounded aggravation. "That isn't a question; that's an insult, and it should not be allowed!"

Jarvis bent forward, concentrating hard. He held his forefinger straight and rigid directly in front of his barely opened mouth.

"No, perhaps the tone was a little condescending, and in that sense, not appropriate," he said with a quick sidelong glance at me; "but the question itself is fair. Overruled," he said, nodding to himself, as he drew his arms back from the bench.

"It did not occur to you—after what you say she said—that you ought to cancel the trip and stay with her?" I asked incredulously.

He dismissed it without apology, as something almost beneath notice. In the world in which he lived, obligations had to be met. She was the one who had had the affair, the one who now wanted him back; he had a prior scheduled appointment—the rest could wait.

"It was an important business meeting. I had no choice."

"On a Saturday?"

"Yes."

I knew about the meeting; I had checked.

"The meeting was over by six."

"I had other things I had to do."

"You were married twice before?"

"Yes."

"The first marriage ended in divorce?"

"I'm afraid so."

"There was a rather unusual provision in the divorce settlement, wasn't there? A provision under which your ex-wife agreed never to talk about the marriage, or the reasons for the divorce?"

He made a show of indifference. "Whatever the terms of the agreement, it's something the lawyers did."

"I see. Your second marriage—that did not end in divorce. Your second wife was killed; an automobile accident, I believe?"

He threw an irritated glance at Judge Jarvis, as if he expected him to intervene.

"Yes, that's true. She died in an accident. It was a terrible thing."

"Yes, I agree. Drove off a cliff, in the middle of the afternoon, no one else around."

"Your Honor!" Foster was on her feet, both hands on the table in front of her. But all Jarvis did was to motion with his hand that I should hurry up and get to the point, if there was one.

"You paid a lot of money to buy the silence of one woman, and the next one died; but Daphne told, didn't she? Told about the violence, the cruel, unspeakable things you did to her, the ugly perversions that are the only way you can get aroused. That's why she was leaving you; that's why she ran to her friend, to Julian Sinclair, the one man she knew she could trust—not to tell him she was through with him, but to tell him that, finally, whatever it cost, she was through with you!"

Robert McMillan came straight up from the chair, enraged, shouting his denials while, right behind me, Maddy Foster thundered her objections.

"And that's why you did it—why you killed her—why you pounded that knife into her over and over again! Because you couldn't have her, and because with what she knew about you she could ruin you anytime she wanted! That's why you murdered her!" I yelled over the gavel pounding and the deafening courtroom noise. "Because she had the guts to leave!"

Chapter Nine

MY SHOELACE BROKE. It was surprising how such a little thing threw me so far off, made a bad mood even worse. I was a creature of habit, always getting dressed the same way whenever I had to wear a suit. Shorts, then a shirt; and when that was buttoned down the front, starting with the second button first, I did the cuffs. I put on my socks, first the right one, then the left; followed by my pants. When my belt was buckled shut, I put on a tie. It was easy, automatic; I had been doing it for years, I could have done it in my sleep: the tie, the shoes, then the coat. Put the right shoe on first, tie it; then the left. I was sitting on the edge of the chair, my left ankle on my knee, pulling the laces tight, when it happened, when it snapped right in two. I did not have another one; all I could do was tie the two pieces together—make a knot, push it as best I could underneath the laces—and hope it would not show.

I kept swearing at it, swearing at myself, down the elevator and across the cool cement garage floor; knowing all along that if it had not been the shoelace it would have been something else. I was angry; angry at Albert Craven, though he had done nothing wrong; angry at Harry Godwin, the firm's biggest client, though we had not yet met;

angry at television, angry at the trial, angry at the world. When I reached the car, I threw both arms forward and kicked the front tire as hard as I could. Swearing at myself, I tried to rub away the dirty smudge now left on my shoe. I got in the car and began to laugh. It was Saturday night and I was on my way to the Four Seasons Hotel. So what if instead of a beautiful woman, I was having dinner with two old men? I laughed and swore some more.

Harry Godwin had come all the way from Sydney to see me. I did not believe that, but then I did not need to. That was the way it had been put to Albert Craven, and that did not leave me any real choice. By this time I was curious anyway about what Harry Godwin was really like: whether he was the man of Thomas Hobbes's much quoted description, whose life was that "quest for power after power that ceaseth only in death"; or whether, beneath that surface of endless calculation, there was more worth knowing.

I wondered if it had made him a little crazy that no matter how much money they offered Julian Sinclair for an exclusive interview, he kept saying no. It had made me a little crazy that none of the producers and executives, none of the publishers and magazine editors, none of the many people who represented different parts of Harry Godwin's far-flung interests seemed able to understand that the only place Julian Sinclair was going to tell his story was in court, a witness in his own defense. They had offered him finally something well into seven figures. When he would not take it, they started talking to me.

"The answer is no," I said when Harry Godwin began to broach the subject over a drink. The bar and restaurant was crowded with out-of-town visitors and busy, bright faces, the usual well-heeled Four Seasons crowd. Our table was ready, but Harry liked it where we were, at a small table half-hidden by the baby grand piano at which a tuxedo-dressed pianist played an unobtrusive Cole Porter tune.

"We'll be a half hour or so," he remarked, barely lifting his eyes as he sent the maître d' away. Nursing a martini, he looked back at me. His eyes were blue, like Albert Craven's, but at least two shades paler, and without any of Albert's intense curiosity. That was my first, surprising impression: that lack of anything unusual in his eyes; that sense that he was ordinary, average, prosaic. Harry Godwin had no interest, no serious interest, in anything beyond what he did. Everything was put in terms of that. Music, books, painting, the theater—the arts in general—was a resource required to feed the insatiable demand for entertainment. If someone had mentioned the paintings of El Greco, his mind would have moved immediately to the question whether the network had done a show on him and what the ratings had been.

He ignored my answer, dismissed it with a shopkeeper's smile, as he ordered a second martini and began to tell me the things he was certain I did not understand.

"I watched your two appearances, watched them several times on tape. You bring a certain quality the others don't have. It's hard to say what it is. We've had focus groups watch as well. They trust you: maybe it's your face, your manner, the way you carry yourself, the way you speak your words. They wouldn't make a judgment on what any of the others said: they wanted to hear what you said first. Didn't mean they agreed with it, or even liked it; but you have a kind of authority they respect."

There was not much left of Harry Godwin's accent; he lived so many places, spent so much of his time here, that you had to listen carefully to know he was not a native. He drank, however, as only an Australian can: slowly, steadily, one after the other, all evening long, and without any effect you could notice. I could not drink as much water as Harry Godwin drank gin.

"And in that second show, the one you did alone with Bryan Allen, you more than held your own. Held your own! You demolished that stupid son of a bitch! Of course, he's too dumb to know it, and so is most of his audience. That's why they watch him; it's why we put him on: He says what they think and they pretty much think what he says."

He caught the skepticism in my eye, the doubt that it could be as simple as that.

"It's not an act: he's exactly what you see. This isn't university; he isn't hired to give a lecture on physics—this is mainstream America and this is TV. I don't know why people think it should be—or could be—something else. And besides, it's not as hopeless as you might think."

He gave me a glance that he must have used countless times before, the look that told someone they were different, special.

"What we want to do hasn't been done before, but it's going to happen sooner or later. And I'm sure Albert would agree," he said with a sidelong glance at Craven sitting with a blank expression at the side of the table between us, "that it would set the highest possible standard if it started with you."

"You want me to go on television before I give my summation to the jury and give it on the air, argue the case on television?"

"The jury is sequestered. They won't know. And you won't be doing it alone. It will be just like doing it in court. You make your argument—why Sinclair didn't do it; the prosecution makes its argument—why he did."

It was more than some aberration: it was insane.

"That ends it right there. Even if I was willing—which I'm not—Maddy Foster won't do it. She can't."

Harry Godwin put the thin-tapered glass down on the table. Scratching his chin, he bent his head to the side and seemed to ponder the point.

"People have checked on this. It isn't that clear that she couldn't. There isn't any specific rule that says she can't."

"She won't."

He insisted it did not matter. "We have a long list of former prosecutors eager to do it. It's a public trial; everyone is following it. We have people there in the courtroom every day. It won't be hard to make the kind of argument any good prosecutor would make."

"Then you can do the same thing with the defense."

I said this to make final my refusal, thinking that he would realize that none of it made sense and that he would let the matter drop. But he did not bat an eyelash: He agreed that I was right and that they could easily get someone to take my place.

"But we'd rather have you than find someone to play the part. It's a little more authentic; and, as I said before, you have that quality not many of the others have. Everyone is after reality, and everyone is following this trial. There are already shows that use real people—lawyers, judges, witnesses, juries—and this is just the next step in that progression. It's important to catch that first wave, ride it as far as you can take it. Someone will, why not you? It's all set; everything is ready. We're going to do it in a courtroom just like the one you're in. We have a jury, we have a judge; we'll have someone to play Foster's part. And, if we have to, we'll have someone play your part as well."

"What then, after the closing arguments? Are you going to have your fake jury decide whether Julian Sinclair lives or dies?"

I could have asked him the time for all the change of expression. This was nothing more than a programming detail, in principle no different than cutting out a character the audience did not like.

"There will be two numbers the audience can call: one to acquit, the other to convict. They can also vote on the Internet. We'll announce the winner—the defense or the prosecution—and then we'll see if that agrees with the actual verdict in the case. Audience participation is a very effective device. Wouldn't you like to see what the public thinks?"

I shot a glance at Albert Craven, but he was studiously examining the amber liquid in his glass.

"No, I would not," I said, more amused than offended at this strange addiction to giving an audience anything that would make it come back again, in even larger numbers, for what he could show them. He was going to reduce the single most serious public deliberative proceeding—a trial in which one citizen was charged with the murder of another—to a spectacle with as little dignity and sense of importance as professional wrestling or some other mindless escape.

Again it did not faze him; he just ignored it. He ordered another drink.

"After the trial is over," he began as if instead of saying no, I had said yes, "I'd like to talk with you about doing something more permanent with us. We have too many people talking about court cases who haven't spent much time in court. We're thinking of a series— something about famous trials. We'd like to talk to you about helping put it together, choosing the trials we re-create, and about hosting the series. One of the trials we've thought about doing is one of yours."

We got through dinner without any more discussion about the closing courtroom scene he wanted to broadcast before the scene had taken place. He did not seem disturbed that I had turned him down, much less that I had made that refusal emphatic. Harry Godwin never got angry; he was too sure of himself and of his ability to anticipate the direction in which things were headed, to become upset with those who would soon be trying to catch up.

"What you said the other day," said Godwin over an after-dinner drink, "when you had Robert McMillan on the stand. Do you really think he did it? Murdered his wife?"

His eyes were serious, immediate. It was not a question that I had to answer: he could tell from the look I gave him that I had meant it.

He nodded, lowered his eyes, took a long, slow sip and then looked at me again.

"It wouldn't surprise me. McMillan can be a violent man . . . around women."

He said it with such assurance, not the way one would relate something heard secondhand, but as if he knew it directly.

"We did some business in the past," he explained. A grim smile made a brief appearance at the corners of his mouth. "Come to Sydney—after the trial. There's a woman in my organization who can tell you a thing or two about Robert McMillan."

I was staring at him, hard, intense. Julian Sinclair was on trial for his life, every network commentator—none of them with more self-righteous indignation than Harry Godwin's own—telling the world he was guilty; and Godwin is telling me in private that because of something that happened to a woman who works for him, he would not be surprised if Daphne McMillan had been killed by her husband instead?

"It happened in Sydney, five years ago. McMillan was there on business, meeting with some of my people. She—the woman I mentioned—took him to dinner. It was a professional courtesy, nothing more. He made advances; she resisted. He got angry, started to push her around. It got quite ugly. He hit her, hit her hard, tore off her dress; might have raped her if someone hadn't come along."

"But Harry!" Craven protested. "If Joseph had known about this before, he might have been able to use her as a witness!"

Godwin did not see how. The woman lived in Sydney; she was an Australian, not an American; the trial had nothing to do with her. Besides, he had not known that what McMillan had done to her was part of a pattern, a long history of abuse, until those questions had been asked in yesterday's cross-examination.

"What he did with her wouldn't be admissible anyway, would it? He isn't the one on trial."

"Admissible for impeachment," I replied. "Once he denied he had ever used violence on a woman, I could put a woman on the stand who is in a position to say he has."

I asked for her name, but Godwin brushed it off with the vague assertion that there was no reason for her to become involved. I pressed him harder. He insisted that as an Australian national she could not be called as a witness: an American court had no power to force her and she would never do it on her own. She was a married woman, he said, invoking the same morality his network routinely mocked in others, and had a right to her privacy.

"But this is all academic anyway, isn't it? I said I wouldn't be surprised if McMillan was the killer because I think he's quite capable of murder; but that doesn't change any of the facts of the case. And the facts, unfortunately, all point to your client, don't they? You'll have to forgive me, but from where I sit your Mr. Sinclair looks to be in quite a bit of trouble."

"Those facts," I replied, trying hard for Albert's sake to keep control of myself, "mean nothing by themselves. Do you think if the jury knew half of what Robert McMillan has done—if I could have found just one woman willing to tell the truth about him—it would mean anything except that McMillan killed his wife? You knew this about him—forget whether this woman who works for you could be compelled to testify—you knew he beat her, that he would have raped her. Why didn't any of these eager investigative reporters of yours ever look into any of that? Why did they spend all their time calling Julian Sinclair guilty, instead of finding out what they could about what Daphne McMillan's husband had done?"

We were not in court, there was no jury; Harry Godwin did not have to answer to me. He did not answer to anyone. With that same vacant commercial smile, he assured me that, first, as he had just told me, he had only just made the connection; and, second, while he ran the business, he did not get involved in the day-to-day specifics—he did not have the time.

"I'd like it very much if you would reconsider my offer. I know you won't," he added with a shrewd glance. "I just want you to know that I think you would be terrific. And I meant what I said: Come to Sydney when this is over and we'll talk at length about what you can do. I'm open to pretty much anything, so give it some thought: what you think we ought to do, what you would personally feel comfortable with. I agree that most of the people we have doing this sort of thing are charlatans and worse, self-promoting fools I would not have represent me on a bet. You could make things better. I'm sure you could. And I was not lying—what I said a moment ago: I don't get involved in day-to-day operations. You come up with an idea for a show, it's yours—I won't interfere; and I can assure you, no one else will either. You can count on it. Ask Albert here: what Harry Godwin says he'll do, Harry Godwin does. So come to Sydney. It will be my pleasure to show you all around."

We rose from the table and I said goodbye. Albert gave me a strange look and started to laugh.

"Good grief, Antonelli; your shoelace is broken. Careful you don't stumble and break your neck."

WHEN I GOT HOME, I took the elevator from the garage; but when I reached my floor, I changed my mind and rode it back down to the lobby. Out in the street, the cool night air cleared my mind. I went across to the small hilltop park, found a vacant bench and tried to forget everything except what I heard and saw all around me. Laughing voices floated vague and voluptuous from the great hotels—the Fairmont and the Mark Hopkins—a few short blocks away. For all its elegance, all its wizardry and wealth, San Francisco on a Saturday night was still a shore-leave sailor's drunken dream, a flashy, hot-eyed woman who might take all his money, but give him the best time he had ever had.

The city had practically been founded on a total lack of inhibition: men came from all over to find gold and get rich, and then spent it in the brothels and bars that lined the first dirt streets. The bars were quieter now, more sedate; and the women rich men wanted were not quite so often the ones they could hire for an hour or for the night. The commercial transactions, the unspoken premise on which more than one marriage began, were more subtle, and perhaps more shrewd. Daphne McMillan had not sold her young body for money; but neither had she married the much older Robert McMillan for anything as honest and uncomplicated as love. She was a breathtakingly gorgeous young woman, and ambitious besides. In a city like San Francisco, to say nothing of New York, beautiful and well-educated young women could tell the world, and even on occasion themselves, that older men who had done something with their lives were more interesting than men who were just starting out and who might, or might not, do something interesting with their own. Everyone was in a hurry to get ahead; what better way to get there than with the advice and counsel of someone who not only loved you but knew something about the road you had to travel and the people who were guarding each gate.

The fog was rolling in. I turned up the collar of my suit coat and pulled it close around my throat. Far off in the distance, the burning lights of Berkeley stretched from the bay's black waters to the dark hills stamped against the eastern sky. Somewhere near the top, the lights where Julian Sinclair lived at least a little longer, flickered with the rest. I wondered how often Daphne McMillan had watched that way in the night, searching for that single light, indistinguishable from all the others, the other side of Berkeley, the other side of the bay. She did not live that far from here, near the top of Russian Hill, almost the first place in the city to see the morning sun.

I wondered what she had thought, about Julian and what he meant to her. She must have been in love with him, but Julian . . . ? He was a throwback, out of touch with his time; he possessed the kind of gallantry that would not permit him to make advances to a woman who was still married to another man.

They could be friends—and they were: better friends than most married couples would ever be; they could spend the night together—and they sometimes did—but always it was, if you believed him, not just innocent, but in some marvelous, quite unexpected way, almost chaste. They shared a bed; he touched her hand; he held her close. They never did more than that. Did he want to? Was it difficult, near impossible, to hold back, to control the urge? The way he talked about those times he had with her, I was almost afraid to ask. There was something almost obscene in the suggestion that not everyone would have behaved the same way.

It was not that he had never been with a woman, or that he had some fear of sex; he did not share any of the moral or religious principles that taught that sex without marriage was a vice or a sin. He knew all about making love with women and, as he admitted quite candidly, he liked it when he did. It was just that he did not think about it very often and, after he had done it, he did not think about it at all. He compared the desire with hunger or thirst, something that, having satisfied it, you went back to what you were doing, what was really important in your life. There was a difference, of course, between hunger and thirst, on the one hand, and sex on the other, though not the difference that most people would have thought of first. Sex, Julian shrewdly noted, was a desire that, if you learned to ignore it, would eventually pass. What did Julian Sinclair think about sex? For the most part, he forgot it.

"I discovered very early—at the beginning, so to speak," he remarked with a burst of candor one of the first times we talked, "that as soon as it was over, all I wanted was to get away, to be left alone. It isn't fair, I know it: to leave a girl with the feeling that you lost all interest in her the moment you were through. But sex is a need—a kind of tyrant in the soul—that once it has you, if you let it, won't let go. It's a little like getting drunk: when you wake up in the morning, the last thing you think about is another drink.

"The psychiatrists, the psychologists—the kind of people who can't understand anyone except as the representative of a type—would tell you, I imagine, that it is an attitude indicative of a man caught in the angel-whore dilemma. It seems not to occur to anyone that the whole notion of the supposedly intimate connection between love and sex is itself a completely artificial creation. Sex as an expression of love? I really rather doubt it. I loved Daphne; I always will. Do I regret that we never made love? Not for a minute. Would I have slept with her if she hadn't been married? Yes; without question, and right away. And if I ever married anyone, I would have married her. But she was married to someone else, and there are some things you just don't do. I didn't spend my days, or my nights, dreaming about what she would be like in bed; but that doesn't mean that I ever doubted that she would be all I wanted and more. She was the best friend—the only friend—I had; and now she's gone, and I miss her and nothing that we didn't do could make me miss her more. It might even, in some strange way, have made me miss her less. That's how much I loved her; that's how much she loved me. How did she give that expression? Every time she looked at me, I saw it in her eyes. Was I in love with her?" A smile, wistful and full of regret, moved bravely over his mouth. "Perhaps, or perhaps it was something even more than that."

I looked back across the bay, searching vainly the distant candle-light hills. She must have looked across, each night from Russian Hill, wondering perhaps if she really understood him, and whether it could ever work. The things she wanted, the ambition that drove her; the reason why she married whom she had—what did Julian Sinclair have to do with any of that? She must have understood that for all the encouragement he may have given her, the things she prized had no meaning for him. A part of her would have admired that, the way he stood above the things that others strove for; but another part of her must have thought that he was also, in some fashion, looking down on her. She was too much a modern woman not to wonder how long before what she now saw as detachment she would start to see as contempt. When she was with him, when they were alone, talking in candid whispers about how things could be, I imagine she forgot all those reservations, lost all thought of the future in what she felt, what they both felt, right now.

Or so it seemed to me; but then, as I reminded myself while I headed home, all I knew, or thought I knew, was only guesswork. I had met her only once, and had not liked her; thought her much too glib and far too ambitious with her flashing smile, waiting with breathless anticipation to make some new provocative remark. It tasted a little too much like cheap revenge to wonder what she would have thought about the misplaced outrage now directed at the man she loved, wrongly accused of her murder; but I could not help myself: I did it anyway.

Chapter Ten

"THE DEFENSE CALLS Julian Sinclair."

The silence in the courtroom was heavy, profound; not a breath taken in or let out. Instead of a trial, you would have thought all these tight-packed spectators were witness to an execution.

Julian raised his hand and swore the oath. He started toward the witness chair, hesitated, turned and took a long look around, as if he wanted to impress upon his mind the moment his trial began. The other witnesses, everything they had said; the different exhibits entered into evidence—those were things that other people did. And whether they had told the truth, or whether, like Daphne's husband, they had lied, it might affect the jury's verdict, but it could not affect who he was and what he wanted to be. I do not know whether he believed that what he had to say would change anyone's mind. All I know is that it did not matter. He could not help what anyone believed, only what he did. He took the stand, and with his head held high, sat forward, waiting for me to begin. I started with the only question that mattered.

"Did you, or did you not, murder Daphne McMillan?"

"I did not."

He said it with such confidence, such serenity of expression, that I was tempted to stop right there. Julian was telling the truth; it was obvious on the face of it—no one could look like that and lie. Perhaps I should have done it, but I did not trust my instinct: the risk was just too great. I moved closer, ready with the next question.

"How long had you known her, Daphne McMillan?"

"We first met when we were both working in the district attorney's office in San Francisco."

"Would you describe to the jury the nature of your relationship?"

I moved off to the side, watching the faces of the five men and seven women who would soon decide whether the young man talking to them was a murderer or not. They seemed puzzled. He was not what they had expected; though precisely what they had expected they probably could not have said. But they clearly found it odd that someone accused of what was tantamount to slaughter, could look them straight in the eye—never once look away—and talk with such calm intelligence about what he felt.

For the first time, I began to think Julian Sinclair might have a chance. I had practiced law more than half my life; been in more courtrooms than I could count; seen—or so I thought—everything there was to see, but I had never seen anything even remotely close to this. He was looking right at them and he was talking to himself; holding them, entranced, while he spoke out loud the dialogue within. It was like watching an actor who, from the moment he comes onstage, dominates the scene. Standing there, just a few feet away, I had become a character of such secondary importance that I could have left the courtroom, let the doors swing shut behind me, and no one—not the judge, not the crowd, certainly not the jury—would have noticed that I had gone. When he finally finished, told them how they had been friends from the beginning, and how that friendship had gradually turned to love, I had almost forgotten why I was there.

"You loved her, and she loved you; but you remained friends only—nothing more?"

Julian leaned forward. His golden brown hair, long at the collar, glistened in the light, making him look even younger than his years.

"She was married. Nothing was going to happen while she was. Her life was complicated enough. It was important—important for her—that she not have to lie; that she could tell the truth when she was accused of infidelity." He paused, a grim expression in his eyes. "She was often accused of things like that—and worse."

"By her husband?"

"Yes," replied Julian, his eyes flashing. "She wanted to leave him; she had tried to leave him before. That night—the night she died— she had already decided that she was not going back. She was tired of being afraid."

"Afraid? But she was an intelligent, well-educated woman; a lawyer, a prosecutor in the San Francisco district attorney's office. If she wanted to leave her husband, why did she not just file for divorce? If he threatened her with violence, she certainly knew how to get a court order to make him stay away from her. We've already heard testimony from her husband that for a time they had been separated. Why would she have been afraid?"

A bitter smile lent a tragic cast to Julian's expression as he shook his head in self-reproach.

"That's what I kept telling her: that she could go to court, get a restraining order—call the police the first time he came too close. She told me about all the women she had seen brutalized by men who were under court orders to leave them alone. She told me that nothing could stop him when he became enraged. I knew about some of the things he had done to her already: locking her in closets, leaving her there for days at a time, making her think she was going to die. I should have known she was right; that he'd never let her go, that he'd kill her the way she said he had done before!"

The dull noise of the crowd began to gather, getting ready to explode. With a single, baleful glance, Conrad Jarvis forced it back into a dying, dim murmur. His reddish brown freckled eyes moved immediately to Maddy Foster, tall and patient, waiting to make her objection.

"Hearsay," she said, her husky voice all the more effective for not being much more than a hushed whisper.

"State of mind," I retorted with a quick, dismissive glance back over my shoulder. It was one of the law's subtle distinctions, in this case the difference between what Daphne McMillan believed—why she might have been in a state of fear—and whether it was true.

Jarvis thought about it. He looked at the jury and explained what they could, and could not, do with what they had just heard.

"The statement by the witness about what Daphne McMillan said to him is hearsay: what someone tells you someone else said to him. The law allows hearsay into evidence, but only when it falls within one of the well-established exceptions to the rule against it. One of those is the 'state of mind' exception. I am allowing the statement that . . ." He turned to the court reporter and asked her to read the statement back to the jury.

"'. . . that he'd kill her the way she said he had done before.'"

Jarvis looked back at the jury. "You may consider this statement as evidence only for the purpose of what the person who said it thought, what she may have feared. You are not to consider it with respect to the entirely separate question of whether that statement was true."

The moment Jarvis was finished, I asked Julian a question that would make that dry distinction all but impossible to remember.

"That 'he'd kill her the way she said he had done before.' What did she mean by that? Whom did she think he had killed?"

"His wife, the one who drove her car off a cliff. She said he told her he had done it, and that he would do the same thing to her if she ever betrayed him or tried to leave."

This time the objection was more forceful. Foster was furious at what I had done. Jarvis sustained her objection the moment she made it, but nothing could now erase it from the jury's mind.

"In other words," I went on as if I had never been interrupted, "she was afraid for her life. What happened that night, the night she came to your home, the night she died? Her husband had gone to Los Angeles on business: Is that why she thought it was safe to leave?"

Julian shook his head. "He told her he was going to L.A. and that he would not be back until the next day, but she did not believe it."

The jury was watching Julian intently. He looked down at his hands, that same bitter expression back on his mouth.

"He found out that she had been seeing me. She told him that we were friends, that we had not been 'intimately involved.'" Julian's eyes opened wide as he suddenly raised his head and looked at me, eager to explain. "That's why it was important—what I said before—that she did not have to lie, that she could tell the truth.

"He told her that she had to see me that night to tell me she could not see me again, that she was breaking it off, that she had decided to make her marriage work. She knew he would be waiting there when she got home."

"But why did she think that? What did she think he was going to do?"

"Take his revenge; do something awful to her for ever having thought she could leave him for someone else. That's why she stayed, why she did not go back that night." Julian's voice made a small choking sound before he could finally finish. "I told her that she couldn't go back; that he might really kill her this time if she did."

The jury, those twelve sets of anonymous eyes, were, if I read them right, sympathetic, willing to believe, or at least to credit the possibility, that Julian was telling the truth: that he did not do it, that he did not kill her; that someone else—her husband—had instead. There were cases that were decided on a look, a word, a gesture, something that for reasons a jury could not later explain made one witness become believable and another one not. We were close, I could feel it; a few more questions, we might be there.

"What time did she get there?" Lowering my head, I moved the few steps to the jury box and waited.

"A little after eight. We talked for hours. She was so scared, upset."

"You convinced her not to go home, but to stay there that night with you?" I asked, raising my head far enough for a sidelong glance.

"Yes, that's right. I told her I'd take care of everything, that it wasn't safe to go back. Monday morning, we'd make arrangements through a lawyer—the police, if we had to—to get her things out of there."

"But you went to bed and she stayed up." I let my eyes wander down the row of jurors' faces, giving them time to consider the full importance of what was being said. "When she was found that morning, when the police arrived, she was still dressed. Why, if she was leaving her husband, if she was going to be staying with you," I asked as I faced him straight on, my fingertips still touching the wooden railing of the jury box, "why, if that had been decided, didn't she sleep with you?"

"Because she hadn't left him yet," he answered without pause or hesitation. "She was still married, and everything she did," he added with a look of utter certainty, "was dependent on that simple fact. Yes, she was going to leave him; yes, she was not going back; but she was as much in fear of him that night as she had ever been. She could not put him out of her mind. And until she did, she wasn't free. She could not know—neither of us could—how much of what she felt was because I made her feel safe against him, or what she might feel when she was no longer burdened with that awful, dreadful fear."

"You went to bed, but you went to bed alone. She stayed up?"

"I went to bed around eleven-thirty. We had been talking for hours. She came with me, sat on the edge of the bed in the darkness, talking to me in that quiet voice of hers until I fell asleep."

"Did you wake up during the night—hear any noise?"

"No, nothing. . . ." The shadow of a doubt flashed across his eyes. "Yes, maybe . . . No, I don't know. There may have been something. Maybe I was dreaming, or maybe, because of what happened—the shock of finding her in the morning like that, what had been done to her—I've started to imagine that I must have heard something, woken up, heard nothing else and gone back to sleep. The honest answer, I suppose, is that I just don't know." Julian's eyes narrowed into brutal self-recrimination. "I should have heard something; I should have been awake—I should have saved her!"

One of the advantages of treating everyone with evenhanded fairness, with raising objections only when you have to and always in a decent, respectful voice, is that it makes it so much easier to convince a jury that your first burst of outrage is honestly and deeply felt. Maddy Foster stood just to the side of the counsel table, her thick ankles spread shoulder width, her broad-spaced eyes firmly set. Each side of her tight closed mouth was marked with a short indented perpendicular line, giving the lower part of her face the slightly wooden aspect of a puppet's jaw. When she began to speak, her voice was harsh, strident, nothing like what it had been before.

"Well, Mr. Sinclair, I must tell you I found your testimony, and especially that part about the nature of your relationship with the victim, Daphne McMillan, charming, quaint, really quite . . . incredible. Why wouldn't you have slept through her murder? You seem to have slept through her life."

She stepped forward, her head bent down, watching him with a mocking gaze.

"You were in love with each other—or you thought you were—or something. And you spent as much time together as you could, but you never, as they say, 'did anything about it'? It was, you want us to believe, an entirely 'platonic' affair?"

Julian's head snapped up; his eyes luminous, intense.

"Not as that phrase is commonly understood."

Maddy Foster was still moving forward. She stopped in her tracks, a jagged, bewildered grin slashed across her face.

"Not as that phrase is commonly understood?"

"The absence of anything physical," explained Julian. "We had not made love—I think that's your point—but it was not because we thought ourselves above it. We thought we should wait."

Foster nodded eagerly, as if that was exactly the answer she wanted.

"Yes, precisely. How old are you, Mr. Sinclair? Thirty-two?"

"Thirty-three next month."

"Thirty-two. And Daphne McMillan was what? Twenty-nine?" She turned her head to the side, and with a knowing smile looked at the jury. "She often came to your place, didn't she?"

"Not often. Once every week or so."

"You said earlier that she came whenever she could; whenever—I think this is the way you put it—she thought it was safe. So let me rephrase the question since you insist on being so precise. Part of your training as a lawyer, I suppose: this insistence on redefining every-thing I ask—"

"Your Honor," I objected, throwing up my hands in a show of frustration.

"Ms. Foster—"

"Yes, Your Honor," she said without any sign of contrition as she kept staring at the witness. "She often came to see you, didn't she? As often as she could?"

She did not care about his answer, and she did not wait until he had given one.

"And there were occasions when, instead of spending part of the evening, she spent the night—isn't that correct, Mr. Sinclair?"

"Yes, she did."

"In the guest room," she added with a smile that called him a liar.

"Sometimes; sometimes not."

"Sometimes, sometimes not," she mocked. Her smile twisted into an angry, sinister doubt. "So sometimes she did not sleep in the guest room; sometimes she slept with you?"

"Yes, that's right."

She crossed her arms in front of her. Her eyebrows rose majestically.

"But you never made love!"

"No, we did not."

She raised her chin, and then, looking past him as if the memory of what had happened to Daphne McMillan was almost more than she could bear, began to shake her head. She hurried to the counsel table, where she picked up a document from inside a file.

"This is a hotel receipt," she said, handing it to him. "That's your signature at the bottom, your credit card that was billed?"

"Yes," he replied, giving it back.

"You spent a three-day weekend, with Daphne McMillan, late last fall, at this hotel in Carmel. But you didn't touch her, did you? Because she was a married woman, and you didn't—what was it? Oh, yes, 'didn't want to complicate her life'?"

She did not let him answer, but took him quickly in another direction, trying to catch him off-guard.

"You found her body in the morning—the jury has seen the pictures of her slashed to pieces, slaughtered, blood all over. You found her there, and then you wait hours before you bother to call the police?"

"An hour," Julian corrected her; "perhaps a little longer."

She had taken two steps toward the jury. She wheeled back.

"You called your lawyer first, isn't that correct?"

"No."

"No?"

"I didn't have a lawyer. Mr. Antonelli was a friend, someone I trusted. I was half out of my mind," cried Julian, sitting bolt upright in the chair. His eyes were frantic, intense. "Finding her like that. I didn't know what to do. She was lying there—looking at me with those dead, empty eyes—the front door wide open. I didn't know when it had happened: hours or just minutes before. I knew she was dead, and it made me crazy with grief. I was on the floor, next to her, holding her, telling her it was going to be all right, rocking her in my arms as if she were just asleep. Did I call the police? No, I didn't even think of it; I didn't think of anything but her. She was dead! What did I care what happened next! I don't know how long I held her dead body in my arms: minutes, hours? Finally, out of sheer exhaustion, I picked up the telephone and asked if Mr. Antonelli could come help."

Foster dismissed it as the predictable fabrication of a murderer practically caught in the act.

"You don't deny that the kitchen knife was yours?"

"You don't deny that you had her blood all over you?"

"You don't deny that you waited before you called the police?"

"You don't deny that you called a lawyer first?"

The questions came with all the speed and force of an artillery barrage, running so close together that if Julian had tried to answer, no one would have known what that answer was. She did not care about that: the answers were not important, the questions were—the deafening insistence that each fact was undeniable, and that each fact was evidence that he was guilty, that he killed her, that there should not be any doubt of that in anyone's mind.

"You were having an affair with her, and she came there that night to tell you that it was over, that she was breaking it off—"

"No, that's not true!"

"She was breaking if off, going back to her husband, wasn't going to see you anymore—"

"No, that's not—!"

"You couldn't stand that, the idea that she was rejecting you, so you killed her; took that knife, followed her outside, grabbed her, dragged her back inside and stabbed her to death, didn't you?"

"No, I did not!"

"Stabbed her seventeen times, stabbed her until you were covered in her blood and you finally quit! Then you left her there, crumpled up on your living room floor. But you did not know what to do next, did you? You tried to wash the blood off, but you realized—didn't you?—that it wouldn't work, that there was too much blood everywhere, that you could never get it out, that the police would know it was you. That's why you didn't call them, why you called a lawyer first—because you made up this story, this strange, unbelievable tale, that someone else did it: her husband came there in the middle of the night, killed her while you were sleeping and you did not hear a thing! Made up this story because after the way you killed her, after what you had done in all your rage, it was the only chance you had. That's right, isn't it? You killed her—murdered her in cold blood—that beautiful young woman you could not have anymore!"

"No, I did not," replied Julian, clutching the arms of the chair, staring every bit as hard at her as she was at him.

A thin, caustic smile twisted slowly along Maddy Foster's broad full mouth. "No one believes you, Mr. Sinclair; no one at all."

I had kept Julian on the stand all morning; she had him there all afternoon. He had not lost his composure, and despite the constant badgering, Foster had not forced him into a mistake. But as I watched the jury watching him, I knew that the prosecution had achieved the result it wanted. The willingness to believe that I had seen start on their faces when Julian held them spellbound with his story of how he and Daphne had fallen in love and been content with barely touching, had disappeared and become once more suspicion.

Julian said he had not slept with her, said they never would have slept together until she was free of her husband and her marriage. Maddy Foster had played on it every way she could. It was not just the questions, but the look, the doubting, half-laughing skepticism in her eye, as she waited while he answered each thing she asked. Here was this gorgeous young woman, she seemed to say; an overnight sensation on talk show television; throwing herself at him, spending every evening with him she could get away, sometimes spending the night—and nothing happened? It was ludicrous, inexplicable. Julian Sinclair was young, intelligent, handsome as the devil; and yet, somehow, oblivious or indifferent to what anyone else must have wanted most.

There were only two alternatives, Foster seemed to tell the jury with each sidelong glance. Either Julian Sinclair was lying or he was telling the truth, but either way he was not someone they could trust. Because if he was telling the truth—if despite those long nights which sometimes became long weekends alone, he had never once made love with her—his conduct was not just inexplicable, but abnormal. He was the kind of person you could never really know, the kind who might commit murder.

It was insidious, and it was effective, this thought that Julian was not like everyone else. To those twelve anonymous jurors, nothing about Julian Sinclair made sense. On re-direct, I had to show that it did.

"The woman who raised you—the only mother you ever knew—died two years ago, if I'm not mistaken. What was the cause?"

It was nearly four o'clock. The prosecution had just finished cross-examination. Julian was still alert. He had answered every question thrown at him, but with this question, his demeanor changed. He lowered his eyes and bit down on his lip.

"They said it was heart failure. I think she was just worn out."

"From . . . ?"

"A lifetime of drugs and alcohol and abuse."

"What happened to your father?"

Julian bent forward. His hands, clasped together, dangled over his lap.

"I never knew my real parents. My mother—the woman I always called my mother—raised me alone."

"You mentioned drugs, alcohol . . . ?"

"For as long as I can remember, it was one thing or the other—usually both."

"Did she ever get help?"

"It never worked; at least not for very long."

"Isn't it true that from a very early age, you pretty much raised yourself? That you worked while you went to school; that all the way through college and law school, you did what you could to take care of her?"

A bleak expression in his eyes, Julian, letting his silence answer, waited for what I was going to ask next.

"You mentioned abuse?"

"My mother was in the habit of being taken advantage of by men."

"And was it that experience—watching men come in and out of your mother's life, that made you so determined that you would never do anything like that to anyone else? Never take advantage of what someone felt? Was it that—what happened to your mother—that made you treat Daphne McMillan with—what shall I call it?" I asked, staring hard at the jury. "Old-fashioned decency and respect?"

Chapter Eleven

Albert Craven slumped into the gray upholstered chair. Brushing his thumbs back and forth against each other, he gazed out the window at the sun-spattered buildings on the other side of the street.

"I watched it. Can't say it was the best thing I ever saw." His mouth twisted down at the corners, intensifying an attitude of pensive contemplation. "It would have been more interesting if you had watched it with me." A sly sparkle started in his pale blue eyes. His head rolled in my direction. "Except then I would not have heard a word anyone said, what with all your swearing."

He stared again out the glass pane window, fascinated, as it seemed, by the way the light changed colors as the narrow streak of sunshine moved away. He took a deep breath, then let it out, a sigh like a last regret in the mid-morning silence.

"It's amazing how much has changed. A few years ago no one would have thought it possible, what they did last night. A man is on trial for murder, but that's not enough! People have to see it on television or, I suppose, they don't think it's real."

Albert Craven's eyes narrowed to an intense focus as he appeared to search for what it all might mean.

"Eighty-four percent say he's guilty. I read it in the papers this morning," I explained.

Albert shoved himself up in the silk-smooth chair. With slow reluctance he turned away from the window and the changing light outside.

"Everyone gets to vote on everything these days. There are no rules anymore. Forget right and wrong. It's all a question of what the public wants. That's what television has done. We change our minds the way we change the channel: if we don't like what we see, what someone is trying to tell us, we look at something else. One thing is for certain: whatever you are looking at, it won't take any effort to understand it and it won't last longer than a fraction of a minute."

Albert Craven's eyes glistened with a kind of gleeful remorse, angry at the blatant stupidity of what he described, and yet amused at his own performance.

"It was on for two hours, which means that when you take out the time for commercials, a trial—a trial that is now in its second month—was collapsed into the space of—what?—an hour and a quarter?—an hour and a half? They did just what Harry said they would. Each side put on their witnesses in the same order Foster and you have done in the trial; and the words—at least as far as I could tell—were all the same. But what a difference when things get that abbreviated! Julian did not kill Daphne McMillan. I know he did not. But if I had not met him, if I had not been in court, if all I knew was what I had seen on television and what I saw last night—I would have gone to bed absolutely certain they had the right man and that you, my friend, were fighting a losing cause."

"At least the jury didn't see it. Thank God they're sequestered."

Albert twisted his head to the side, a troubled expression in his eyes. The light outside had grown pale and gray as the clouds scattered under the sun.

"Too bad they weren't sequestered the day of the murder. I had the impression that the jury did not quite know what to make of Julian. I've never met anyone quite like him; what must those people think?"

Drawn back to the window, Albert scratched his throat. Something kept nagging at him, a thought he could not finish, a question that he did not know how to ask.

"You're back in court this afternoon?" he asked without moving his eyes away from the window.

"Jarvis had some other things he had to take care of this morning. We start again at two."

"Does Julian read the papers? Does he watch what they do to him on television at night?"

He was still gazing toward the window. His voice was a low, heavy whisper, as if the words, spoken somewhere earlier, were now echoing back.

"Eighty-four percent," Craven repeated to himself. "That's what's happened to us: it's how we decide everything from the random, uninformed opinion of the moment, except, I imagine, Julian, for whom it would not mean anything at all."

A strange, enigmatic smile crossed Albert Craven's wise and worldly mouth. He brought his eyes back around to mine.

"That's what they can't understand about him—that he doesn't take his bearings by what other people think. It is one of the great ironies of the age, isn't it? That with all this talk about diversity, about respecting our differences, the one thing we won't tolerate is anyone who doesn't think just like us."

I started to rise from my chair, but he stopped me.

"Have you talked to Julian yet about what he wants to do?"

There was something nearly tragic in his look. It gave me a sense of foreboding. My stomach tightened and I felt that sudden terrible emptiness that comes with the knowledge that something has happened and that nothing will be the same again.

"When the jury doesn't acquit him, when the only question left is death or life in prison. I have a very difficult time thinking that Julian Sinclair will have any interest in a life like that."

As I drove over the Bay Bridge on my way to Oakland, Albert Craven's solemn pronouncement reverberated in my mind like the dismal certainties of a death foretold. For the first time, I began to think seriously about what would happen if Julian Sinclair was convicted for a murder I knew he did not commit.

The sun blinked through the crisscrossed girders between the upper and lower decks as the traffic edged slowly along, every driver trapped in a one-way moving mass. Albert was right: the world had changed, all of us becoming, without our quite knowing how, the thoughtless parts of some great unguided machine. He was right about Julian, too. It was hard to think of him as a prisoner, locked up, a faceless statistic in the regimented existence of a thick-walled penitentiary. What would he do if he had that choice to make, to die and end it, or grow old without the possibility that he would ever be free? He had been so persuasive that day I heard him arguing in his class that there was no more principled reason to oppose the death penalty than life in prison. But this was real; this was not academic. This was the question that put nearly every other question in the shade: Whether it was better to live or to die when life meant living like a slave.

I did not raise the question that day, or the one after that. I did not ask Julian anything until the jury had reached its verdict.

The prosecution spent two and a half hours—from the time we started in the morning until we stopped for lunch—reviewing with painstaking precision the evidence that pointed—"unmistakably," in the view of the relentless Maddy Foster—to the guilt of Julian Sinclair.

More than competent, it was nothing short of masterful, the way Maddy Foster built the case for conviction.

"We know how Daphne McMillan was murdered. We know where she was murdered and we know when she was murdered. She was murdered with a knife, a knife the defendant admits was his. There is no such thing as a decent murder, but some murders are more violent than others, and, let me assure you, there has never been a murder more brutal than this. He cut her throat like someone slaughtering an animal, ripped it open with that knife, right down to the bone. But that was only the beginning. Was she still alive, if only for a few seconds, when he began to plunge that bloody knife deep into her stomach, not once or twice, but over and over again, seventeen times before he was finally finished, before he finally ran out of rage? Was she still alive, trying to scream, but nothing would come out, only the death rattle of the blood gurgling out of her throat—still alive when he thrust that knife into her again?

"No one disputes that that is how Daphne McMillan died. No one disputes that she was murdered in the living room of the defendant's home. The walls, the carpet, the furniture were covered in her blood. And no one disputes that Julian Sinclair was there when it happened, sometime around midnight on the night Daphne McMillan came to see him for what would be the very last time."

Maddy Foster stood still, her large frame immobile. The silence in the courtroom was tense, profound. Her mouth twisted into the agonizing certainty of a shocking truth.

"She went there that night to tell him that it was over, that she was not going to see him again. She did not know she was going there to meet her own death."

Foster lifted her chin a bare fraction of an inch and moved her head a quarter turn to the right. Her eyes were cold, insistent, unforgiving. She looked at the jury, raised her arm and pointed behind her to the counsel table where Julian Sinclair sat next to me. She was pointing to us both.

"There has been a calculated effort during this trial to convince you that Daphne McMillan went there that night because she was running away from her husband, and that, because she was, her husband, and not the defendant, must have killed her. Let me say right at the beginning that as trial strategies go, this was brilliant in its conception and, as always when Mr. Antonelli is involved, brilliant in the execution."

She glanced briefly at the floor, moved a single step forward parallel to the jury box, stopped and looked up. Her eyes were even less forgiving than before.

"But we're here to deal with facts, not acts of the imagination. Robert McMillan has a spotless reputation, but in private he's a beast? What evidence do we have for this? Statements we're told his wife made to the defendant, statements which for some reason she made to no one else. Robert McMillan bought the silence of his first wife and murdered his second. How do we know this? The defendant tells us so. Robert McMillan told his wife she had to go there that night and break off the affair, then followed her and murdered her himself. It must have happened that way—why? Because Mr. Antonelli says it did. And what evidence does he produce to substantiate this charge, this accusation that the dead woman's grieving husband is a murderer and a fraud? None, none at all; nothing, not a scintilla of evidence to prove that Robert McMillan was within a hundred miles of that house when the murder happened!"

Maddy Foster swung her broad shoulders away from the jury box. Cold, implacable, she subjected Julian Sinclair to a scrutiny that was withering and intense.

"Why did he do it?" she asked in a way that invited the jury, watching behind her, to ask that question themselves. "Why did Julian

Sinclair, with his gifted, brilliant mind, one of the brightest of his generation, commit, not just a murder, but a murder so awful? Why did he murder this beautiful young woman he insists was his great, good friend?"

She let the question hang in the air like some dark secret she had only just discovered.

"Why did he murder her when she came there that night, when she told him it was over? He told you himself—if he was telling the truth."

Her eyes brightened, became more alert, more energetic. She began to move rapidly, gesturing with her hands.

"If he was lying, then that's another matter. He's guilty if he's lying, because he swore to tell the truth. But if he was telling the truth, then he's guilty then as well."

She stopped, her hands crossed in front of her, clutching her upper arm. A thin smile, defiant, triumphant, enigmatic, danced across her mouth. I sat there, like everyone else, riveted, stunned by this strange, unexpected juxtaposition, mystified as to what she was going to do next.

"If he never touched her, if they spent all that time together, if they spent the night, if they shared the same bed and nothing happened— if they never once made love—because—what was it he said?—he wanted her, but not until she was finally free of her husband and her marriage—what must he have thought, that after all that waiting, all that sacrifice of every normal impulse and desire, all that 'old-fashioned decency and respect,' he was never going to have her, not even once? She was going back to her husband; she was never going to be with him! What do you think happened to Julian Sinclair's 'noble purpose,' his sense of who he was, when she told him that? He must have felt like a fool. He thought their life was all poetry and verse, and she's going back to the older man with all the money! In his mind, at that moment, she deserved to die. In his mind, that brilliant, gifted mind I don't pretend to understand, he killed her and thought he was doing the right thing. She was not the angel he thought she was: She was a whore!" cried Maddy Foster as she wheeled back on Julian, sitting calm and impassive in his chair. "That's why you did it, isn't it? The anger, the rage, at finding out that it was all for nothing, that the woman you had put so high up on a pedestal was giving you up to go back to another man's bed!"

It left me nearly speechless, those final few minutes of Maddy Foster's closing argument. All those sleepless nights imagining everything that either side could say and I had never thought of this. The stunning thing was that, like every well-told story, it made so much sense. The relationship she had herself ridiculed as 'platonic' on cross-examination, a claim of innocence that was the best proof Julian was a liar, now explained what had led him to murder. It hit the jury with all the force of a revelation. The only question was why they had not seen it before.

I stared down at my hands, conscious that every eye was on me. Maddy Foster was sliding onto her chair; Judge Jarvis was waiting for me to begin. The prosecution's words echoed in my mind. I tried to concentrate, to think of something I could say. A strange smile settled on Julian's mouth.

"It's always all about sex," he said in a solemn voice so quiet that it took me a moment before I knew I had heard him right. Then I was on my feet.

"It's always all about sex," I announced with an air of defiance. "That's all we think about. It's the only thing we think important. Sex is everywhere, you can't avoid it. Try to find a movie that does not have people taking off their clothes, a program on television where sex isn't the only thing anyone talks about. It was not that long ago that a married couple in a movie had to sleep in twin beds; now couples, married or not, are shown naked without so much as a sheet. It was not that long ago that you could not utter any kind of profanity on television; now half the things said are laced with obscenities. I am not here to argue the virtues—or the vices—of unfettered, or irresponsible, free speech; I am here to remind you of the effect all of this has had on the way we think and the way we act and the way we decide, as in this case, whether someone will live or die.

"We've become the prisoners of our own impulses, driven by our own desires, taught to believe by all the things we see around us that the greatest thing that could ever happen to us is to be like one of those famous celebrities we all read about who sleep with someone different every night. Everywhere you look, that's what you see—it's all you hear. Be honest with yourselves, if about nothing else, about this: Before this trial ever started, before you stepped foot inside this courthouse, called for jury duty, you knew—everyone knew—that this case was all about murder and this murder was all about sex.

"What else could it be?" I asked as I unbuttoned my coat and put both hands on my hips. I stood in front of them, my feet spread wide apart. "A married woman—and not just any married woman, but a young, beautiful woman who was on her way to becoming a television star—involved with an unmarried man, found murdered at his bachelor home high up in the Berkeley hills, no one else around, the blood, from all the lurid reports, ankle deep. You came in here and swore to be impartial; you came in here and swore to listen to all the evidence before you reached any conclusions; you swore to do what the law requires. You swore to do all that and no one believes you will, because no one believes you can.

"You can't be impartial; you can't be fair. No one could, after being told for months on end that Julian Sinclair murdered Daphne McMillan and that her murder was all about sex. Curious the way that word both titillates and alarms. It's thrown at us from every direction, we can't avoid it; yet it remains a secret and, sometimes, guilty pleasure. We can't hear enough about it, when it involves someone else; we're outraged when the talk is about us. It's been all about Julian Sinclair and Daphne McMillan since the morning the crime was first reported.

"'They were having an affair!' That was both the premise and the conclusion of the argument all those wonderfully fair-minded people on television kept shouting over each other. And all of you believed it."

I moved to the end of the jury box and looked back at the courtroom, where the crowd waited, hushed and expectant. Julian sat perfectly still, following each word more with the studious eye of the scholar than with the tense, frightened attention of someone on trial for his life. I think he had no conscious sense of himself, no thought for anything except getting his mind around the argument that in my own feeble fashion, I was trying to make.

"All of you believed it," I repeated, moving my eyes back to the jury. "You believed Julian Sinclair was guilty before the trial began because that is what everyone said; and we believe that—don't we?—what everyone says. Everyone said he was having an affair and he was guilty because of it, and you believed it.

"The prosecution tells us first that Julian Sinclair was lying when he said that though he loved Daphne McMillan, and she loved him, they had not slept together, and would not have until she was free of her husband and her marriage. He was lying; they were having an affair; she wanted to break it off, and in a rage he killed her. But then the prosecution tells us that perhaps Julian Sinclair and Daphne McMillan never slept together. But she still wanted to end their relationship. He kills her because, though he had never slept with her, it was the only thing he had ever really wanted, and he was in a rage because now he knew he would never get it.

"He slept with her, he didn't sleep with her, but either way he killed her, because—don't you see?—either way it is still all about sex. It has to be about sex. Without sex there is no motive, and without a motive, blaming Julian Sinclair for the murder of Daphne McMillan makes no sense and the prosecution knows it. That's why the prosecution cannot admit so much as the possibility that what Julian Sinclair told you is the truth. The prosecution thinks it inconceivable that anyone could love someone and want only what was best for them; inconceivable that Julian Sinclair could have treasured the time he had with the woman he loved and not think it was a sacrifice, a form of indebtedness that could only be repaid in bed. She owed him, but she would not pay; and when that happened, Sinclair, like Shylock, had to have his pound of flesh. That in all its tawdry elegance is the sum total of the prosecution's case."

I looked back to where Julian Sinclair sat alone. There was nothing furtive or secretive in his eyes, nothing to suggest that he would so much as think of not telling the truth. But then I had never thought of him as a murderer, and those who had thought of him that way perhaps saw in those remarkable eyes of his not honesty, but a lack of conscience.

"Julian Sinclair swore under oath to tell the truth. There is a point where you have to trust yourselves. You have to decide whether a witness is someone you can believe. There is no one now to decide that for you. That loud strident chorus that filled the airwaves with all its expert opinion before the first witness was called has fallen silent: yours is the only voice that matters. It is easy to call for a conviction, to claim to know what happened, when you are not the one who has to decide if someone will live or die.

"At the very beginning of this trial, I described to you what almost a thousand years ago was called trial by ordeal. You remember—hot iron in your hand, guilt or innocence determined by whether, three days later, your hand had blistered or perfectly healed. Remember what you thought when you heard it—how cruel and barbaric it seemed? But are we really any better? They believed that everything was, or could be, decided by God; we believe that everything is determined by our own lowest instincts, in this case by sex. But just as there were people then who did not give a thought to God when they were hot in pursuit of their own carnal desires, there are still some people today who believe there is something more to being human than what the prosecution would have us believe. You saw him, you heard him, you made a judgment about him as you listened—I saw it in your eyes. Do you really believe that Julian Sinclair could have been driven into a murderous rage because Daphne McMillan told him she was going back to her husband and because he had lost any chance he had ever had of getting her into bed?"

I threw an angry glance at Maddy Foster, sitting somber at the counsel table. She bent her head to the side with a look that dared me to continue.

"Daphne McMillan was not killed by Julian Sinclair. She was killed by her husband, Robert McMillan. He could not stand the thought that this woman he had tortured into submission was in love with someone else. He killed her, and if you don't acquit Julian Sinclair, you'll not only send an innocent man to his death or prison, you'll let the real killer go free!"

At the end, when I was finally finished and sank exhausted into my chair, I did not feel what I usually felt: a sense of relief that it was over and that there was nothing now but to wait. Instead of a burden lifted from my shoulders, the weight seemed even more oppressive. Like a deepening depression, the more I struggled against it, the darker everything seemed. Instead of trying to cheer up Julian, Julian tried to encourage me.

Within a certain limit, that is to say. Julian would not indulge in false hopes. He knew as well as I did—perhaps better than I did, because, though he was the one on trial, his powers of detachment were greater than mine—that the verdict could go either way. He had known from the beginning what he was up against. He was under no illusions about what might happen. He knew that with the best will in the world it would be impossible for any jury to forget everything they had seen and heard. Not once did he complain about it, not once did he suggest it was unfair. On the one occasion I remarked upon it in his presence, he reminded me that after what had happened to Daphne, he did not expect to find much fairness in the world.

"That was extraordinary," he said about the closing argument after Jarvis had instructed the jury and we were alone. "And you did it off the top of your head, without a note; took what the prosecutor said and for the next two hours turned it upside down. Of course it was not off the top of your head at all, was it? Reminds me of the Whistler case."

I did not know what he was talking about. My mind was too cluttered with all the things I wished I had done a different way, things I wished I had said and things I wished I had not said at all.

"Whistler?" I asked with a blank expression. I should have pressed harder when I had Robert McMillan on the stand. I should have been better prepared, dug deeper into his past. It would have helped if I had had something more specific to use against him, something about which I could have proved he had lied.

"Whistler—the famous painter. He was in a lawsuit over the fee he had charged for a painting he had done. The lawyer on the other side asked him if he did not think the amount excessive for what Whistler had admitted had taken only a day to paint. Whistler replied: 'A day of painting, but years of preparation.'"

I barely heard him. I kept thinking about the trial, going back to the beginning, running through it to the end. If I had done everything right, if I had been able to show conclusively the past misconduct of

Daphne's husband, would it have changed what they had thought about Julian Sinclair? They were the kind of questions that could drive you crazy, the kind you never ask, because you don't have to, when you know your client is guilty, or when you know you have won.

We sat in the small windowless room reserved for lawyers and their clients, safe from the prying eyes of passersby, assaulted by our fears. My fears, not his. Julian kept praising what I had done, explaining the effect it produced and examining the way it had been done. It seemed he always had to be teaching something, helping even someone as unwilling as myself to learn. We stayed there for an hour, two, until the bailiff knocked on the door.

"Jury has stopped deliberations. They'll start again in the morning."

Julian stayed at my place that night. The next morning we went downtown to my office and waited by the phone. The call did not come that day or the next. On the evening of the third day, they finally reached a verdict. We were told to be in court at ten o'clock the next morning, when the verdict would be announced.

Chapter Twelve

WE COULD NOT EAT in a restaurant; we could not go out on the street. Julian's face was everywhere, printed on the front page of the late edition of all the papers, flashed on every television screen. The news had raced across the country: The jury in the Daphne McMillan murder case had reached a verdict and would announce it tomorrow morning in open court. There was only one night left to speculate about what that verdict would be. By this time tomorrow, television and public attention would move on to another gruesome murder and another round of intense debate about whether someone obviously guilty might beat the charge in court.

"Do you want to watch what they're saying about us?" I asked Julian after we had finished the dinner that had been brought to the office.

He shook his head. "I don't watch television very often. I used to watch Daphne when she was on, mainly so I could tease her about it after."

It was a little past seven. Under the fading August light, the gray buildings on the other side of the narrow city street shimmered a soft reddish gold. The slanting rays of the dying sun, pouring through the tall office windows, caught the side of Julian's face, giving it a vibrant, youthful glow. He had barely spoken through dinner, nor had I tried to draw him out. He had spent the days waiting with me for the verdict, and the nights at my place on Nob Hill. Tonight he was going home. As we both understood, it might be the last night he ever could.

"Daphne had an instinct for what other people wanted her to be. She did not have to think about it—there wasn't any premeditated calculation—she just knew. It's what happens to almost everyone: we're all, one way or the other, the creation of what we think other people think. That's how we become what we are, isn't it? Imitation. We model ourselves on what we see others do. Which others? The ones who seem to be the ones everyone else wants to be like. It's always been like that, but the difference was that until television—and before that, the movies—there were all sorts of different models, different types—different every place you went. Now, everything is the same, and that makes it," he added with an enigmatic look, "almost impossible for anyone to become something individual, unique. I used to tease her a little about that," he remarked in a quiet, wistful voice.

"And you, Julian: What model did you have? What did you try to imitate?"

Julian's eyes, dark, mysterious, full of things I did not understand, without looking away seemed to race all around. He appeared to study me, as if, even now, after all the time we had spent together, after all we had been through, there were still things about himself he thought it best to keep hidden.

"The past," he said finally. "Leaving the place you were born and raised, where you had no reason to think there was any way of life better than that, learning about another way of life so that you had something to compare—that was the way people first learned to think for themselves who and what they wanted to be. But space has collapsed, places have become the same. The only thing left is to read about the way things were once, long ago in different places. But only," he cautioned, "if they're written by those who had some understanding of how people at the time thought about those things themselves."

Julian turned away from the outside light. For a long time he did not say a word. I had the impression that he was coming to grips with what might happen to him after tomorrow. I kept thinking about what Albert Craven had said: that the thought of Julian Sinclair locked up in prison, treated like an animal with no mind of his own, seemed worse, more cruel, than death.

"I suppose there is a certain irony that my favorite story as a boy growing up was *The Count of Monte Cristo*," he said with a brave grin. "I did not kill Daphne, and I think you know it, but the chances are that tomorrow morning I'll be found guilty and either sentenced to death or given life in prison. You must have wondered which one I would choose. I remember what we talked about that day at lunch, about that man you knew who had been in prison for thirty years, the one who would not have chosen death under any circumstances." In a single fluid motion he rose from the chair. "If I were guilty of Daphne's murder and the punishment were up to me, I would choose death, because whoever murdered her deserves to die. But I am innocent and for that reason I choose life, because it's damn difficult to escape once you're dead!"

I DID NOT SLEEP at all that night, and in the morning felt tired, depleted, as worried as I had ever been. Julian's fate had been decided, and there was nothing that I could do. It was like waiting for the dealer to turn over the card, the card that had already been drawn, the card that could not be replaced, the card that would decide whether you had won the fortune that would change your life, or had lost everything you had. Julian sat next to me in his dark blue suit with such an air of polished confidence that anyone who had just walked in would have thought that he was the lawyer defending me and that whatever the verdict, he would be in another courtroom tomorrow, starting another trial.

"Has the jury reached a verdict?" asked Conrad Jarvis after the jury had taken their seats in the jury box.

I had watched their faces when they filed in, looking for something in their expression that would tell me what they had done. They came in with their heads bowed, moving slowly, one behind the other. None of them looked around the courtroom; none of them looked at me.

The jury foreman rose from her place in the back row. A middle-aged college graduate with large, sympathetic eyes, she had shown more interest in Julian than had some of the others, stole a look at him, perhaps to see his reaction, during the prosecution's summation. I felt a surge of hope.

"Yes, we have, Your Honor," she replied in a firm, steady voice. She looked at the judge and waited.

"And on the sole count of the indictment, murder in the first degree—how does the jury find: guilty or not guilty?"

On the judge's instruction, Julian and I stood facing the jury. Instinctively, I slipped my hand around his arm.

"Guilty, Your Honor."

I felt Julian's arm tense, and then, a moment later, relax. But when he turned to me, he could not hide the bitter anguish in his eyes.

"You did everything you could. It isn't your fault. Don't ever think it was."

Julian was taken into custody and a date for sentencing was set. Outside the courthouse, I started to wave off the questions shouted by reporters, but then had second thoughts. They demanded to know what I thought about the verdict.

"Bryan Allen and all the others like him should be delighted."

"Delighted? Why?"

"They said from the very beginning, starting the day after Daphne McMillan was killed, that Julian Sinclair was guilty. Now they can say they were right."

"You make it sound as if you think it's their fault, their responsibility for what the jury decided!"

"You have enough people shouting two plus two equals five and after a while you may not find too many people left willing to say it's four."

A young woman with ravenous eyes thrust a microphone in front of my face.

"This was a death penalty case. Are you going to try for life in prison?"

I remembered at that moment what Julian had said, but instead of repeating it, I gave them another reason for what I was going to do.

"One day, the real killer of Daphne McMillan is going to be caught. And when that happens, all of you who were so quick to condemn, so eager to have your say on television, had better hope Julian Sinclair is still alive, because if he's not, what are you going to do—blame each other?"

Disgusted, depressed, ready to give up the practice of law rather than watch another innocent man condemned before his trial started, I went back to the city and locked myself inside my office. I would not answer the telephone; I ignored each knock on the door. For a while, I sat quietly at my desk, staring straight ahead, trying hard not to think. What had happened was so terrible, an outrage that I had not been able to prevent and could now do nothing to change, that it had destroyed the last illusion I had: the belief that the courtroom was the one place safe from the world's insanity. With bleak, despondent eyes, I gazed at the shadowed, shifting light outside, remembering how much better things had seemed at the beginning, when I had thought that if I ever lost a case it would only be because the defendant was so guilty that even I knew it.

I had seen lawyers lose cases they should have won, lawyers who were lazy, incompetent, out of their depth; lawyers who did not care what happened as long as they got paid. I had heard all the time-honored excuses, the easy rationales, the glib assurances that the criminal courts were filled with criminals, and if one you happened to represent was not guilty of the charge on which you took him to trial, he was guilty of something else; and if, by some miracle, you got him acquitted, it was only a matter of time before he would be back in court, his hands bound behind him, waiting arraignment on another crime. I had known from the beginning that I could not practice law like that, that I could not live like that. I could not trivialize the one thing I thought important. The law held everything together, and worse than any criminal was the lawyer who forgot that he was there to guard it.

How grand, how noble, it had all seemed in my vanished dream-twisted youth, those early days when I still believed in what lawyers and the law could do; how hollow, how false, it sounded now, when I had lost a case I should have won and Julian Sinclair was on his way to death or something worse. Angry, frustrated, beside myself with grief, I grabbed a book that lay open on my desk and hurled it across the room.

"Damn everyone! Damn me!" I cried. And then, as that sad and futile imprecation echoed back at me, I did something I had not done for so long that I could not remember when I had last done it before. I started to cry, and once I started, I could not stop. Bent forward, my elbows on the desk, I held my head in my hands as the hot wet tears ran down my face.

After the first few attempts to get me to answer the telephone or the door, I was left alone until late in the afternoon, when Albert Craven knocked twice softly and called my name.

"It hasn't been a very good day, has it, my friend?"

He patted my shoulder and then settled himself into one of the two chairs that sat on each side of a small table across the room from my desk. Standing in my shirtsleeves, I thrust my hands into my pockets, looked at him for a moment, and then, shaking my head, looked away.

"It was not your fault. With you at least, he had a chance. The jury was out three days. Anyone else, with the evidence against him, they might not have been out an hour." As my eyes came back to him, he paused before he added: "We're both too old, and we've known each other too long, for either one of us to pretend that that doesn't matter. It matters a great deal. Yes, the verdict is still the same; but you forced them to think twice about it. No one else could have done the job you did, or even come close. I've seen you in a lot of cases, but I've never seen you better. Julian knew it, too. You could tell it in his eyes. That was the first thing he said to you, wasn't it? After he heard the verdict. I saw him turn to you. I could not hear it, but that was it, wasn't it? It's what Julian would have done—think of you and how it would affect you, before he thought of himself. He knew—he's far too intelligent not to have known—what the verdict was going to be. The way he held himself . . . I don't know if I could have done that, seemed so—not exactly indifferent, but unaffected by what happened. I must be wrong about this, but I wondered whether he did not almost enjoy it, showing himself, perhaps as well as others, how well he could handle the worst thing anyone could do to him. I had the feeling he had been getting ready for that moment for a long time, perhaps as early as the morning he woke up to Daphne's death.

"Do you remember the line in *Henry the Fourth*: 'As if he master'd there a double spirit of teaching and of learning instantly.' That was Julian Sinclair," said Albert in a solemn voice as he rose from the chair. "What a loss. You almost saved him. And in a way that makes the tragedy of it even worse. No point ignoring that fact. I came in here to make you feel better; all I've done is make us both feel worse. Nothing we can do about that. Let's you and I go out. If we don't get drunk, at least we'll have a decent dinner."

Without protest—without, really, a will of my own—I followed Albert Craven down to his car. Exhausted, all my emotion spent, I felt a little like a child or a tired old man, aware of what was immediately around him and not much else. Albert talked and I listened, though if he had asked me, I could not have told him what he had just said. The words ran together into a long continuous sound, the foreign strange language of a kind and friendly face. I was falling back into memory, back into a dimly remembered past. I wanted to start all over again, lead my life some other way; do it so that I did not have to face the dismal future of someone who, however close I may have come, had failed.

"I don't think I would have felt this bad if I had picked up that knife from next to Daphne McMillan's body and killed him with it. We talk about being brave in the face of death, but we all want to die in our sleep. Or at least die without warning so that we can escape all the fear. Julian may spend fifty years—he's that young—with nothing to look forward to, nothing to dream about, nothing except when it's going to end. And I'm going to have to live with that every day for the rest of my life—that he was innocent, that I was there to defend him, to protect him, and I did not. If it's the last thing I ever do, I'm going to prove he did not do it and that McMillan did."

Anyone else would have tried to offer words of consolation, told me that I had done my best, which was all that anyone could ask; told me that while I had every right to be angry and upset, the innocent were sometimes convicted and all anyone could do was try to make sure it did not happen again. There was much to commend in that kind of advice. The innocent were convicted, and it was certainly important to do everything you could to keep it from happening in another case. It was also dangerous and self-defeating to become so obsessed with something that had happened that you lost the ability to think about much of anything else. There is only so much of the future anyone should sacrifice to the past. All of that was true, but it meant as little to Albert Craven as he knew it meant to me.

"If I were you, that's what I would do: prove McMillan did it, save Julian's life. What could be more important than that? I'll do anything I can to help."

I had a lot of reasons why I liked Albert Craven, and now I had one more. We were both of the age to know that things did not always work out for the best. The closer you got to the end, when death changes faces and instead of a vague distant possibility becomes the daily companion of your thoughts, the easier it becomes to grasp in all its joyful sorrow the tragic sense of what it means to be alive. Some, like Julian Sinclair, seem to be born with it, the knowledge that time is fleeting and that nothing lasts; most of us only learn when it's too late to live the way we always should have.

ALBERT CRAVEN had lived in San Francisco all his life. He drove through the narrow, steep city streets by the kind of instinct not permitted to recent arrivals or visitors from out of town. Talking all the time, gesturing with his hands, gazing out the window at whatever caught his eye, he steered the black Mercedes through the crush of downtown traffic, heading a few blocks south of Market to the comfortable, and for him, familiar, surroundings of the Four Seasons Hotel.

The bar was packed. Heads began to turn as soon as we walked in, among them a few of the vaguely familiar faces of network reporters who had covered the trial. A couple of them set their ice-filled glasses on the bar and started toward me through the crowd. Albert was a step too quick. Before anyone could get to us, we were ushered to a table in the far corner of the restaurant where no one could follow. Albert sat facing the restaurant and, beyond it, the piano and the scattered tables in front of the bar. I sat with my back to everyone, grateful that only Albert would know just how miserable I felt.

The bar was crowded to capacity, full of laughter and eager greetings shouted through the noise. The restaurant had only just started to fill up. A few well-dressed couples sampled the wine they had ordered while they studied the menu, or, having made their selection, flashed brief smiles of satisfaction.

"I feel like champagne," said Albert, "but that might be misunderstood." He looked past my shoulder, beyond the dining room, to the gathering at the bar. The grim smile on his rose-petal mouth became cheerful and defiant. "On the other hand, serve the bastards right. Drive them crazy guessing what we're celebrating about!"

When the waiter came, I decided Albert had a point. While his eyes were on the wine list, I ordered a bottle of their best champagne.

"Confusion to our enemies!" Albert toasted after the bottle was uncorked.

"And freedom for Julian Sinclair," I added in a quieter voice.

In rapid succession we drank down three straight glasses, a race to reach the fortress against reality that only madness provides. Things started to look better than they had in weeks; the trial, the verdict, nothing more than a temporary setback, a challenge made to be overcome. My head was whirling with the vague enchantment of my own inevitability, the drumbeat certainty of victory distant but already in hand; everything that had been lost, lost only so it could be won. If we had not stopped drinking and ordered dinner, I would have staggered out into the night listening to my own applause.

"You'll never guess who just walked in," said Albert, his eyes suddenly sharp and alert. We were nearly finished with dinner and I had recovered some of my self-possession.

"Perhaps they won't see us. Their table is on the other side, close to the front," he said with a hopeful glance. I could not guess whom he meant.

"Harry Godwin," he reported as he hunched forward. "And he's not alone. He has Bryan Allen with him, and a couple of women. There is someone else with him, too—Robert McMillan." Albert's eyes darted across the room. "They haven't seen us," he said with evident relief. "Maybe they won't. I'm genuinely sorry about this. It never occurred to me Harry might be here. I thought he had left a couple of days ago."

I turned around, searching until I found them, sitting at their table, the five of them, having what to all appearances looked like the time of their lives. There was half a glass of champagne left. I tossed it down and, with Albert moving quickly to catch up, marched over to Harry Godwin's table.

Godwin had not seen me coming, but when he looked up and saw me, he greeted me with all the warmth of a long-lost friend.

"Joseph Antonelli! What a wonderful surprise! And here's Albert, too!" He was on his feet, shaking hands. "Of course you know Bryan," he remarked cheerfully as Bryan Allen smiled and nodded. "And I believe you know Robert McMillan," he said in a more formal tone. There was a slight embarrassment in his voice, an acknowledgment of the awkwardness everyone must feel.

Bryan Allen had not stood up, but McMillan did. He grasped my hand firmly; a little too firmly, I thought—as if he wanted to impress, or perhaps intimidate me, with his strength. He did not say anything and he showed no expression, but despite that, there was something ruthless in his eyes, like someone who knew your secret fear and was not just willing, but eager, to exploit it. I got my right hand out of his and quickly turned to Harry Godwin.

"Let me introduce Bryan's wife, Marci," he said as I exchanged a greeting with a woman I guessed to be about the same age as her husband and, from what I saw in her gentle, gray eyes, at least twice as smart.

The other woman there, considerably younger, worked for Harry Godwin. Her first name was Rachel; I did not catch her last. She had an Australian accent and, though her appearance was not otherwise remarkable, she had haunting dark eyes.

"We just did tonight's show," said Bryan Allen, his jaw held at that same belligerent angle that was so familiar on the air. "Robert—Mr. McMillan—was the guest. You can watch it later, if you like. It's broadcast live on the East Coast, but we tape-delay it out here. Thought people would be interested in hearing his reaction to the verdict; how he feels about finally getting close to closure in his wife's tragic death."

I looked at McMillan, sitting between the two women on the far side of the table.

"I think perhaps I will watch that. What did you say, Mr. McMillan? How did you feel when you heard the verdict? What was the first thing that passed through your mind when you heard the word 'guilty' pronounced this morning in court?"

McMillan looked at me with a smile full of self-assurance.

"What did it feel like, knowing that you have just gotten away with murder? Knowing that you killed your wife and that someone else has to pay for it?"

The smile was frozen on his face; his eyes were deadly and full of warning.

"For God's sake, he lost his wife," said Bryan Allen with disgust. No one paid attention. They kept looking at me, and looking at McMillan, wondering what was going to happen next.

"You still want me to do a show?" I asked Godwin, as I stared hard at McMillan's cold, defiant eyes.

"We'd certainly like to talk—"

"How about a whole series devoted to killers who got away with it, murders that got blamed on someone else. We could start with the murder of Daphne McMillan. We'll show highlights of what he did tonight, how he told the world how much he loved her and how much she loved him, and then we'll show what he really did." I turned abruptly to Harry Godwin. "Instead of staging the trial, showing before it ever happened what everyone wanted to think it was like, we'll stage the crime. But it won't be fiction, we'll show what really happened: how he followed his wife to Julian's home, how he killed her!"

I shot a glance at Bryan Allen. "And I'll bet you anything the ratings will be a hell of a lot higher than what you and this murdering liar got tonight!"

Before I could say anything more, Albert grabbed my arm and led me away, explaining over his shoulder that it had been a long and difficult day.

Chapter Thirteen

THE TELEVISION TRUCKS that had circled the courthouse during the long weeks of the trial had started leaving the day the verdict was announced. On the day set for sentencing, the only reporters there to cover it were the ones who wrote for the local papers and for the wire services. There was not sufficient suspense in the question whether a convicted murderer would spend the rest of his life in prison or wait on death row ten or twenty years for his execution to appeal to a television audience taught to expect something new and different every few seconds.

The courtroom had the feel of a hotel ballroom on a Sunday morning, the only traces of last night's fevered excitement a few limp streamers and a dust-covered floor. The court reporter moved her fingers with blank-eyed dull repetition; the bailiff stared straight ahead, stifling a yawn. Two guards brought Julian into the courtroom with the same bored efficiency with which they had moved a thousand faceless prisoners before. Maddy Foster, who had argued with such passion in her summation, glanced at the case file, closed it and leaned forward. She picked up a pencil, tapped the eraser on the legal pad she had in front of her, then turned it over and began to tap with the point.

There was nothing left of the tension that had built through the trial and culminated in the verdict, nothing of that sense of combat in which words were weapons and only the winner would survive. It was over, the game had been played; only the losers cared what happened next, and perhaps not all of them. With a stoic reserve that was both admirable and infuriating, Julian Sinclair had said to me the night before: "Save me if you can; don't think twice about it if you can't." In court he refused to ask anything for himself. Instead, he posed a dilemma that challenged what the jury had done.

"If I had killed her, if I had done that, then you ought to sentence me to death because I would without question deserve to die; but I did not kill her, and if you kill me now, think what you will have to regret when you finally find that out."

Maddy Foster seemed caught short by what Julian had said. From the mouth of any other convicted killer, those words would have sounded defiant, disrespectful, a last gesture of contempt for those who sat in judgment. But Julian had spoken in a voice serious and strangely sympathetic, as if he realized that all of them—the judge, the jury, the prosecution—were as much a prisoner as he, bound by circumstance to do exactly what they had done. As Maddy Foster watched him, studying him closely, I thought I saw the shadow of a doubt rise from the depths of her eyes. She was there to ask for the death penalty, and nothing anyone said could change the decision to do that. But she did it now with a certain obvious regret, a burdensome task she would have preferred not to perform.

I argued, or tried to argue, that Julian's life should be spared because even if the jury was right, even if he was guilty of this unspeakable murder, it was evident on the face of it that it had been a crime of passion, that it had not been done from some cold-hearted motive of advantage or revenge. On the prosecution's own case, there had not been any planning, any thought-out scheme. There was no compelling reason to sentence Julian Sinclair to death, and there was more than one reason to spare his life. Julian had given one of them; I gave another.

"With a mind like his, who is to say that even during a life in prison he may not do some good."

We both did our jobs, Maddy Foster and I; we both played our parts to the end. Nothing that we did made any difference. The decision about what would be done with Julian Sinclair, whether he would live or die, had been made long before now. I suspect it had been made that day he took the stand, the day he talked to that jury as if all twelve of them were as serious and as intelligent as he was. The most important things that happen in a trial sometimes leave no record at all. Julian Sinclair was different. Most of those who were in attendance during each day's proceedings had never seen anyone quite like him. They knew what he was accused of doing; and they knew, including even that supposedly impartial jury, that hardly anyone thought he was innocent—and yet he was not what they had expected. He seemed too decent, too intelligent, to have done anything like that.

There was nothing dramatic in the way the sentence was pronounced. Conrad Jarvis did not engage in any of those rhetorical beatings judges sometimes lavish on the condemned. Far from anything vindictive in his voice, there was a sense of deep regret, as of something valuable and promising now lost, when he pronounced those final words:

"Life imprisonment without possibility of parole."

Julian did not tense or shudder. There was no show of emotion.

"Thank you, Your Honor," he said with the same formality as a lawyer at the end of a proceeding.

I DID NOT SEE Julian Sinclair again for more than three months. For weeks I studied the voluminous transcript of the trial, searching for some reversible error, something that might form the basis of an appeal. It was a fool's errand, and I had known it from the start. An appeal lies only on those issues of law on which the trial court has ruled. In all the decisions that counted, Conrad Jarvis had ruled in favor of the defense. There was not going to be a new trial. The only way to get Julian Sinclair out of prison was to prove that her husband had killed Daphne McMillan instead, and I had no idea how I was ever going to be able to do that.

Three months does not seem like much time on the outside, but it must have seemed like three years to Julian Sinclair, locked up with the other new arrivals at San Quentin. I was eager to see him, but I hated coming here, to the tan high-walled prison that sat next to the bay right at the end of the Richmond–San Rafael Bridge. It seemed to taunt the inmates with their own confinement, tease them insane with the near proximity to freedom and civilization, the highway used by thousands a few short yards away.

There are over six thousand inmates in San Quentin, six hundred of them slowly losing their minds on death row. Julian had told me that. There were eight hundred guards and five hundred support personnel to keep them under control. Had that same ratio of roughly four and a half to one been adopted in the early grades of school, then who knows how many would have wound up here. The entrance requirements, at least for those who had killed someone, were in their own way almost as stringent as admission to one of the better schools. Murder, by itself, was not sufficient. You had to have been sentenced either to death or, as in Julian's case, to life without possibility of parole. If you were in San Quentin because you killed someone, you were not getting out.

"In a real sense, the lifers are the elite," explained Julian. "I don't mean because of what they did to get here. It doesn't have anything to do with having what the outside world might think of as a reputation. They know they are here forever, and they learn fairly quickly how to get what they can out of the life they have."

We were sitting in a windowless room, the only furniture two wooden chairs and a small square table. The double neon light overhead lent a ghastly greenish glow to the dark shadowed cement walls. The room felt close, claustrophobic; the air dank, musty, and not enough of it.

Julian looked different. His brown hair was cut close and he was dressed in the dull uniformity of prison garb, but it was more than that. He had lost weight, his face had become hollow, gaunt; his eyes had drawn back in their sockets, giving him the brooding aspect of someone guarded, detached and—dare I say it?—dangerous. It was probably nothing more than an intensification of the instinct of self-defense, the primitive and necessary response to a condition of existence in which you could never feel entirely safe. Whatever the prison authorities tried to teach about inmate life, that must have been the first thing every inmate taught himself: that he could never relax, never let down his guard, never fully trust anyone.

"Life is different here," remarked Julian as if he had read my mind. He was still filled with that same intense curiosity, that same inexhaustible desire to know everything about the world in which he lived, even if, or perhaps especially when, that world was as strange, as alien, as this.

"It isn't like being on one of those Southern chain gangs, doing hard labor breaking rock. If you're here for life you have the run of the place. There are two men to a cell and you're part of the general population. Everyone has a job; everyone gets paid. The curious thing is that even here in San Quentin, the pay structure follows the great American principle of economic inequality. That's quite remarkable, when you think about it, that two men—both of them serving the same sentence for the same crime—should make a substantially different hourly wage. Ignore for the moment that the highest wage isn't going to make anyone rich; consider only the huge differential between getting paid a dollar an hour or eight cents. You would think because we're all locked up, fed the same thing at the same time, always subject to other people's rules, we would all get paid the same—that is to say, if they decided to pay us anything at all. We're prisoners, after all—slaves. But what you have instead is capitalism run rampant, everyone who works eager to make more!"

Julian bent forward on his elbows, his eyes glittering with pleasure at having grasped the inner meaning of what at first had seemed a paradox.

"What they have done here—whether by accident or design doesn't matter—is to apply the principles of the market as a way to keep everyone in line. It is what, if I'm not mistaken, modernity is all about. How do you keep everyone from killing each other, taking what does not belong to them? What is the incentive for leaving everyone else alone? Property, or rather the ability to acquire it in peace. You need the law, and someone to enforce it, to make sure no one steals—but if everyone knows the law is there, everyone will concentrate all their energy trying to get more. It is the basis of the whole argument, isn't it? That freedom and capitalism go hand in hand? But notice," he went on with a sly, knowing grin, "the prison authorities grasped something the people on the outside don't want to admit: it works just as well with slaves; it doesn't require freedom at all.

"Thousands of men here, inmates of a prison, but except for the ones on death row, they all have jobs. The lifers, because they're here longer, acquire all the seniority. The more they make, the more they have to spend. They can buy things in the commissary; they can order out of certain catalogues; they can buy a radio, a television. So there is this powerful incentive to do your job well and move on to something that pays even more, and—this is the genius of it—there is a tremendous incentive not to make trouble, and not to let anyone else do so either. Because if that happens—if there is a fight, a riot in the yard—there is a lockdown and all those privileges are lost. And when that happens, the lifers don't like it; they don't like it one bit. Curious, isn't it? That in prison it is the murderers who have the greatest interest in law and order."

Julian caught his breath, looked at me with a vaguely apologetic smile, then lowered his gaze and began to laugh in that sad, uncertain way that bitter, lonely people do. His eyes suddenly came up. He stared at me with a strange intensity.

"I may not be able to survive this much longer."

Even as he said it, he was beginning to reproach himself for his weakness and irresolution. Pulling away from the table, he forced himself erect. He smiled bravely and, as I thought, with something like impatience.

"Don't pay any attention to me. I haven't really talked to anyone since that last day in court, when I talked to you."

He must have wondered how long he could stay sane, how long he could keep the keen edge of his intelligence from being dulled and blunted and finally defeated by the crushing, mindless repetition of prison life.

"The law may save me yet."

Startled, I tried to hide the bitter disappointment I felt. I had gone through the trial transcript more times than I could count.

Convinced that there must be something there, something I had missed, I had had two other lawyers work their way through it as well.

"I haven't been able to find anything yet," I began my carefully rehearsed speech. "But I'm going to—"

Julian cut me off. "I told you there wasn't anything there. There weren't any mistakes of law; certainly none that would have affected the outcome of the trial. You think this is your fault, don't you? You think you should have done something different, something that would have made it come out right."

There was a slight change in his expression. His eyes, which had never left me, seemed to come back into a sharper focus.

"It isn't your fault. No one could have done as well. I was convicted before the trial began. It's that electronic lynch mob I was talking about. You at least made them stop and think about it a moment before they got the rope."

He was smiling to himself, remembering when he had first said it, that day we met, when he had had so much fun telling Daphne on national television that she might want to wait for the trial before she started telling everyone how guilty the defendant had to be.

"The law may save me." He dropped his hands in his lap and leaned back against the chair. "The job I want here, the one I think they'll give me, is in the law library. It's run by a retired librarian, a woman who knows I taught at Berkeley. I can work as an assistant, helping inmates with their legal work." With a baleful glance, Julian shrugged. "Not quite like joining the firm, but at least it's the kind of work I was trained for."

An enigmatic smile, the look of someone who has a secret he cannot yet reveal, began to form on his mouth. He seemed confident, self-assured, as careless of the future as he had been that day he had gone off to his fencing lesson after we had had lunch at the faculty club on campus.

"There are certain legal issues I want to understand more thoroughly."

I started to say something ordinary, banal; something about how it was good to stay busy, to use his legal training, to use his mind.

"Issues I need to understand for the time when I'm finally out of here."

I did not know what issues he meant, but I thought I knew what he believed would set him free.

"I won't give up on that," I said earnestly. It was important that he have a hope to cling to, a reason to stay alive. "One way or the other, I'm going to prove McMillan murdered Daphne. I've already started. I'm—"

"I know that. I know you won't quit until you do. But that could take a long time, longer than I can wait."

"Then how? What do you propose . . . ?"

Then I saw it in his eyes, and I knew what he intended. My first reaction was that it was impossible, but then I wondered why he thought it could be done.

"Escape? From San Quentin? How?"

The glance he gave me made me think that he was more amused by the possibility than serious about the attempt. Julian had always been a dreamer, always a romantic. What else would he think about in prison but ways to get out? Swinging around to the side, he crossed his leg and with both hands grasped the corner of the chair. The look on his face became yet more enigmatic, more intense. His eyes darted all around that barren, distressing room. He bent closer over the corner of the chair. His eyes followed as his foot began to trace a lazy short half-circle in the air.

"There is someone named Phillips over on death row. He uses another inmate's medication to make himself violently ill. He's going to be executed, but that doesn't mean they can just let him die. They have to take him to the hospital. There are three they can take him to: one in San Francisco, one up in Novato, the other, closer, in San Rafael. A guard—unarmed—rides in the back of the ambulance. The prisoner is shackled of course. The reason the guard is unarmed is so the prisoner has no chance to get his hands on a weapon. An armed guard rides in front. A SWAT team rides in a separate car. What Phillips wants to do—the reason he keeps making himself sick—is to have people on the outside shoot the guards and break him out. It has not worked. Too much firepower, I suppose."

A grudging smile darkened his mood. "That guard—the one who rides in back—if he had a gun and it got taken away, he wouldn't have a chance. There's a policy here of no negotiation. That's what they told you when they let you in here today, isn't it? If you're taken hostage, they won't try to negotiate your release. They meant it, too. You can't be in this place a week without hearing what happened in the sixties when George Jackson tried to escape. His lawyer—some radical who sympathized with Angela Davis and the Black Panthers—got a gun inside by hiding it in his tape recorder. Remember how big they used to be? He's in a conference room with his client. Jackson hides the gun inside a black Afro wig. He has the gun on his head. When he gets back to the cell block, he grabs one of the guards and starts shooting. A couple guards were killed. Every new guard who comes here is told all about it, and told that if they are ever taken hostage, all they better do is duck when the bullets start flying, because if they're not immediately released that is what is going to happen. Prisoners know it, too; which is the reason, I suppose, that it has only been tried a few times since.

"Take someone hostage, try to bargain with another person's life—you ought to be shot. The only way to escape prison is just to walk away."

He made it sound so easy, so simple: I wondered for a moment if he had forgotten where he was. Julian saw the confusion on my face and seemed to enjoy it.

"There was a prisoner in H unit—that's down the hill. It was like one of those escapes you see in a movie. He made a rope out of the bedsheets and climbed out the window. The difficult part came next. He had to get over two fences, each with concertina wire—razor sharp—fifteen feet apart, and do it between two towers, each one with a guard inside. He used the same bedsheet rope to protect himself against the wire, but he could not have gotten away with it if one of the guards had not fallen asleep. Strange that no one seems to have asked how he could have known that would happen," remarked Julian with a wry grin. "He was never caught. I don't know what happened to the guard."

His eyes were full of mischief and his voice full of adventure. It was like listening to the boyhood fantasies of a young man still outside.

"But the best way is what I said before: just walk away. It happens here more often than you would think; more often than the people who run this place would like you to know. San Quentin isn't all maximum security. There are different levels of that. Level one is really no security at all, nothing but the inmate's own good sense. At the end of your sentence, when you have only a year or so to go, you get to live at what they call the ranch annex. It's where the prison grows some of its own food. You live in dormitories out in the open fields. All you have to do is walk away if you feel like it. Of course, if you do that and you get caught, you have to serve time for escape in addition to what you owe on your sentence. But they do it, some of them; usually because of a woman, something that has gone wrong they think they have to fix."

Did I need to remind him what his own sentence was, that there would never be a time when he would be scheduled to get out?

"Of course they don't let everyone go live at the ranch annex. You can't go there if you have any history of violence, or if you have ever tried to escape from any jail or prison."

Julian faced forward and planted both feet on the concrete floor. He began to search my eyes, to see if I had even started to figure it out.

"I admit these may seem like insurmountable difficulties for someone serving a sentence of life without possibility of parole, but as we both discovered during my trial, no system is ever quite perfect. Perhaps one day I'll find myself over at the annex with only an open field to cross between me and Highway 101 heading north to San Francisco."

A wistful smile stretched across his mouth, as he rose from the simple, prison-made chair. "Stranger things have happened," he said, holding out his hand to say goodbye.

I told him that I would come back, that I would see him again, that I had meant what I said about doing everything I could to prove that he had not murdered Daphne McMillan and that her husband had. He stood in front of me, his eyes clear and determined, his shoulders straight. He might have been one of those young gallant British lieutenants who flew every day against the Germans when Britain fought alone. There was that same understated courage, the same easy willingness to take on whatever fate had in store. I had done well right to the end. I had kept all my emotion in check: I had not given in. But I was seeing him now in the double aspect of the young man at the end of a life that had shown such astonishing promise, and the prisoner at the beginning of a long and heartless captivity; a young man who, in terms of what he could have been, might probably be better off dead; a young man who might well grow old in prison, dreaming of the open fields he could never cross.

"Julian," I said, grabbing him by the shoulders, trying to force him to understand how awful I felt. "I'm sorry, I . . ."

He pulled away, gently removing my hands. "No, it's all right. But do one more thing, if you would. Don't come to see me again. Not until I write and ask you to. This is my life now. I have to come to grips with that. I have to learn to live as if I'm never going to see or know anyone on the outside. A long time ago I read something I never forgot: 'It isn't what happens to you in life that matters; it is the way in which you face it.'"

I left San Quentin almost certain that I would never hear from Julian Sinclair again. It was only because he had not wanted to injure my feelings that he asked me to wait until he wrote, rather than tell me that he was turning his back forever on me and everyone he had known. And who could blame him? Nearly everyone had turned his back on him.

The November rains had come and the air smelled fresh and sweet and clean. When I reached the Golden Gate Bridge, the sun broke through the clouds, bathing San Francisco in a soft, golden light. Across the bay, high up in the Berkeley hills, the house where Julian Sinclair had lived and Daphne McMillan had died, was, like their memory, buried in a dense gray mist.

Chapter Fourteen

Robert McMillan became my own private obsession. Newspaper clippings, investigative reports, rumors I picked up on the street—I kept a file on anything that might lead me to the kind of evidence I needed to prove what he had done. I called in favors all over town. Someone whose son I had once helped got me the accident report on McMillan's second wife's death. She had driven off a cliff on the highway that twists high above the Pacific south of Monterey. There was nothing left of the automobile and nothing left of her. There were no skid marks on the road, which seemed strange, and might have led to the suspicion that something had been done to the car had the police not learned that she had been drinking heavily at her home near Pebble Beach and had driven off in anger after being told she should stop. That is what Robert McMillan told them and the police had no reason to question anything he said.

"I told you once that what his friends described as eccentricity, I thought something closer to a streak of insanity," said Albert Craven one night at dinner a week or so after I had visited Julian in prison. "Now I'm sure of it. He's dangerous, perhaps the most dangerous man I've ever known. He's murdered at least one woman, perhaps two—there is nothing he won't do."

Albert raised the cup to his lips, held it there in front of his mouth, his eyes serious, undaunted.

"And now, I'm afraid, he's coming after us."

I thought he was being overdramatic. What could Robert McMillan do to Albert Craven, or to me?

"The firm has lost three clients already. I expect before this is over we'll lose more." Albert reached for my arm across the table. "Don't worry about it. I'm not," he assured me with a confident eye. "It's always good to find out who your friends are: who you can count on and who you can't."

"Harry Godwin?" I asked. "Did he . . . ?"

"Harry? Oh, hell no." Albert threw out his hand, gesturing for the waiter. He ordered both of us a drink. "Harry will never leave. He's loyal to the bone. And besides, you forget, Harry made his fortune on scandal. Leave the firm because we said Robert McMillan killed his wife? If we didn't already represent him, he would leave who he had and come to us. Which reminds me. He called today. He wants you to come for that visit you promised."

"I never promised him that."

"He's renewed the invitation. You should go. You should get out of the city for a while. You could use a little change of scene. And if I'm not mistaken, there was someone you wanted to talk to, a woman who works for Harry. And maybe after everything that has happened, you might want to consider again that old adage about the necessity sometimes to fight fire with fire. Harry wants to talk to you about doing something on television, something in which you would have a great deal of control. Anyway, there it is, an offer which you can take or not as you choose. But there isn't any harm in talking to him about it, and you might enjoy Sydney. It's the summer down there now."

"What about the business you've lost because of this? I could leave the firm. There isn't any point in you paying a price for what I do."

"A price? I should pay you. These same cringing cowards, so desperate to stay in McMillan's good graces, afraid that after some passing expression of his displeasure over what happened to him at the trial, think if they don't sever our relationship, he might sever theirs with him. Can you imagine what fun it's going to be after you prove Julian innocent and McMillan a murderer and a liar, when they come crawling back, claiming it was all just a tragic misunderstanding? Can you imagine how good it's going to feel when I tell them that we're so busy I could not possibly consider taking on another client, and that even if I could, I'd rather be dead than dirty the firm's name by representing them? It's one of the reasons why at my age I know I'm not going to die: because it would not be fair if I didn't have that one chance to tell them to go screw themselves. So don't even think about leaving the firm. You can't. Not before you prove Julian innocent and I get to do that. You owe me that much. That," he added with a sly grin, "and the bill, which I am sure will be outrageous, for this night's dinner."

Each week the file on Robert McMillan grew thicker and more diverse, with everything from the published financial reports of the companies he controlled to the society page clippings of the gatherings he attended with the rest of the city's business and social elite. There was nothing in the photographs taken of him within the first year of his wife's murder that betrayed any lingering sense of grief. It was still the same almost aggressively handsome face and the same firm athletic smile. There was nothing introspective in his eyes, nothing to suggest that he spent much time thinking about the past. Even in those still photos, he seemed to dominate and draw toward him everything around him. He looked like a man who thought he owned the world.

The file grew larger, and the chance of catching him, of proving what he had done, seemed with each passing day to become more remote. He was a man without a conscience, a man who would never be driven by remorse to confess to anyone, even someone he trusted, what he had done. He had confessed to Daphne, but only to tell her that what had happened to his second wife could happen to her.

I felt defeated, depressed; locked in a battle I could not win and could not quit. The determination that had at first been accompanied with a certain heartfelt enthusiasm began to turn into something closer to a sense of duty, an obligation. It was the gradual and perhaps inevitable transition to a state of passive observation, of watchful waiting, of dying hope and resignation. There were other cases, other trials, new responsibilities that required my attention. The day would come when Julian was less an urgent necessity than a memory too painful to think about.

And then, two days before Christmas, while I was doing some last-minute shopping, I caught sight of Robert McMillan on a corner, waiting for the light to change. He was standing next to a striking, well-dressed woman. They were each holding bright-colored shopping bags filled with packages wrapped in silver and gold. She was younger, much younger, in her early thirties at most, with sleek long legs and a face like money.

In the jostling crowd behind me, someone remarked with a guttural laugh, "Someone should sue the bastard." I looked around to see two shrewd-eyed men in business suits nodding in agreement as they headed up the street in the opposite direction. From the tone of their voices, I guessed they were talking about someone with whom they had both had dealings. The light changed and as the crowd surged forward, I nearly tripped as I tried to get close to where McMillan and his new friend would pass. Close enough to touch him if I had wanted, I stared right at him, but he never saw me. He was too engrossed in the glittering young eyes of the woman moving next to him on the other side.

It hit me as I stepped onto the corner sidewalk. They were right, those two perfect strangers who had been talking with such gleeful malice about someone I did not know. Sue the bastard: it was the American way, every lawyer's dream. A civil suit had a different set of rules than a criminal case. So what if I could not prove beyond a reasonable doubt that Robert McMillan was a murderer and Julian Sinclair was not. In a civil action the burden of proof went all the way down to a preponderance of the evidence, which meant having just a little more—fifty-one percent, if you wanted to quantify it—than the other side. If I could get McMillan into court in a civil case . . . But how? There had been cases when someone acquitted of murder in a criminal case became the defendant in a wrongful death action brought by survivors of the murder victim, but Julian Sinclair had been convicted. Even if I could find a relative willing to sue on Daphne's behalf, that conviction would be used to throw the case out of court. I would never have the chance to use a civil trial as a search for new evidence.

There had to be a way. I started walking, following blindly the direction of the crowd. The air was cold, crisp, a perfect late December. Cars and buses, cabs and trucks, honked their sulky horns and made their strident noises. On each corner, between a shaken silver bell tinkle, clear, sharp voices echoed gratitude for every dime or dollar given; while every face that gave it beamed with inner pleasure at the cheerful sadness of another Christmas to remember. Two blocks, three, moving at a steady pace, bright lights everywhere, a thousand different sounds translated into a single song, and I did not see or hear anything, only that speech without grammar that kept beating in my mind, something I knew, something I had forgotten.

"Don't sue the bastard," I said to a stunned red-dressed Santa Claus as I handed him a twenty. "Make the bastard sue you!"

"Merry Christmas," he said with a look of shared madness before he turned and shook his bell at the people coming up the street behind me.

The weight had been lifted from my shoulders. I could scarcely wait for morning when I could tell Albert Craven my scheme for getting McMillan back in court. That night at home, I spent hours reading up on the law of slander. It was one of the few actions in which the normal economic calculations of costs and benefits did not apply. If someone damages your reputation, the only way to restore it is to bring a lawsuit and show that what had been said was false and malicious and that the one who said it was a liar. All I had to do was make a public statement that Robert McMillan had murdered his wife and let another man be punished for his crime. The failure to sue me then for defamation would be tantamount to an admission.

Albert Craven was not sure it would work.

He found me down the hall from his office in the library, poring over the major reported cases. It was Christmas Eve. The firm was closed for the week. Everyone was on holiday but us.

"I thought I might find you here. I got your message last night," he explained as he dropped into a chair on the other side of the long library table.

Dressed in one of his expensively tailored suits, Albert looked around the labyrinth of bookshelves that twisted into the dim recesses of the cavernous room. He stroked his small chin, the expression in his narrowed eyes one of shrewd appraisal.

"Maybe we should sell all this—the whole damn thing: the books, the furniture, the building even; go back to the way things were at the beginning, when there were just four of us, jammed into a couple of tiny rented rooms over on Montgomery Street. I used to take the trolley over to the courthouse and use the library there. Now we have a library larger than the one the courthouse had then—have our own librarian—and it isn't a hundred feet away and I never come. Half the lawyers who work here, I'm not sure I've ever met. I have of course— met them, that is—but I'm not sure I would recognize them if I ran into them on the street."

Ordinarily, I liked listening to Albert Craven compare the present with the past, but today I was impatient to know his reaction to how I proposed to draw McMillan out.

"But you have more pressing matters on your mind," he remarked, smiling at the pile of open volumes and the several notepads spread out upon the table. He pulled himself up from the lounging position he had assumed and began to speak with businesslike seriousness.

"The difficulty is that what you propose to say about him, you have said already. You accused him to his face during the trial, and it was repeated in all the papers. If I remember correctly, it was the lead story that night on television, at least the lead in the coverage of the trial."

I started to speak, but Albert lifted his left hand and briefly shook his head.

"I understand, of course, that things said during a court proceeding carry immunity from an action for defamation. But if you simply repeat now what you said then, McMillan can dismiss it as the lying complaint of a lawyer who can't accept defeat. He'll say that he isn't going to waste time dignifying it with a denial when he already denied it under oath at the trial, the same trial that found Joseph Antonelli's client guilty of that same murder."

Albert caught the look of eager anticipation in my eye. "What is it? You have something else up your sleeve, don't you?"

I had been here since seven in the morning and it was now close to two o'clock in the afternoon. With my shirt collar unbuttoned and ink all over my hands, I felt a little like a third-year law student getting ready for a week of finals at the end of the term.

"Have you eaten anything, Antonelli?" suddenly laughed Craven. "My God, it's Christmas Eve. If you're planning to stay here through New Year's, I'll have something brought in. What is it?" he asked, his eyes bright and alert. "What do you think you have?"

"I don't say anything about the murder—not directly. I accuse him instead of a long history of abuse of women."

I crooked my arm and swung it around the corner of the chair. A smile Albert must have thought feverish raced across my mouth.

"It hit me last evening, watching the faces of Christmas shoppers. A young couple was standing in front of Neiman Marcus, window-shopping, talking excitedly about something they saw; and I realized how trusted we are when we're with someone we love. That's why anything to do with sex that does not involve love is always a kind of betrayal. You can kill someone and claim self-defense; but if you force, or try to force, a woman to have sex; or if you have sex with another woman while you are supposed to be faithful to someone else—what defense could you ever have for that?"

I slapped both hands hard on the table and got to my feet. My joints were tired from sitting. I stretched my arms and then began to walk slowly back and forth.

"If I accused him of the murder again, I'm sure he would do exactly what you say: dismiss it as something that has already been settled. But if I talk publicly about the things he has done with women, what choice does he have but to sue me for defamation? And once he does that, I get to depose him; which means I get to ask him questions under oath about almost anything I want. And that means," I added as I wheeled around and grasped the back of a chair with both hands, "that

I'll know a lot more about him than I do now. Maybe that will give me something I can use to prove that he murdered Daphne after all!"

There was another problem, and Albert pointed it out at once.

"No newspaper will ever print it. They won't take the chance that in addition to going after you, McMillan will file a libel action against them. . . . Oh, I see: You've decided you want to go to Sydney after all. You want me to talk to Harry Godwin because if you're on the air, you can say anything you like." His eyes became knowing, shrewd. "And because if the network gets sued, Harry has someone who works for him who can testify that what you say is true."

Albert put his hands behind his head and chuckled. "It's what the world has always suspected: Even on Christmas Eve there is a lawyer somewhere whose only thought is how to start someone suing someone else. Which reminds me," he remarked as the smile on his face softened. He rose from the chair and reached inside his jacket pocket. "This is for you. Merry Christmas."

He handed me a narrow, flat rectangular box, wrapped in ribbon. I was embarrassed. I had not gotten anything for him.

"It was a spur-of-the-moment thing. I knew you would be here, working all day—the way I used to, and probably still should—and I remembered . . . Well, never mind, just open it."

It had scarcely been the spur-of-the-moment purchase he claimed. The box was from Cartier and the fountain pen inside—a black ribbed barrel trimmed in silver—was the most gorgeous thing of its kind I had ever seen. My flustered tongue-tied incoherence was all the thanks Albert required. He lifted his wispy eyebrows and rolled a mischievous eye toward the ink-smudged pages filled with my illegible scrawl.

"I thought you could probably use a new one," he said dryly and to his own vast amusement.

THREE WEEKS LATER, in the middle of January, I boarded a midnight flight out of San Francisco. Fourteen and a half hours later I arrived in Sydney and entered a different world. Like most Americans, I had not thought much about a place I had never been. The Australians I had met in the United States, with the possible exception of Harry Godwin about whom I still was not sure, had all been cheerful and outgoing, with a rugged easygoing outlook on life, eager to talk, and more than willing to drink without any apparent effort far into the night. They were brash adventurers, tough-minded people who in the face of danger took their own bravery as no better than what anyone in the same circumstances would have done. It was British understatement without British reserve. They were the most likeable people on the planet, and I knew next to nothing about the way they lived.

Australia is larger than the United States. On a twenty-two-hour flight from Sydney to London it is six hours before you stop crossing over land. It is larger than the United States, but with not much more than half California's population: eighteen or nineteen million people, of whom a sizable proportion live in either Sydney or Melbourne and most of the rest in cities strung along the eastern shore.

The Australians call it the lucky country, because, though it has fought some of Great Britain's wars, it has no hostile neighbors waiting on the other side of some shifting territorial boundary to take back land on which it claims some dubious right. It is an island, the largest in the world; a continent floating in the temperate southern sphere, where the northern light breaks the solitude of winter and Christmas comes on a December summer day. It was the lucky country because the ones who first came here, whether the convicts brought in chains, or the officers who ran things thousands of miles from any higher authority, built a place without the burdens and the privileges of a landed aristocracy. It had certainly been the lucky country for Harry Godwin, an orphan immigrant from England, who shipped over in the early days of the war and became one of the most powerful and influential men in the world.

The woman sent to meet me at the airport seemed vaguely familiar.

"We met in San Francisco," she reminded me as we walked to her car.

"You were at the Four Seasons, having dinner with Harry Godwin and Bryan Allen," I said, starting to remember. "It was the same day the verdict came back in the Sinclair trial. I'm afraid I wasn't in a very good mood. I said some things I probably should not have said, not in front of you and Harry, anyway."

Rachel Burke smiled. "But you should have done, and I'm rather glad you did. I was quite ready to applaud. Bastard tried to rape me once. He deserved everything you said and a damned lot more besides, if you ask me."

She announced this with a kind of cheerful defiance. Despite what had happened to her, she certainly did not seem to think of herself as a victim. Her eyes were fixed on the flat highway in front of her as we drove toward the city. I guessed she was in her mid-thirties, not beautiful in any obvious, striking way, but the more you were around her the lovelier she seemed, with fine delicate skin and eyes remarkable for their depth and tranquillity. I noticed that she was not wearing a ring. She had been a married woman, according to what Harry Godwin had told me, when Robert McMillan had attacked her in a Sydney hotel. It was not any of my business to ask, and another question was pressing much more urgently in my mind.

"Why were you there? At dinner that night? Did you know McMillan would be there? Or did Bryan Allen just bring him along after they had done the show?"

She seemed slightly baffled by the tone of incredulity in my voice.

"You mean because of what he tried to do? Yes, well, it wasn't as if he had done what he wanted, was it? Americans don't always seem to hold their liquor. He was crude and obnoxious; he made advances. I told him what I thought of what he was doing. I told him I was married—I'm not anymore," she added with a quick, sidelong glance. "I told him he had to stop. That really seemed to set him off. He started grabbing at me, ripping at my clothes, screaming things that, shall we say, lacked all imagination. So I stopped it. That's all that happened, nothing more. So, no—I didn't mind he was coming to dinner. I rather looked forward to seeing what he would do when he found me there, instead of just Harry alone."

I had missed something. When she said he had stopped it, she meant the attack, the attempt to rape her, but she made it sound as if it had not required any more effort than hanging up a telephone or turning down a written invitation.

"You 'stopped it'?"

Her chin came up; a smile glittered triumphant on her mouth.

"I know a little about self-defense. I grew up with two brothers. Have you ever noticed how quickly a man's mood changes when you hit him hard in the balls with your knee? The last thing our friend Robert McMillan wanted to think about was sex. But if you'd like to take me to dinner, I'm free," she added without a pause.

She laughed at the look she caught on my face. "Don't know if you're more afraid to say no, or to say yes. I wouldn't worry much if I were you. I'm usually reasonably safe," she added as her eyes, quiet and contented, moved back to the road.

Chapter Fifteen

"AMERICA CONQUERED the world. There are no more ideals, no more religion, no more morality. There is only technology."

Sitting behind the long rectangular glass table that served as his desk, Harry Godwin peered at me through lazy half-shut eyes. The immense corner office on the top floor looked out on the harbor, from the famous Sydney Bridge, where a group of fearless tourists were climbing slowly to the top, to the chalk-like headlands that formed the narrow gate to the Tasman Sea.

"I know what everyone says: that the tabloids and the network, that everything we produce is responsible for the coarsening of the culture and the corruption of morals."

Godwin waved his hand, amused at the false bravado of an insect that did not know it had lost its sting.

"What culture they might mean, I'm not sure I know. And corrupting morals? How? By giving people what they want to watch? Suppose I closed down the network tomorrow. Do you think for one bloody minute that would change anything? I did not create the American obsession with sex and violence and with instant gratification: I just learned to understand where it was going—what people wanted—a little bit ahead of some of the others." Godwin rolled his eyes. "Culture! This from people who think some fat thug chanting some vicious cop-killing rhyme is engaged in an act of artistic expression, a musical creation no different than what in their time Mozart or Beethoven had done!"

I had spent three days in discussions with Harry Godwin and some of his people. This was one of the first times we had talked alone.

"And just how much classical music can we expect to see on the network next season?" I had the temerity to ask.

Harry Godwin was blunt, plainspoken, but too powerful, too important for people to speak back to him the same way. He gave me a look that must have silenced more than one person who had something to lose from his displeasure. I ignored him.

"How much Wagner, how much Donizetti, how much . . . ?"

He sprang out of the circular steel chair and bounded across the room to a set of rosewood bookshelves. Standing on his tiptoes, he reached a thin volume on the top shelf.

"I did not go to university," he felt compelled to tell me as he thumbed the pages. He sat down on the thick leather arm of a square black chair that, along with three others, was arranged around a glass coffee table just below the book-lined shelves. "I never went to school a day in my life. But early on, I learned to read. The printers taught me," he said, having found the place he wanted.

There was an almost childlike pride in his eyes as he recalled his boyhood achievement.

"In those days, way back before the war, print was set one letter at a time. A man who was a printer then, though he may have started out like me, an orphan without any education, learned to do something most presumably well-educated people today not only can't do, but would not think important: to read slowly, with great care and precision, not one word at a time, but one letter. I knew printers then, old men who had been doing it for forty, fifty years, who could repeat from memory whole passages—whole pages—from books whose print they had set years before, at the beginning of their careers. I used to listen to them talk among themselves about what they had read, and if they spoke highly of something—which wasn't all that often—I would find it and read it myself. This, for example." He eyed the book he held in his hand with a glance of brief nostalgia. "One of them had set the type for the first English translation. Seems impossible, doesn't it?" he added with an inward smile. "That you can live so long that someone you knew when you were a boy, a man who was then probably as old as I am now, should have in his youth set the type for something Tolstoy wrote?"

Godwin opened the book to the place where he had kept his thumb. "This is what I wanted you to hear. It's the point I wanted to make, when I said I just see where things are going, that I didn't have anything to do with how things got to be what they are. This was written in 1910, the year Tolstoy died:

"'Medieval theology and the moral corruption of Rome poisoned only their own respective people, and hence only a small portion of humanity; today electricity, railroads, and telegraphs are corrupting the whole world. Everyone appropriates these things; they cannot avoid appropriating them, and everyone is suffering in the same manner, forced in the same degree to change their way of life. Everyone is being put in a situation in which it is necessary to betray what is most important in their lives, to betray an understanding of life itself, to betray religion.

"'What are machines supposed to manufacture? What are telegraphs supposed to transmit? What are schools, universities, and academics supposed to discuss? What kind of news is supposed to be conveyed by books and newspapers? What is supposed to be accomplished by millions of human beings who are drawn together and subjected to a higher power? For what purpose are hospitals, doctors, and pharmacists supposed to prolong life? . . .'"

From the shadow of that book-lined alcove, Harry Godwin looked at me across the bright, sterile, sunlit room.

"All the books, the serious books, talked about it before the First World War—that's what I learned listening to the printers talk about the books they read letter by letter—the way civilization had been changed by technology and the machine, how no one believed in anything anymore except the importance of their own position and whatever worldly possessions they had managed to acquire."

Godwin closed the book and held it on his lap. He tapped the cover three times, paused, then tapped it once more.

"And look what has happened since, the way that technology keeps building on itself: the telegraph replaced by the telephone; radio, then television; the railroad as good as replaced by cars, trucks—the airplane, the missile. If civilization was in danger of destruction—if it had been destroyed already, before the First World War—what now, with all of this? I don't know. It's beyond my grasp. All I know is that whatever got unleashed on the world, it's much too late to do much about it now. The world demands comfort, security, entertainment: all the things Tolstoy thought would make us all less human. Perhaps he was right. He was a great man, and I'm not. Someone else can worry where all this is headed and what it means. I'm just in the business of giving people what they want, and if they ever want Mozart and Beethoven and Wagner and Donizetti, I'll give them that. But right now they want more of crime and punishment and so, if we can reach an agreement, I'll give them you."

Godwin replaced the Tolstoy volume on the top shelf where it would not be seen except by someone who knew already that it was there.

"Come along with me," he said in a casual voice as he opened the door and started toward the elevator down the hall. "I'll take you to my favorite place for lunch."

Harry Godwin drove a very expensive car, a pearl gray Bentley, but he drove it himself. There was no limousine waiting to take him where he wanted, no driver waiting to open the door. Visiting the network offices in New York or San Francisco, always working, he would sit in the leather-lined backseat, studying under a reader's lamp program ratings and budget projections, the shifting numbers that were the lifeblood of his business, while someone else drove. But this was Sydney, and Sydney was home.

Instead of a restaurant in the financial district downtown, he headed into the park and followed the curving tree-lined road out to a promontory where he stopped the car. Clutching a small brown paper bag in his hand, he led me along a footpath to a ledge carved into a rock beneath the spreading foliage of an enormous tree with a thick, wide trunk that twisted around itself like braided rope.

"Mrs. Macquarie's chair," Harry Godwin remarked after he sat down and opened the bag. He removed two sandwiches wrapped in old-fashioned wax paper, the kind that, because it was not made to adhere to what it covered, began to flap open once he lifted them out of the bag. "You have a choice," he said with a droll expression. "Ham and cheese or ham and cheese."

Godwin bit into the sandwich without enthusiasm. He did not care what he ate, as long as it did not take too much of his time.

"It's called Mrs. Macquarie's chair because this is the spot, as far out into the harbor as the land goes, that the wife of Lachlan Macquarie, the governor who came after Captain Bligh, used to come to and sit. I'll tell you a secret: it's where I came, too, when I first came to Sydney, and for a long time after that. It was my first Australian home. I would sleep out here, when the weather was fine. It was a lot better than sleeping in the back of the old brick warehouse where I first got work. And you have to remember how exciting it was, for a boy my age, in the years of the war."

While he took another bite of the sandwich, he gestured with his arm toward the inlet that ran along the shore behind us to the right. Four ships of the Australian navy were berthed at the long dock.

"That's Woolloomooloo. There were a lot more ships then, American, British, coming in and out, day and night; sailors everywhere. I used to hawk newspapers among the Yanks that came ashore. I learned pretty quick to shout whatever news from the States might be inside."

Slowly, as if he were reluctant to let go of what he remembered now about the past and his own origins, his eyes came back around, not to me, but to the placid gray waters lapping against the rocks below us.

"When I left England, I didn't leave anyone behind. I never knew my mother or my father: I didn't have any relations; I was too young, and too poor, to have any friends. It was all a great adventure, coming out here, the war on, the first time I had been on a ship. But when I got here, I'd never felt quite that lonely in my life. There was nothing familiar to me, nothing I knew. I may not have had much, living orphan-like in London, but I had learned to make my way. When you don't have parents, when you come into the world a stranger—I'm not saying I would recommend it to anyone—but there are certain advantages. You don't have any expectations, it never occurs to you that there is anyone on whom you can depend, you never think that anyone depends on you. In that sense, the world becomes your own creation: it's whatever you choose to make it.

"Mrs. Macquarie would sit out here for hours. What was she thinking, watching the waves wash in from the ocean, ten thousand miles away from home and everything she had known, knowing she might never be going back, that she might have to live the rest of her life in this flat, inhospitable place surrounded by water and with scarcely any fit to drink, scorching summer heat and as many bugs and snakes as you'd ever find in Africa? It's a wonder she didn't go a little mad, and perhaps she did, though I doubt it."

He looked at me with a smile that while it made a show of imitating the affectations of superiority, was not entirely without certain deeper pretensions.

"She was an Englishwoman, after all, and an Englishwoman would never allow something so self-indulgent. She may have been out here all alone, but she was still part of England."

Godwin finished the sandwich, carefully folded the wax paper into a square and placed it back inside the brown paper sack.

"That's the truth of it—what you Americans have such a hard time understanding about us. You've forgotten all your old ties to Britain because you broke them. We never have, and perhaps we never will. See that over there?" he asked, pointing directly across the harbor at a large white house that perched on the rocks just this side of the Sydney Bridge. "That's the Governor's House. It isn't any museum. We still have a governor, the Queen's own representative. We elect our own government, we're a separate nation, but a nation that in some sense remains one of the Queen's dominions. Tell you the bloody truth: if I wasn't who I am—didn't have all this infernal business all the time—that's the job I'd like: be the Queen's own governor, live in that house over there. Fair distance traveled from when I first came here, during the war, when Elizabeth was still a girl and her father, King George, was on the throne.

"I'm an Australian, but I'm British to the bone. I was lonely when I got here, but I still had that: that knowledge that every Britisher, orphan child or not, was still part of that family. I love the Queen. It isn't the pageantry, the palaces—it isn't even the tradition, though there is some of that. It's having someone you always love and respect who teaches you life's lessons about courage and honor and right conduct and good manners and how you're supposed to behave. Americans don't have that. You used to, with some of your presidents, but no more. And that's the problem, isn't it? You don't have anyone to look up to, no one to set the example that everyone wants to follow. It's one of the reasons Americans have become so stupid. No offense," he added without any change in his determined, even-minded expression. "There are exceptions. But, taken as a whole, in terms of what some people might still call culture, what would you call it, if not stupidity institutionalized? That's why the network has done so well there," he remarked without apology or the slightest sign that one might be in order. "Why do you think so many people like to watch what we show them? Because it makes them feel comfortable with themselves, with the way they think."

Harry Godwin stood up. With his hands on the small of his back, he rose up on his toes, the way he had when he reached for that book in his office. He stayed there, as high as he could go, balanced against the wind that blew off the harbor, rustling through the leaves with the dry breath of summer. A sly, crooked smile inched along his mouth until it reached all the way across.

"But at Albert's prodding, I've repented. Instead of giving the Americans what they want to see, we'll try this once to give them what they ought to hear. We'll give them you."

He bounced twice, to see how high he could reach, then came down off the balls of his feet and stood planted flat.

"Albert was bloody angry, that's what he was. Called me in the middle of the bloomin' night to tell me what he thought of what we'd done. But I suppose you know all about that, don't you?"

With his arms crossed in front of him, he kicked at a thick-rutted root that ran only half-buried in the dirt. He raised his head just far enough to see me. He was surprised at my puzzled expression, and knew immediately that he should not have been.

"Didn't tell you, did he? Should have known. Albert would not go telling that sort of thing to another, especially when what he was saying, he was saying on that other man's behalf. Called me right after Bryan Allen began his nightly diatribe against your client, Sinclair. Told me it was damned unfair, that the least we could do was give you a chance to give the defendant's side of it. I thought it was a good idea. I'm not in the business of convicting anyone, innocent or guilty; I'm in the business of building an audience. If giving both sides a chance to have their say will help do that, I'm all for it."

Harry Godwin took the wax paper from my hand, folded it into the same square he had done before, and tucked it into the bag.

"He was angry that time, but he was livid that night we had dinner and I told you about what we were going to do: have a televised version of the trial they would not let us cover."

"I was there," I reminded him. "Albert didn't say a thing about it. I was the one upset, remember?"

"I'm afraid I remember more than you," he replied with the look of someone who had made a lucky escape. "After he dropped you off, Albert came back to the hotel. He told me that your client wasn't guilty, and that if he was convicted much of the blame would be on the heads of people like me. He said we were no better than an 'electronic lynch mob'—the phrase seemed familiar, but I couldn't remember where I had heard it before. Was it you? He was furious, Albert was. I thought he might have a coronary. Then he threatened me and I bloody well knew he was serious. I've known Albert—what?—thirty, forty years, and I'd never heard him threaten anyone before!"

Albert could not have done what Harry Godwin said. He was the least violent man I knew. And even if he had such an inclination, the thought that at his age he would threaten harm to anyone was so outrageous, so perfectly ludicrous, that I could not help myself—I laughed.

"Albert? That's impossible!"

"Swear to Jesus he did. Said if I didn't do something to try to make it right, I'd have to find another lawyer. Said he couldn't in conscience continue to have the name of his firm linked with ours. That hurt pretty bad, I have to tell you, after all the years we've been together."

There was something sad and funny and a little tragic in the thought that as they came to the end of their long, successful lives, the money they had both worked so hard to earn meant nothing when it came to wounded feelings and the bitterness of pride.

"He actually threatened that, did he?" I replied, trying hard not to laugh again. "Is that why I'm here: so you two old reprobates can become good friends again?"

"Of course not. You're here because it's a good idea, a solid commercial possibility. If there is an audience for people like Bryan Allen, who think everyone who gets arrested is guilty, there is an audience for Joseph Antonelli, who thinks that some of the guilty don't get arrested and that they're the ones should be hung. That's what you want to do, isn't it? Reopen old cases, starting with one of your own; redramatize what happened, with the police investigation, the trial—show how someone innocent got convicted and how someone guilty got away. Listen, if there is anything the public likes better than convicting someone before they've had a trial, it's getting mad as hell at people who made a mistake."

Harry Godwin wanted to walk. We left the promontory and Mrs. Macquarie's chair and followed a path along the water, where dozens of passenger ferries plied back and forth, toward the opera house and the curving steel bridge. The bay was quiet, still, serene inside the broad circle of what, within the lush green boundary of the park, seemed like a lagoon. We cut across the grass of the Royal Botanical Garden and found ourselves in the middle of what to an American eye was strange, tropical vegetation. High overhead, hanging upside down from trees stripped bare by their voracious hunger, brown furry bats that were not bats at all, but flying foxes, slept undisturbed through the hot afternoon. With an Alice in Wonderland quality, a sign just inside the entrance at the other side invited visitors to walk on the grass. The garden belonged to everyone who came there, it was yours to use, to love the treasures it contained, to make them in that sense of love and feeling your own. That is what it said, and, having come to know a little about the people who lived here, I believed it.

"You're convinced he's innocent, this young—and brilliant, from what Albert tells me—Julian Sinclair? Life without possibility of parole," added Godwin to his own obvious displeasure. "There are no limits for Americans in anything, even, or perhaps especially, revenge. You're worse than the Italians! Sorry, no offense," he said with a matter-of-fact expression. He stopped, smiled, turned and faced me. "A friend of mine in Rome, a man I've known almost as long as I've known Albert—we were in a restaurant once, he pointed to someone he said he had always hated. When I asked him why, he wasn't particularly embarrassed to admit that, as he put it, 'I've hated him so long, I can't remember.' We don't have capital punishment in Australia, and it would be a rare case where someone was sent to prison without a chance of someday getting out."

He started walking, moving at the same no-nonsense pace he had assumed from the beginning. Harry Godwin did everything with an eye to efficiency.

"And you're certain Robert McMillan did it? Certain enough that you want me to stand behind you if he files an action for slander? I don't think he will, you know. He may be an American, but he isn't stupid. He isn't stupid at all. He won't start a lawsuit he knows he can't win. He tried to rape Rachel—I think that still qualifies as abuse of women."

I was starting to have difficulty keeping up. It was hot and getting hotter, a blank white heat that quickly became debilitating, though not, apparently, for Harry Godwin or any other Australian who passed us from the opposite direction. Shirtless middle-aged men jogged by barely breathing. Women pushed strollers with children who wore caps, while their mothers wore none. In a broad open space, a game of cricket was under way, a round of polite applause from a dozen people watching as an over-the-head straight-arm delivery pitched the ball one bounce to the wicket.

"From what Rachel told me, he didn't get very far."

Under the spreading branches of a banyan tree with an odd twisting trunk like the one above Mrs. Macquarie's ancient chair, Godwin found an empty bench. His eyes drew close together as he stared at the city skyline looming over us, just blocks away. His suit coat, carried under his arm while he walked, now lay across his knees.

"From what Rachel told you, you probably think McMillan got the worst of it. But if you'd seen her that night, her eye cut, her mouth all bloody, you wouldn't have been so easily convinced. She gave him a knee all right—she's a bit proud of that—but he made her pay for it, the wretched bastard. He hit her good. I did not think it at the time, but after what you told me about him, looking back on it, I imagine he might have killed her, beaten her to death, if someone had not come along."

Nearly as old as Albert Craven—in his late sixties, if I was not mistaken—there was a hardness about Harry Godwin, a physical tenacity that Albert had never had. It was the difference between being born into a life of modest wealth and reasonable privilege and being born into nothing at all, forced from birth to fight for everything you got. It was the difference between what they would have done if they had happened on the scene and discovered what McMillan had done to Rachel Burke. Albert Craven would have called the police and, if he had the chance, given McMillan as stern a lecture as he had ever given anyone before; Harry Godwin would have beaten McMillan unconscious or been beaten trying.

"I'm the one who made certain McMillan came that night to dinner. I was supposed to be back here in Sydney, but when I found out that Allen had arranged to have him on the night the jury brought back the verdict, I decided to stay the few days until it happened. That's when I had Rachel fly over. I wanted to see what he would do, how he would react, when he walked into the Four Seasons expecting to see me alone and found Rachel there with me instead."

A cockatoo shrieked high above in the tree. Unimpressed, a black-and-white ibis pecked with its long curved beak around a gnarled gray fig tree a few yards away. Stretching both legs out in front of me, I crossed one ankle over the other. I could see McMillan's face, the silent taunting in his eyes, when he grasped my hand.

"He didn't react at all, did he?" I asked, as I watched, high up in the tree, other shrieking cockatoos join the first. "Either he did not remember her, or she was someone he could barely recall having met."

For a moment, Harry Godwin seemed to take what I had said under advisement.

"You're right. There was no reaction, at least nothing like what I would have expected. Though, now that we're talking about it, I'm not sure what it was I did expect. What could he have said? What could he have done, except to pretend that the whole business never happened? I imagine that's what I would have done, had I ever been stupid enough to put myself in his position. But there was something beyond what you describe, and I have to tell you, it convinced me that you were right, that your client Julian Sinclair was innocent, that McMillan killed his wife. At first, it was the strange look in his eyes. I could not quite define it, only that it seemed odd and out of place. The jury just come back that morning with the verdict in the case, the man accused of murdering his wife had just been found guilty. I thought it must be fatigue, the kind of feverish look people get when they've gone about as far as their adrenaline can take them. First the trial, then the verdict, then the hour-long interview—it would be enough to exhaust the inner resources of anyone. But even then, I knew better than to believe that. After we finished dinner, McMillan—it was just extraordinary what he did—he asked Rachel, for God's sake, if she wanted to go somewhere with him for a drink. He had just told the world how he never loved anyone the way he loved his wife, Daphne, and that he knew he could never love anyone that much again, and all he can think about from the moment he sees Rachel is how much he wants to get her in bed. That's what that look meant. It was lechery, and something more than that, something deep and disturbing about making a woman submit."

"What did he do when Rachel said no?"

"She didn't say no. She asked him instead if he thought he would have better luck 'the second time you try to rape me?'"

"Good for Rachel. What did he say to that?"

A look of disgust swept across Harry Godwin's eyes. "He smiled, the way, as I remember, he smiled at you: calm, confident, as if he had everything under control. He looked right at her, or rather, I think, right through her. 'Isn't that what you wanted?' he asked with that insufferable smile still on his lips."

Godwin got to his feet and took a long look around, his eyes grim, determined.

"Let's go back to the office and put the finishing touches on our agreement. I wish you would do the show on a regular basis instead of just once in a while, but do the show: perhaps you'll change your mind after you get a taste of it. Say anything you like about Robert McMillan and anyone else—but especially about him." He gave me a sly glance. "And if you're in any doubt about how far you can go, you can always use Bryan Allen as a standard of what the network demands in the way of moderation."

Chapter Sixteen

I SPENT THREE WEEKS in Sydney, and would have stayed longer if I had not had to get back to San Francisco for a trial. Beneath the invariable cheerfulness of the Australian, there was something sad and mysterious that, as an outsider, I did not understand. Was it the absence of what an American took almost for granted: a future filled with great expectations and a past that made us struggle with our own imperfections? Australians seemed to live more in the present, and perhaps for that reason enjoy more of what they had. It would have been hard to imagine that the harsh and strident, in-your-face talk-show television that Harry Godwin had done so much to popularize in America would have found an audience in the country he called home.

"And now America is about to be blessed with the Joseph Antonelli show. Who says Harry Godwin is trying to ruin the American civilization?" taunted Albert Craven, his pink face aglow. Sunk into the thick soft chair behind his heavy oversized desk, his hands folded neatly in his lap, he watched out the window as a muted shaft of sunlight broke through the gray morning fog.

"When do you do the first one?" he asked, still smiling at his own remark.

"First they have to come up with a name," I replied. "And if the discussions I heard among what they call their 'creative people' are any indication, that could take years. And, no, it won't be called 'The Antonelli Show.' They would not say so, but I think they think it's too Sicilian. They want something that makes an immediate connection with what the show is about."

"Any good ideas?"

"Me? No. But the best one I heard was something one of their publicists suggested after we had all had a couple of drinks late one night in a pub: 'Them What Was Screwed!' I thought it had a certain ring," I said as Albert's face turned a bright shiny delighted shade of pink.

"Did she say it like that? With that kind of accent? Like what's her name—Eliza Doolittle in *My Fair Lady*? 'Them What Was Screwed!' How wonderful!"

"Harry and I like things that sound the way real people talk," I said, cocking an eye.

"Harry and you? How real people talk?"

Albert pulled his head back and raised his eyebrows. A look of vast amusement entered his eyes as he twisted around in the chair and stared at me straight on.

"How quickly we give up all standards when it's a question of fame and fortune on television."

He drew himself up and changed expression. Reaching inside the top desk drawer on the right, he pulled out an envelope that had been opened some time before. He tapped the envelope against his fingers.

"I shouldn't have opened this, but it came while you were gone, and because of the return address . . ."

Without another word of explanation, he handed me the envelope. The return address was San Quentin.

"He wants to see you," said Albert. "He doesn't say why. But he does make the rather curious remark that he wants to see you 'one last time.' What does he mean by that? Do you know?" asked Albert, a worried look in his gentle blue eyes.

I opened the letter and read it through. From the tone of it, I thought the answer to Albert's question lay in Julian's almost archaic sense of manners and morals. He was serving life in prison for a murder he did not commit, and he was afraid he might have wounded my feelings. I folded the letter, placed it back in the envelope and, because it had been meant for me, put it in my pocket.

"Julian thinks he might have been a little abrupt the time I was there. The rest of it, that business about wanting to talk to me about something else, I don't know what that might be. I'm glad he wrote. I want to tell him what I've done with Harry Godwin, what I'm going to try to do to try to draw out McMillan. I'll call San Quentin and schedule the visit—this Saturday, or as soon as they'll let me."

I had less than an hour before I was supposed to be in court. I was nearly to the door when I remembered.

"Did you have a chance to check on what McMillan did at Stanford?"

"Yes. There wasn't much. It was what you might expect. He had too much money to worry about where he might finish in his class. His grades were a bit above average, though his senior year, which is when he got engaged, there was a noticeable improvement. It seems he got serious, and there is no doubt that when Robert McMillan put his mind to something, he did it quite well. He became a womanizer, and then a murderer—all that is true—but he was never, at any time, a fool. There is one other thing," Albert called after me as I turned toward the door. "He has one thing in common with Julian. They both learned how to fence. McMillan was the captain of the fencing team at Stanford his senior year. Julian did not take it up until later, though, did he? He probably didn't have time, working the way he did, while he was still in school."

Nearly four months had passed since that day I left San Quentin, almost certain I would never see Julian Sinclair again. He had now been locked up, an inmate in a prison, for more than half a year. I remembered what I had been told by older men when I was younger that the days moved more quickly the fewer of them you had left; that the autumn years went dying in a fading light while the long night of winter waited just behind it with a cold, frozen sun. But Julian Sinclair was still the age when the future whispered in your ear the promise of immortality, when everything you ever dreamed, everything you ever wanted, still beckoned with a smile of your own achievement. More than half a year in prison: it must have seemed a lifetime since he had been free.

He was pushing a cart loaded with books when the guard brought me into the prison library. His back was turned to me as he stopped and with a slow, fastidious manner began reshelving a dozen thick volumes. I took a chair at one of five or six tables scattered in an open area between the stacks of law books kept at one end of the narrow building and the main library. The library was on the main courtyard. The windows in the back looked down on the baseball field and, beyond the walls of the prison, to an inlet of the bay. The building itself seemed nothing like what you would expect to find in a prison. Six enormous wooden crossbeams, three feet thick, bolted at the ends with iron straps, made the peaked ceiling look like something in a mountain lodge or a rural school. A mural of Yosemite, eight feet by twelve, hung high on the wall at the end, painted by some forgotten inmate, long since dead.

An inmate with a strange three-letter tattoo spoke briefly with Julian, then listened in an attitude of respectful attention to his reply. Two others, both Hispanic, eyed each other with deep and hostile suspicion as they waited their turn to ask something of the former law professor turned librarian's assistant. Julian said something to the two of them together. I was too far away to hear what he said, but there was a certain marked severity in his expression, the way a parent or a teacher might address two truants. Duly chastened, both of them lowered their eyes, and then, when he finished, nodded their agreement. Only then did he listen to the question each wanted to ask.

If I had seen him outside this dismal place, I would have thought he looked tired, distracted, as if he had spent too many late nights working on some brief he had to finish. But here, in the close quarters of this prison, that look of his seemed grim, ascetic, the effect of a permanent change of condition. It was not the look of someone who had resigned himself to his own captivity. There was something unconquerable and invincible just below the surface of his eyes.

He saw me out of the corner of his eye just as he finished with the second Hispanic. He did not smile, or nod, or give any other sign of recognition. Instead, he turned back to the shelves and put the last two books away.

"Thank you for coming," said Julian with an odd formality when, a minute later, he slid onto the chair across the table from me.

At first I could not understand the strange reserve, the way, instead of looking straight at me, his eyes darted in one direction then another. I felt my own manner start to stiffen, to take on the role of the attorney making the obligatory prison visit, to forget that we had been friends and, more than that, that he had been one of the few people I admired and even, if the truth be told, a little envied. Then I understood. He was embarrassed. It had not showed the first time I had come to see him, but then he had only just got here. He had not had time to realize the full implications of what he had become. It was like finding someone you had not seen in years—someone who when you last saw him had everything a man could want—living in the streets. I knew better than to tell him that the change was unimportant, or to utter any of the other words of comfort and assurance that, with all the best intentions, only remind those who have fallen how far they fell.

"That fellow you were talking to had a strange tattoo—'NLR.' Are those his initials?"

Julian came alive. Like someone astonished at the idiocy of the world, he slowly shook his head.

"He'd tell you those were his mother's initials, if you asked. Then he'd tell you that it's just an odd coincidence that maybe a hundred other inmates have mothers with those same initials. NLR stands for 'Nazi Low Riders.' They don't know what it means, either—except that they're white and racist and proud of it. Bizarre, isn't it? Prancing around prison, insisting on your own superiority, and the only people who believe it are other people who are just as stupid as you. But don't imagine that hatreds in prison are as monotonous as racism. Did you see the two Hispanics? I had to tell them that if they wanted my help with their appeals, they would have to leave their mindless animosities outside. This isn't as easy as it may sound," said Julian, his eyes becoming more keen, more curious, as he talked. "They're both under an obligation to fight each other with fists or knives anytime they come in contact. They are sworn enemies. Why? Because one of them comes from the north side of Fresno, and the other comes from the south. That's the dividing line, not just for Fresno, but the whole state of California. It's like most historical quarrels: no one knows why the line was drawn there, or, for that matter, why any line was drawn at all. It was probably because the white and black prisoners had each other to hate and the Hispanics felt left out. One of them probably thought, 'Okay, if we can't fight one of them, we'll fight ourselves.' It's like kids picking sides for a game—'Everybody over there, you're on that side; everybody over here, you're on this.'"

"But they all come to you?" I asked, watching the way the eagerness of his intelligence made him forget everything else.

"Just the ones who have a legal issue they think should be explored;

the ones who don't have a lawyer on the outside, or don't trust the one they have."

He began to relax. With his right hand he grasped his left upper arm, kneading it with his thumb. He looked at me without the need to look away.

"A lot of them shouldn't be here. I don't mean because they didn't do something that deserves punishment," he added with a quick, dismissive gesture. "But some of them shouldn't have been given sentences of such severity for the crimes they actually committed. Bad judges and worse lawyers. It's criminal," he said with deliberate irony, "some of what goes on out there. Makes you wonder who has been teaching these people, doesn't it?" he went on, enjoying the added, double irony of his own situation.

The light in Julian's eyes stayed there a moment longer and then began to dampen. He grew thoughtful, serious, intense. The awkward embarrassment was gone and would not come back.

"When I wrote you, I was not sure you would come." He made a kind of desperate, helpless gesture, as of one grown too conscious of the easy habits of dishonesty. "No, that's not true. I knew you would. It's that I didn't know that you would want to. I didn't have the right to talk to you the way I did the last time I saw you. When I told you I didn't want you to visit me here again unless I asked you, I think you know that I thought I had to cut off all contact to survive this place. I suppose I've always had a tendency to overdramatize my life."

A pensive smile filled with a strange nostalgia slipped across his handsome mouth. It was the look seen more often on the aging faces of much older men, staring back at the years of their youth, the years they took themselves so seriously, and seeing in it the first beginnings of the sad comedy of their lives.

"When you're young, it's easy to dream of tragic endings. . . ."

Slumped in the chair, his hands folded on the table in front of him, Julian studied his long, tapered fingers. "When you're young"—the words echoed in my mind, hollow, false, ridiculous. He was looking back at his life as if he were old, decrepit, the memory of what he had been the only way left to remember who he was—and he was barely more than thirty! Was that the real hell of this place, serving a sentence of life without possibility of parole: that all the days you lived were all the same, which meant you lived the same day over and over again, that the only thing you could remember was the life that stopped the day you came inside?

"I asked you to come because I need a favor," said Julian, leaning forward. "I need someone to be my executor. I have no family, no friends I could ask. I wonder if you might be willing."

"Your executor? Of your estate, in the event of your death? Is that what you're asking?"

"Yes, exactly. I'm afraid I took the liberty of using your name already. I can always change it," he added quickly. "There were forms I had to fill out. Simple enough, usually: next of kin, the person to be notified if something happens to you inside—if you have a medical emergency, or if you die. Someone has to be notified. Someone has to decide what to do with the last remains—that kind of thing. Would you mind?"

Julian turned, threw his near arm over the corner of the chair and tossed his head to the side.

"The first day I was in the general population—the first day I was out in the exercise yard—one of the Russians came at me with a sharpened fork. The Russians have the reputation of being the dumbest ones here. Lucky for me, he was no exception. He wanted to show everyone how tough, how vicious he could be, so instead of sticking me in the back, he came straight at me. All I had to do was wait until he pulled his arm back and lunged ahead. He was so off-balance that when I stepped to the side, he flew right past and landed on his face. Never touched me, stuck himself in the stomach instead. That must have hurt.

"He would have been put in solitary, what they call here administrative segregation, and might have been charged with attempted murder. I took the fork and hid it in my pants, while a couple of the others got him to his feet and helped him walk away. What else was I going to do? Let him be caught, put away in solitary confinement, prosecuted for another crime to add to his sentence?" Julian's eyes narrowed, became more intense. "Let him brood upon the fact that he had been made a fool of, tried to kill someone and missed? Let him spend time planning his revenge? He did not have anything against me: he had never seen me before in his life. I was just the new one in the yard, someone he could use to make his reputation. So I saved him, and by doing that I saved myself. The reason is pretty basic. Most of the people in here learned a long time ago—on the streets—that the only rule of survival is to kill anyone who tries to kill you first. What they learned from what I did, was that the rules of revenge don't apply to me. That all I want is to be left alone. It's curious, isn't it?" asked Julian with an eager, penetrating look. "Among even the worst criminals there is still a basic sense of justice. A man tried to kill me. Instead of retaliating, I helped him hide his crime. And now everyone—especially that Russian—thinks he has an obligation to protect me."

Perhaps Julian was right, and it was some sense of justice that had brought about this change in his treatment by the others here, but I suspected that it was something more basic even than that. Julian was different. They would have known it the moment they saw his reaction: how he had without the slightest hesitation made himself one of them—and better than them—by joining, as it were, the very conspiracy of his own murder. They would have trusted him with anything after that, especially their lives.

"When I started taking fencing lessons, I never thought it would save my life."

At first I did not think I had heard him right. "Fencing lessons saved your life?"

"Balance, agility, learning how to anticipate the next move. When he came at me, I saw it all in slow motion. It was almost funny, he was so incredibly awkward. Turn to the side, one quick step away, and he's flat on his face. I think that is the real reason I helped him, that I hid the weapon: It was all so one-sided. Which reminds me," he went on, as his eyes suddenly brightened. "There is an issue I wanted to ask you about. Remember at the beginning of the trial—I think it was your opening. Remember what you said about the way the question of guilt or innocence used to be decided: trial by ordeal? Grasping a piece of red-hot metal, seeing how it healed; or being thrown into the water to see if you were innocent by whether you drowned? You loaned me Maitland's book, remember?" He paused, scratched his head. "I returned it, didn't I? Yes? Good. But I never had the chance to talk to you about something in there that caught my eye. There was another kind of trial by ordeal, another way to 'appeal to heaven.' Remember trial by challenge? If someone was accused of a crime—say, murder—that man had the right to challenge his accuser, which sometimes meant the witness, the one who said he had knowledge that you did it. The accused then called him a liar, dared him to let God decide in his favor, and then, the challenge accepted, the two of them would fight to the death. The question I have is this: If I had challenged Robert McMillan, if we had fought to the death, whether we had used pistols at twenty paces, or fought with—"

"He was the captain of the fencing team at Stanford," I interjected, caught for a moment in the rush of Julian's strange enthusiasm.

"Yes, I know. Daphne told me all about him." He looked past my shoulder, his eyes dark, ominous. "It was one of the things he liked to talk about: how good he had been." Julian's eyes came back to mine. "You saw how he cut her, the force he used. That was not done just with the hand and wrist; that was done with the arm and shoulder. He used everything he knew when he murdered her."

It had not occurred to me. Until Albert Craven told me, I had not known that Robert McMillan had any training, much less experience, in the intricate movements of a knife or any other sharp-pointed instrument. Could I have used it at the trial; argued that instead of killing his wife in a rage, he had done it with cold-blooded vindictive precision? Why had Julian not told me? Was it that he did not think it important, or that he had not thought of it at all?

"The question is not whether the law would now permit it—dueling is a crime—but what would the punishment be if by their own free agreement two men fought a fair fight to the end? Would the survivor be charged with murder, or manslaughter? Make it more difficult," he continued, clasping his hands behind his neck as he studied me closely. "Suppose that Robert McMillan, guilty of murder, fought a duel with me, and I killed him. He murdered Daphne, I was innocent; but the law, instead of protecting me, protected him. Am I still guilty of murder, or even manslaughter, if, having exhausted all the law's own remedies, I made my last appeal, that once famous appeal to heaven? Would a jury convict me on the facts of the case? Or do you think, whatever the law might say, the jury would decide there was something higher than the law?"

Julian Sinclair was an inmate, sentenced to spend the rest of his days in prison, yet he made it sound as if this were not only a realistic possibility, but that the choice was entirely his whether this bizarre set of circumstances would somehow be set into motion. I reminded myself that he was back in a law library, even if one as small and limited as this, and that he had spent years in a classroom on both sides of the desk, taking up legal questions that would not likely be encountered in two lifetimes of actual practice. And so I smiled and pronounced my academic analysis on that remote and unlikely possibility.

"I imagine a jury would be more than sympathetic."

"Has there ever been a case like it?"

"None that I can think of; though you do have cases where a defendant, having endured years of abuse, is acquitted after putting an end to it by what, by any other definition, is murder. But on the facts of your . . . hypothetical? All I can say is that it would be an interesting trial, one without precedent."

Julian smiled and politely but firmly disagreed. "There must be cases—in France, when dueling was still practiced, but it was illegal. I wonder how they handled it, what the punishment was—whether it was punished at all?" With a desultory gesture, he waved his hand at the stacks of law books on the shelves behind him. "It isn't a bad library for its size, but there are only American cases. I could never find the answer here. I could find it in Berkeley, though; I'm sure of it."

The excitement in his eyes as he talked about the finer points of some ancient, long-forgotten foreign law, gave way to the sober recognition of his present condition.

"I always took that for granted, having everything I needed close at hand: the school, the library, other people with whom I could talk. I look over there now at night. . . ."

"You can see it? Your cell is on the side of the bay?" I asked, almost alarmed at what seemed to me the added cruelty of the close yet impossible proximity of freedom and the life he had known.

"Not from my cell, but when I'm on the staircase, going up or coming down. I always pause, for just a moment, and look across. It reminds me of all the things I want to do. I'm on the top tier of North Block, five stories up. There are a thousand of us, two hundred to a tier, two men to a cell with a ceiling barely tall as my head, five feet wide and eight feet long, if that. I share it with an old man who has been here close to half a century and would not hurt a fly. He killed his wife in a moment of madness: he came home early one day and found her in bed with another man. He had that old-fashioned sense of honor, the notion that a woman who did that to her husband did not deserve to live. They could have put him on probation and he would never have hurt anyone again in his life. It's what I said before: It's criminal, much of what goes on in the criminal law. But he's good company, though he coughs halfway through the night; just old age, I guess. But, yes, I can see the bay on the other side, when I'm on the steps. I can see my house, or rather where it is on the hillside, near the top. It's too far away to pick out from all the others there. It is that view that keeps me going, the knowledge that everything out there is still the same, that it is waiting for me to get out."

It was nearly time to go. I promised again that I would get him out of there and then I told him briefly about what had happened in Australia in my meetings with Harry Godwin. Julian was appreciative, the way he always was for something you had done, but I could tell that he thought none of it much mattered.

"Robert McMillan is not a man that can be embarrassed," he said succinctly, and though I did not want to agree, I knew he was right. Still, there was nothing for it but to try.

"McMillan thinks he's invulnerable. He won't worry about what might happen to him. All he'll think about, if I can just draw him out, is what he can do to me. He thought he could hurt us by taking business away from the firm. That did not work. What is he going to do when I have everyone talking about him on television? At some point, he'll have to come on the show, take me on face-to-face. We both know he can't stand to have anyone else even appear to be in control."

"You may be right about him and the way he thinks," said Julian. "But whatever else you might get him to say on television in front of a few million people, you'll never get him to confess. And without a confession, I'm never getting out of here—at least not while I'm still alive."

Chapter Seventeen

Bryan Allen was taking a few days off and the network thought it would be a good idea to have me fill in as the host of his show. It was the best possible experience, they insisted, to get ready for hosting a show of my own. It was a disaster. I made all the mistakes that might be expected of a novice and then some. I stumbled over my words, asked the wrong questions of the wrong guests and, as Allen's producer patiently explained, let them talk too long.

"It's our fault," insisted Erskine Rhodes as he walked toward his office in that shuffling, slightly bowlegged way. "But, really, it wasn't all that bad," he said in the indulgent tone of someone who has witnessed some of the great television failures of all time. "It's our fault," he repeated, trying to lighten my spirits. "No, I mean it: tomorrow will be much better. The first time is always tough. But we made it harder than it should have been. I wasn't thinking. You're used to going one-on-one. That's what you do in court, isn't it?" he asked as he opened the door to a cluttered, cubbyhole office.

A three-foot stack of papers covered the only other chair in the room. He dropped it on the floor beneath a bulletin board covered with tacked-up messages. He poured me a mug of thick black coffee from a grimy pot, gestured toward the chair he had just cleared off and plopped himself down behind a desk that, completely out of keeping with everything else in the room, was meticulously neat. A spiral notebook sat open, clean and waiting next to the telephone. A ballpoint pen and two sharpened pencils formed three parallel lines that started an inch to the right of the notebook. A blue ceramic mug with the words "The Bryan Allen Show" embossed in gold letters held a half dozen pencils, two ballpoint pens and a pair of scissors. It was order surrounded by chaos; it was a room that corresponded to the schizophrenia of a world divided between what went on in front of the camera and what went on behind it.

"Look, when you have a witness on the stand, you ask him questions, right? It's just you and him—or her. I don't know anything about what goes on at a trial—just what I've seen on television—but you never have a whole group of them—two or three or four—all trying to talk at the same time. You never have to interrupt one of them to see what one of the others thinks about something the first guy just said, right? It's my fault: I should have thought of that and I didn't. Tomorrow night, we have two guests scheduled. We were going to have them on at the same time—Bryan likes to have people mix it up: It keeps things going, especially when you have a couple who really hate each other, and boy, let me tell you, these two tomorrow. . . . Anyway, we'll put them on back-to-back instead."

The suggestion wounded my vanity. I began to protest, to insist that though it had not gone very well tonight, I had learned from it and would do better tomorrow. Rhodes pushed back until the chair was tilted against the wall. Grasping his wrist with his other hand, he held it against his forehead. His pudgy mouth moved back and forth, wrinkling his nose.

"You really didn't do too badly." He pulled his mouth over to the side, biting on the inside of his lip as he considered what had happened and what he wanted to do. "The show you're going to start this summer is going to be all about the law—killers that have gone free, people that have gone to prison for murders they didn't commit. The network is all excited about it. It's the kind of real-crime, real-life stories people love. Tonight you didn't have any of that. Bryan isn't specialized. We do whatever has the public's attention. Some weeks it's a murder, other times it's politics. Maybe there isn't much difference. Tonight it was the latest bombings in the Middle East. We weren't doing you any favors putting you in the middle of that. It's my fault. If I had had any time to change it, I would have. We thought we'd have time to put together the right kind of package. Then Bryan suddenly has something he has to do; suddenly he's got to have the week off." Rhodes hesitated, gave me a meaningful look and laughed. "Probably met somebody and decided he had to get away for a while."

Rhodes picked up the ballpoint pen and wrote himself a note.

"Starting tomorrow, and for the rest of the week, we'll do nothing but legal type stuff. There's got to be a trial, a murder out there somewhere we can do something with."

Rhodes thought of something else. Quickly, he jotted another note on the open page.

"Constable. Know her? Paula Constable. Oh, that's right," he said before I could open my mouth. "You were on with her once yourself. A year ago, maybe a little longer. The case of that guy supposed to have murdered his wife. Only been married a few months and he cut her up into little pieces," said Rhodes with no discernible suggestion that there was anything unusual in his ability to remember a show, one of hundreds, that long ago. "Wonder whatever happened with that?" he remarked with indifference as he wrote down something more. "Constable," he said, looking up, full of confidence. "You know her; you've been on with her; you both talk the same language. It should work. Trust me. Don't worry about tonight: Tomorrow you'll be terrific."

He looked around the room, reluctant, as it seemed, to look directly back at me. His mouth, almost plastic in its malleability, twisted all around. He tapped his fingers on the desk, then stopped; sat quiet for a moment; then, with a coy expression, finally looked at me. But a second later he looked away again, smiling now while he scratched at something just behind his ear.

"Okay, look: you weren't very good tonight," he said, grinning broadly as he waved his soft, fleshy hand back and forth. He was looking straight at me, his eyes friendly and alert. "But it's nothing we can't fix. You're a quick study; it won't take you any time to learn. Watch what you see on TV. Why would you think it's something you couldn't do? I'm going to give you some tapes to take home. Watch them. Don't pay any attention to what anyone is saying. Actually, you might be better off watching without the sound. Well, better not do that, because the main reason I want you to watch them is to see how long things take."

He nodded at the blank look in my eyes. He knew the source of my confusion.

"You ever listen to talk radio? No, of course not. Why would you? You should, not to hear what they're saying—they're not saying anything, it's all just noise, and attitude. That's the secret; that's the key. Those aren't discussions—calm, thoughtful deliberations—they're the shouted opinions of people who like to shout. It makes them feel good, it makes them feel important. It's the attitude, it's us against them. That's what turns them on. And it's always done in quick, short bursts of sound.

"Watch the tapes. Put a clock above the television set and watch the second hand. Bryan never lets anyone talk for more than twenty, thirty seconds, and not very often as long as that. You think that isn't very much time? On television, it's a lifetime. You're used to reading things in books—that's a problem."

Erskine Rhodes drew his mouth into the form of a long whistle, held it for half a second, then whipped it back into a harsh, abbreviated grimace.

"I had to learn it; so can you. I was a history major in college," he said, scratching behind the other ear.

His head flopped from side to side; he clenched his hands into fists, let go, then did it again. There seemed to be some part of him always in motion. When he stayed still, even for just a moment, you wondered what was wrong.

"I used to read a lot—after college; but not anymore. Takes too long. I'm too busy," he offered with a look that was not an apology, but the beginning of a more important observation. "Everyone is too busy—too much to do. Don't ask me why that is, I only know it's true. The only way to keep an audience is to make everything short and to the point. Watch the tapes, time them the way I said—you'll see. Bryan asks a question—takes a couple seconds; guest answers—five, ten seconds at most. Watch something else, though," he added, a shrewd expression building in the small eyes that seldom lacked a sense of calculation. "Watch how many times the camera changes angles while the same person is talking. It's something television learned from the movies. You remember the old days—did you ever see any of those shows that they used to do then? No one would watch that stuff today: two or three people talking, always looking exactly the same. Go to a movie . . . better yet, rent one; watch at home so you can do the same thing with the clock. I wanted to be a screenwriter once—I still write a few things for the show. You write a scene for a movie, maybe they're talking for two, three minutes, but what you're seeing changes every couple seconds. That's the problem with books:

you have to keep staring at the words. It takes too long to read; too much concentration. People don't have time for it. Television doesn't require them to do anything but watch and listen—watch, mainly. The motion is the message—the attitude they see. You aren't working in front of a jury—they have to listen, they don't have any choice. They have a decision to make that's pretty serious. In television you're working in front of an audience made up of people who are tired, probably half-asleep; the only reason they're watching is to take their mind off all the other things in their life that require work. So tomorrow, when someone starts talking longer than they should—cut them off. Tell them you think they're an idiot—do what Bryan does: give them that look that says, 'Please, what kind of idiot do you take me for?' A gesture—any gesture—is always better than words."

Though I felt like a fool doing it, I did what Erskine Rhodes suggested and studied the way that television broke both words and pictures into short segments. I watched for hours, mesmerized, until two or three in the morning, measuring in growing astonishment how quick, how fast-moving, everything had, quite without my knowing it, become. It seemed insidious, the way the motion of the pictures dominated the spoken word. And I had not noticed—though, like everyone else, I had watched my share—how it shifted things out of all proportion. After what had happened to Julian Sinclair, I had understood something of the effect television could have on the way people thought about things they did not know; but I had not tried to think about the cause. I remembered what I had heard some judge say some months before, that the shows on television, where some dressed-up judge decides disputes, had changed the way people behaved in his court, lessened their respect for the formalities of the law. Now everyone had a complaint and came screaming about their right to be heard.

No one read books anymore that were serious and took some

effort. What they did read, the things touted as the next great book of the year, was written in the same abbreviated, fragmentary speech I heard shouting at me from the screen. And what was I now doing, but joining everyone else who measured everything in terms of mass appeal? For some reason, Albert Craven found it amusing.

"Actually, I thought the show last night far better than anything Bryan Allen has ever done. You at least let people talk. And they both had interesting things to say. I especially liked what that one fellow—the one who wrote that history of the Middle East—said about the Crusades. It's curious how everyone in the West now takes the view that it was some war of conquest, trying to take away from the Muslims what was rightfully theirs. What was it he said? He quoted Jacob Burckhardt—there's an historian worth reading—something about . . . Yes, I remember: 'The difference between the Crusades and the conquests of Mohammed . . . consisted in the fact that this time it was not a matter of the world, but of a venerated spot. Hope is not essentially directed at worldly possessions . . . but at the safeguarding of the most sacred relic. Thus their aim exalts the crusaders, while, after a short, holy, sacrificial war, the Mohammedans are debased by greed for more gain.'"

Albert Craven smiled like a schoolboy who has mastered his lesson.

"You remembered that from last night?" I asked, and if I did not sound more surprised, it was because I had learned that there really was no limit to his ability to do things I could not imagine.

"I was so intrigued by it, I spent half the night looking through my copies of Burckhardt until I found it. You should read him. Gives you a rather different perspective than what we're used to. He saw it all coming, machines and mass production and what industrialization would produce: mass movements of every description, the appeal to public opinion, the frenetic dissatisfied character of modern life, how everything would become, in his word, 'provisional.'"

Albert was sitting in my office, come to bolster my spirits after last night's debacle, though he would never have admitted any such thing. He had just dropped by, he said, to tell me how much he had enjoyed the show.

"Yes, yes, I know you think you let him go on too long; that the moment he started to quote from anything, much less something as obscure as the unread works of a nineteenth-century Swiss historian, Allen would have cut him off with some snide remark that no one cares what someone said that long ago. But those were two serious people you had on last evening, and it certainly would not hurt any-one to listen to what they had to say. You let them talk; Allen would have tried to make them fight. Why should you feel that it was some-how a failure because you didn't interrupt, didn't force them into the banalities of the sound-bite language we've taught a whole generation to talk?"

Urbane, imperturbable, as capable as anyone I had ever known of elevating a conversation, whether at a partners meeting or at the din-ner table, Albert seldom displayed irritation and never showed anger. But when I began to recount the reasons why I had to speed things up if the show was to have any chance of success, he began to grow im-patient.

"God damn it!" he muttered in a rare indulgence in profanity. His head snapped up. With a look of utter mystification, he searched my eyes. "What conceivable difference does it make whether the show, when it finally starts, is a success or not? Have you forgotten why you're doing this? Are you so caught up in what you think other people may think—one of Harry Godwin's focus groups—that in-stead of worrying about how you're going to get Robert McMillan to make the kind of mistake that might make it possible to save Ju-lian's life, you're now intent on becoming the latest great new thing on television?"

Albert shook his head. With conscious irony, he allowed himself a smile.

"Maybe you're right; maybe the only way to draw McMillan out is to make yourself into another Bryan Allen, become like him, a jerk!" The smile broadened, became more relaxed, more a part of his normal, unflappable self. "Well, we all need something to which we can aspire. And you're off to a good start," he went on, almost gleeful. "In twenty-four hours you have gone from two serious scholars who disagree on principles while remaining remarkably civil, to—I can hardly wait to watch—Paula Constable and two other lawyers whose practice, as far as I can tell, is now pretty well restricted to television."

"But you haven't heard the worst part," I jibed at him as he rose to leave. "An hour on television, and not a single woman called the station to try to get my number."

Albert gave me a droll look. "I think you have to be either quite famous, or quite young, for that sort of thing to happen. And while you might get that famous . . ."

We looked at each other across the room, remembering for a moment, but without much regret, the years we had lost and could never get back.

"Which for some reason reminds me that I had a reason for this visit—beyond the natural desire to associate with someone from television. I got a letter from Julian. This one was addressed to me," he explained as he came back across the room and, with his hand on the corner of it, stood next to the chair. "It's a response to the letter I sent him concerning his estate."

I made no response and Albert went on to explain that there were certain, not complications exactly, but contingent possibilities. In addition to becoming the executor of Julian Sinclair's estate—something that carried no responsibilities except in the unlikely event of his death—he wanted me to become his trustee. The responsibilities of that position would begin almost at once. There was nothing difficult involved, and Albert, as he quickly reminded me, could easily take care of most of it himself.

"I'm what in the British tradition they call a solicitor. That—and I mention this because that other brand of lawyer, those barristers, never get it right—is someone who knows the law inside and out; brings to it not only great intelligence, but a really stunning erudition. We're the ones who get everything ready, do all the serious work, so those other proud peacocks can impress each other with how well they speak other people's words. The trustee—I'll explain this slowly so that even a courtroom lawyer might understand—looks after the estate, always from the point of view of advancing the trustor's interest. Yes, I know you had this in law school," he added with an irrepressible grin; "but that was so many years ago it's a wonder you can even remember that you took the course. Now—pay attention—in this instance there really isn't much to it. Mainly, it's a matter of preparing the right forms—I'll be glad to do that—and each year paying the taxes."

"What taxes?" I wondered aloud. "He doesn't have an income—I mean: eight cents an hour working in the prison library?" Then I remembered. "The house. Of course. But what are we supposed to do with it? Is there a mortgage that has to be paid? Should we sell it— then do what with the money?"

Albert became quite serious, the way he always did when the interest of a client was at stake. The easy banter, the shining eyes, the quick contagious smile—all of it was gone, vanished behind the meticulous precision of a man set on business. He sat down, not comfortably as before, but perched on the edge, rigid and alert.

"He owns the house free and clear. Unusual, that; but there it is. It's his forever, as long as the taxes get paid. He has no income, as you quite properly point out. He has some money in savings, but not enough to last."

Albert bent forward and narrowed his eyes into a look I had seen before, but only when he talked about Julian Sinclair. It was admiration, but something more than that, a kind of wonder.

"He really is a genius—and not just in that abstract, theoretical way I thought before. It's a remarkable combination, really; I'm not sure I've seen anything quite like it before. The house—you remember—isn't particularly large, but in that location, with that view . . . I don't know where he got the down payment, but the monthly payments must have been about all he could afford on his salary as a law professor. But he paid it off, more than half a million dollars, from a series of investments he had made in some of those high-tech companies whose stock used to double every few months and that now aren't worth more than twenty or thirty cents. Julian sold it all at the top, and I mean almost the day they hit their highs and began their descent. Let me be precise: this wasn't some lucky guess that could have happened to anyone. He did it with the stock of five separate companies over a period of seven months. How did he know that? How could he know what no one else knew? I lost a fortune in some of those same companies: rode them down in the false hope that each day they had to start coming back. Everyone I know lost money, and a lot of it. And Julian, who had never invested in the market before, made—and how many people do you know capable of this?—not a fortune, but only what he needed. Almost to the penny. He paid off the mortgage; he owned the house free and clear, and with the few thousand left over bought savings bonds. Amazing. Really quite extraordinary. Anyway, he doesn't want us to sell the house, and he doesn't want it rented. He said—read the letter he wrote—that he wants it to be just the way he left it when he comes back."

I tried to think it through, but I was not interested in the economics of what was needed. I had a debt, and this was one way I could start to pay it.

"I'll pay the taxes on it. He ought to have that house to look forward to, though it surprises me a little, that he would want to come back to where Daphne was murdered. That would probably be the last place I'd want to go. On the other hand, what else does he have to call home? Maybe when he gets out, he'll change his mind."

"Julian is willing to let us do that—pay the taxes—but only as a loan. You won't be surprised that he's thought the whole thing through. We pay the taxes, and each year charge him a reasonable rate for interest. When he gets out of prison, he'll pay us with the money he has earned inside, and the rest over time." Albert raised his eyebrows and let out a long sigh. "And if he doesn't get out—if he dies inside—he wants it in his will that the house and all his possessions go to you." Albert's hand shot straight up. "No, he insists on that. And it's his property to do with what he will. Let's just hope it doesn't come to that, that finally we can prove McMillan did it and that Julian is innocent."

All the talk about what under the circumstances seemed the strange obligation of an acting trustee for a man serving life in prison made me feel more acutely the time that had passed since Julian's conviction and how little had been accomplished toward winning his release. Instead of waiting until late in the summer to start, I began the television campaign against Robert McMillan that same night. Paula Constable turned out to be the perfect foil.

Though she was smart enough to hide her disappointment—the last thing she wanted was to jeopardize her chances of more appearances in the future—she could not entirely mask the feeling that in giving me a show of my own, the network had made a mistake, because whatever she thought of me as a lawyer, on television we were not in the same league. It was a lesson she tried to teach me right away. I was not disappointed that she did.

True to his promise, Erskine Rhodes found another murder victim with whom everyone could sympathize, and someone accused everyone could hate. We were not on the air thirty seconds, I had just finished introducing Paula Constable and the other two guests, when she flashed a garish smile and took her shot.

"Must be nice to be able to talk about a murder and not have to defend the guy who did it." She waited, stiff and unmoving, for my reaction.

"The first time I was on the show, I wasn't defending anyone; the second time, I was defending an innocent man."

It threw her off—the way I did not hesitate to make that assertion—but only for a moment. On television, if you did not speak right away, the camera went to someone else.

"That 'innocent man' you were defending is now serving life without possibility of parole in San Quentin, if I'm not mistaken."

"My point precisely," I replied immediately. "Now, about this murder," I said, turning to one of the other guests. I bent forward, focusing all my attention on him. "You've prosecuted a number of important cases. What kind of case does the government have against this woman? She's accused of killing her own two children. What should be done with someone in a case like this? Or do you think it's possible she might be innocent?"

"I doubt there is any chance of that. In cases like this—"

"You doubt there's any chance of that?" I asked, turning up my hands. "Because when two children are murdered, a mother is the one most likely to have done it? Don't you think that logic is kind of odd?" I asked a somewhat startled Paula Constable. "A mother kills her children. It seems so unnatural, it must be true? Is that the way you people think?"

Constable's mouth twisted tight. Her black eyes flashed with defiance, though I am not sure she had quite determined who or what she wanted to defy.

"Of course she did it," said the third guest, a young woman who, like Daphne McMillan, had ambitions beyond the position of an assistant district attorney. "You can tell by the way she cried. She wasn't crying for her children; she was crying out of fear—what she was worried was going to happen to her."

With that, Paula Constable had her decision made for her.

"The fear of the demons inside her that made her do what she did."

Every head turned. The camera followed.

"No woman in her right mind could kill her children. She's a deeply religious woman. Something devil-like, something psychiatry may explain as schizophrenia—forces over which she had no control—made her do it."

She could not help herself; she was too driven by forces of her own. "Which makes what she did rather more forgivable than a man who murders a woman who doesn't want to sleep with him."

"Are you talking about my client—Julian Sinclair? Or the man who really did it—Robert McMillan—who, having murdered two of his wives is, according to what I read in the papers, planning to marry again?"

Constable made a quick, sideways motion with her head, a look of puzzlement in her eyes. Then she understood, or thought she did. She flashed a smile like someone bestowing a gift.

"The new show! The one you start this summer. Congratulations, by the way. I can't think of anyone who could do it better. That's what it's going to be all about, isn't it? Innocent people convicted; the guilty ones who got away? You still think Sinclair is innocent. You have guts, Antonelli—I'll give you that. You may think he's innocent, but no one else I know ever did."

I looked her square in the eye. "Then I'll say it again: Robert McMillan murdered his wife; and he murdered his second wife as well. Mr. McMillan has a long history of abusing women, of acts of violence. And if he cares to come on television and deny it, I'll produce a woman to prove it!"

The next night, I repeated with another set of guests what I had said about McMillan. I did it every night until I had finished the week filling in on the Bryan Allen show. Over the next several months, filling in a day or two at a time, I never failed to throw down the same challenge to McMillan and repeat again that the new network show that would start that summer would feature as the first case the wrongful conviction of Julian Sinclair.

At the beginning of August, with the new show less than two weeks off, I still had not heard a word from anyone connected with the man whom I had called everything I could think of, from a murderer to worse. I was afraid that Julian had been right all along, that McMillan was too smart to get involved in a public dispute. His picture still appeared in the society pages and there was nothing the eye could see in the smiling faces all around him to suggest that anything had changed. In the circles in which he moved, the accusations of a lawyer—a lawyer who had lost—were probably looked upon as a badge of honor. If those glittering black-tie parties were any indication, all my well-laid plans for a public humiliation, a televised challenge that would force him to file suit for slander, instead of causing him harm, had done him a favor. Then, two days before the first show was to air, Robert McMillan sent word that he wanted to see me.

Chapter Eighteen

McMILLAN'S OFFICE was on the fortieth floor of one of the tallest buildings in San Francisco. The receptionist's workstation was deserted, the computer terminals shut off for the night. A few stray lights cut through the shadows that filled the hallways that ran in both directions. I took one of the cushioned modern chairs arrayed on opposite sides of a square glass table and waited. According to the clock on a wood-paneled pillar just behind the receptionist area, it was three minutes before nine. I checked my watch and discovered I was either a minute slow or the clock a minute fast.

The floor-to-ceiling windows gave a view from the Golden Gate to the Bay Bridge, across to the Berkeley hills, where Julian had lived and Daphne had been killed, past the north edge of the bay to Petaluma and beyond. The view was too distant, too remote. It made you forget what was most important about San Francisco: the belief that outside of it nothing else existed. It was the limit that allowed the work of your own romantic imagination. A view like this destroyed the illusion. As I glanced at the surrounding buildings, as tall, or taller, than this, I almost hoped for another good earthquake.

I heard a voice, then two voices talking, coming closer, moving toward me from the end of the long, darkened hall. Two men in their early forties, each carrying a briefcase, headed toward the elevator. One of them pushed the down button; the other caught me out of the corner of his eye.

"Everyone is gone," he remarked with an affable glance. "Anything we can do for you?"

"No, I'm supposed to meet Robert McMillan here at nine."

His eyes darted to the clock. It was five minutes after the hour.

"I haven't seen him since sometime around four."

The elevator door opened and the two of them stepped inside.

"You sure it was nine o'clock?" the same one asked with a shrug, holding the door open a moment longer. "I'm sure he isn't here. And no one said anything about him coming back."

The door slid shut in front of him, and suddenly I felt all alone, a fool caught in a trap. I was not only claustrophobic, but afraid of heights. He wanted me here, alone, at night, on the fortieth floor, with no one else around. My heart began to race; my palms began to sweat. Despising my cowardice, I defied common sense. Instead of getting out of there; instead of picking up one of the telephones on the receptionist desk to let someone know where I was, I walked down the shadowed hallways, searching for McMillan's office.

I found it finally at the end, with a corner view. The door was shut; I opened it and walked in. The light was on at his desk, the only light in the room, and I was certain that he must be there, waiting for me to come to him. I felt more at ease, certain now that I had nothing to fear. The light at the desk was on, but the chair behind it was empty. I looked behind me, and then all around, expecting at any moment to hear his voice telling me he was sorry I had had to wait. The room was empty; there was no one here.

I started to leave, but the lamplight drew me back. There was nothing on top of the desk, just an inkwell and a blotter; but a long credenza in front of the window behind it was cluttered with framed photographs. They seemed to be arranged in a chronological order, beginning as you faced them on the far left side with pictures of a boyhood spent outdoors, followed by the expected progression of a privileged youth. He was on the football team in high school and on the fencing team in college. In the years following his graduation he had apparently traveled to all four corners of the globe. There was a picture of him when he was about thirty on an elephant in India and, when he was not much older, in front of the pyramids in Egypt. There was a photograph—two of them, in fact—taken with the girl I assumed must be his daughter, but nothing with his wives. The photographic history of his life simply skipped over all the married years. The only woman he apparently wanted to remember was the one whose photograph was at the far right corner where the sequence ended. It was the striking, and much younger, woman with whom I had seen him last Christmas, the woman he was going to marry in the fall.

I heard a noise; I turned around. Nothing, not a sound. My imagination was working on my fear. I heard it again; I know I did: it was clear, distinct—a footstep down the hall.

"Anyone there?" I called out, forcing confidence into my voice. "I'm looking for Robert McMillan."

I left his office and headed for the lobby, my eyes darting first one way, then the other. The elevator door was wide open. Someone was here after all. I heard the same sound again, footsteps on the carpet. I started toward the elevator; told myself I was a coward; stopped and went down the hallway that led the other way. A door was open; a light was on. I heard the steps again; I was certain someone was inside. I began to move faster, determined to find out what was going on, what McMillan was trying to do. I was a step from the doorway and suddenly something was shoved right in front of me.

"Sorry," said an older woman who spoke with a heavy accent. The cleaning lady looked at me, afraid that because she had almost hit me with her cart she might be in trouble.

"My fault," I mumbled, embarrassed. "Is anyone else here? Anyone on the floor?"

She shook her head, and then, bent over, pushed the cart loaded with cleaning supplies to the next office.

With one last look out the windows at the burning lights of the city and the bay beyond, I pushed the elevator button and waited. What conceivable reason could McMillan have had to tell me to meet him here at his office at nine o'clock at night and then not show up? Did he think this slight inconvenience would make me regret any of the things I had said about him and what he had done? I could imagine him doing something like this—inviting someone whom he would then stand up—when he was the rich and arrogant schoolboy whose pictures I had seen. But now? It made no sense.

The elevator door opened and I immediately jumped back.

"Sorry, I didn't mean to startle you," said a security guard. "Is your name Antonelli? Mr. McMillan called. Said to tell you he was sorry, but he got hung up. Wondered if you might come out to his house."

"The place on Russian Hill?"

"No, the place he has on the ocean, over in Marin. He had me write down how to get there."

As we rode down the elevator, I glanced at the piece of paper on which the guard had written the directions. Even without traffic, it would take forty-five minutes. I thought about waiting until morning and calling him at his office, but decided not to take the chance that McMillan might change his mind. I had to talk to him, I had to see how close I could get him, when it was just the two of us, to a confession. Ten minutes later I was on the Golden Gate Bridge, heading into the night.

Just a few miles from San Quentin, I turned off the highway and drove along the twisting road toward Muir Woods and the coast. A full moon cast a haunting silver glow out across the Pacific. There was no one on the road. It was one of those moments when California was what it had been at the beginning, a place of solitude and beauty, untouched by the clutter of human invention.

McMillan's place was just a mile or so ahead. I could see the lights burning at the end of a rocky promontory high above the crashing, moonlit surf. Suddenly, headlights were screaming in the rearview mirror. A car was right behind me and closing fast. I pulled to the side to let him pass, but the car kept coming. He was right on top of me and I braced for the collision. I could barely hang on to the wheel as the car jolted forward and then careened off to the side. I was heading straight for the white wooden railing, the only thing between me and the ocean a hundred feet below. I pulled hard on the wheel, but it was too late. There was another impact, another violent collision from the rear. With the awful jagged tearing sound of shattered glass and steel, the car ripped through the railing and I went flying into space. Everything was spinning, turning all around, and then it stopped and I was drifting weightless, my eyes wrapped in darkness, and I could not feel anything at all.

A distant voice kept repeating my name. I tried to answer, but I could not form the words. It struck me funny that the voice would keep on like this, as if there was something I had to do, when I had no desire to move.

"Joseph, you're all right."

It seemed a remarkable thing to say. I felt perfectly fine, completely rested, relaxed, like someone floating motionless on the sea.

Albert Craven was standing over me, a strange, anxious expression on his smooth pink face.

"Doctor, he's opened his eyes."

There were three people hovering over me in a white-walled unfamiliar room. Albert Craven, in one of his dark expensive suits, stepped away, while a man with the cool efficient manner of a physician moved closer. Squinting into a stainless steel instrument, he shined a beam of light into one eye, then the other. The tasteless smell of antiseptic followed the studied movement of his hands. A nurse started working on the other side, pumping a blood pressure cuff tight around my arm. It was a mistake; they had it all wrong: I felt better than I had ever felt in my life. The only thing to do was to get out of bed so they could see I was all right.

It was the strangest feeling, like turning a switch and wondering why the lights did not go on. I was getting up—I could feel it: my shoulder rolling to the side; the movement of my hip; my legs, my feet, swinging free; but I was still in the same position, still on my back, every part of me immobile. I started to panic; I started to yell; but again nothing happened: I could not move my mouth.

"You were in an accident," explained the doctor. "Quite a bad one, I'm afraid. No, don't try to move. You broke your jaw. You were lucky, really; by all rights you should be dead. The car you were driving went off the road. You were apparently thrown clear before it hit the rocks and went up in flames. You broke a few bones—your left arm, both your legs—but nothing worse. You were pretty cut up; that's the reason for the bandages on your face; but all that will heal. In a couple of months, you should be good as new. Anyway," he said, patting me on the arm, "you're out of danger now. We knew the coma was only temporary, but you can never be quite certain how long something like that will last."

How long had I been in a coma? How long since I nearly died? I could not talk; I tried to ask the question with my eyes.

"Four days, but don't worry—you're going to be fine."

After the doctor whispered something to the nurse, he put his hand on Albert Craven's shoulder, and together they left. The nurse injected the contents of a syringe into a tube connected to a needle taped to the back of my hand. "Morphine," she said with a pleasant smile. Her face began to grow indistinct, as I began to drift, across a vast, still ocean I had crossed before.

Every time I opened my eyes, Albert Craven seemed to be there, waiting, until finally, days later, I was able with my one good hand to start writing short notes on a small pad of paper. The first thing I scrawled was that it had not been an accident, that Robert McMillan had done it.

"I could not imagine what you would have been doing driving that late at night on that twisting road on the coast over in Marin. Thank God you were thrown free and that no one else was in the car."

It was time-consuming, frustrating, writing everything with my awkward, slow-moving hand while Albert waited. I felt like a telegraph operator with his mouth taped shut, tapping out a Morse code message to someone standing right in front of him. It would have been worse if Albert had not been so quick to pick up the central thought from the few words I was able to write and take it from there.

"Someone saw the car on fire and called 911. No one saw the accident. No one saw the car go over. As soon as I heard what happened, I told the police where you had gone that night and that I did not believe for a moment that it was an accident. The police made some inquiries—I wouldn't call it an investigation."

Albert knew we were thinking the same thing. "Probably the way he killed his second wife; and just like then, nothing to prove he did it, nothing at all."

I might not be able to prove that Robert McMillan tried to kill me, but it was not hard to understand why he had made the attempt. The wonder was that I had not seen it before, that I had not grasped the simple possibility that he might decide it was safer to murder me than run the risk of a lawsuit in court. In my narrow-minded determination to prove that McMillan had committed murder, I had forgotten that precisely because I was right about him—that he had killed two women—another murder would be right in character. I had told the world that he killed Daphne McMillan and that he lied on the witness stand so that Julian Sinclair would take his place in prison. And now I was about to launch a new series with the real version of what he had done. There was only one way he could stop that show from going on the air.

"The show?" I wrote hastily on the page when Albert came the next day.

Albert was beaming, the sure sign that he had done something masterful.

"Well, actually," he began, dazzled by his own accomplishment, "it was as much Harry's idea as mine. We must have spent an hour on the telephone, trying out the various combinations. I came up with the concept, but Harry—he has of course a lot more experience— added the refinements."

I could not talk; but I could moan my impatience.

" 'They tried to stop this show—but they could not!' That is the lead—quite grabs the attention, doesn't it? The line they're using in all the new promotion. 'They drove him off a cliff—tried to kill him— to stop the story being told. And they succeeded—' notice how that pulls you right back; makes you think someone got away with something—'but only until September!'

"Instead of the summer, you start on television in the fall. As soon as you can talk, Harry wants to get you on camera—in a hospital bed—talking about what happened, how you went to see McMillan, how he tried to kill you. Harry is more excited than I've ever seen him."

WHAT THE DOCTOR said was true. By the end of August I was almost good as new. Though it ached on occasion, and though I had some difficulty pronouncing words that ended with the letter *s,* my jaw worked well enough. My broken arm healed and so did one of my legs; but my left ankle was apparently never going to recover a normal range of motion. Though it was not likely to be all that noticeable, I now walked with a slight limp. I did not need a cane, and it was not painful; it was just there, a minor handicap, a slight deformity thanks to my own stupidity in underestimating Robert McMillan. There was also the disfigurement of my face. The left eye socket had been shattered and the skin ripped apart, but that was being repaired. The bone had been reconstructed and with one more minor procedure, the plastic surgery would be complete. All I would be left with was the limp. Strange, how much I grew to hate it. With each crooked step I took, I was forced to remember that Robert McMillan had again gotten away with something for which someone else had been made to pay the price.

"Beggars mounted," insisted Albert Craven when he caught my downcast expression late one afternoon in early September.

"Beggars what?" I asked, lifting my eyes from the documents by which I was to become the formal trustee of Julian Sinclair's earthly possessions.

"Beggars mounted. It's from Shakespeare—*Henry the Sixth,* I think. 'Beggars mounted run their horse to death.' You have to understand the context," he remarked as he plopped down in the high wingback chair across from me. "'Beggars mounted'—men not born to rule who find themselves in power—'run their horse to death'—they don't know how to rule; think only of their own advantage; destroy the very thing they wanted. I suppose that's why we read Shakespeare: he could tell you the history of the world—or at least of one kingdom—in the space of seven well-chosen words. 'Beggars mounted'—might have had someone just like McMillan in mind. He'll run his horse to death, I guarantee it. It won't be long now; he feels the pressure: He hasn't been seen anywhere in weeks. When you film that spot next week—the promotional piece for the show—when you tell everyone how Julian is serving a life sentence for something he did not do; how they tried to stop you telling the truth about it; how you're going to announce on the first show the name of the man who tried to kill you—if he doesn't try to sue you, everyone will know he's a murderer and that Julian is not. You can't just ignore something like that."

He was trying to revive my spirits, and I felt a little guilty when I had to disagree.

"The beggar mounted," I said with a grateful nod, "may be me; the horse I've run to death, the lengthening list of accusations, not one of which I can prove."

Albert gave me a brief, sympathetic glance; then slapped his thighs and got back to his feet.

"I came in here for a reason, but damned if I can remember what it was!" He laughed. "Anyway, don't worry. It will all work out in the end."

I started to make some reply, a kind reminder that we had both seen too much in our lives to believe that things always ended well. The telephone began to ring insistently.

"Yes? All right, put him on. Yes, this is Joseph Antonelli. Yes, I'm the lawyer who represents Julian Sinclair."

Albert Craven stopped at the door. His eyes were first puzzled, then alarmed, as he watched me, listening, rise slowly from the chair.

"When?" I asked, staring out the window and seeing nothing but a slate gray blackness in front of my eyes.

"How?" I asked, my voice become so quiet I asked again, certain I could not have been heard.

With a deep, despondent breath, I hung up the telephone and looked across at Albert Craven, who had already read it in my eyes.

"Julian Sinclair is dead. He died in a fire, last night, in his cell at San Quentin."

Chapter Nineteen

Julian Sinclair died in a fire, burned to death in his tiny cell along with the old man with whom he shared it. Fire was a frequent occurrence in the cell blocks of San Quentin; sometimes started by an inmate who, suicidal or demented, decided to light his blanket on fire; sometimes started by nothing more than a spark in the dust-laden air. The fire that killed Julian Sinclair started in his cell, but what caused it—whether after years of confinement the old man had lost his mind and done it, or whether it had been an accident—was not the kind of inquiry for which the prison authorities had either the time or the inclination. The death of one inmate meant mainly that there was room for another. The charred remains of two dead bodies were removed and the damaged cell immediately repaired and repainted.

We buried Julian Sinclair in Colma, just south of San Francisco, at a hillside cemetery, where half the people who ever lived in the city must lie buried. Albert Craven made the arrangements. Before he got in trouble with the law, Julian had been too young to think about death, much less where he wanted to be buried; but Albert, much older, had with the sentimentality of a native San Franciscan picked out a plot that looked back toward the city. Julian was buried there instead.

Only four other people attended the service inside the small stone chapel on the cemetery grounds. Two of them were former students from Julian's law school classes; each of them now members of prominent San Francisco firms. An old man hunched over a cane sat quietly at a pew in back. When he shook my hand after the short service was over, he told me that Julian had once done something for his son. A woman in her sixties took my hand and held it gently. She was the law librarian at the prison.

"Julian should never have been there. He didn't kill anyone, did he? I think I knew it the first moment I saw him, the first day he came to work in the library. I've never known anyone like him," she said, a tear in her kind, thoughtful eyes. "I can't believe he's gone."

A few feet away, both hands on his cane, the old man shook his head at what he had heard. Despite his bent shoulders and crooked back, he made a striking figure with his tangled shock of white hair and his proud hawk-shaped nose. When he looked at you, his eyes burned bright and intense.

"He saved my son. My son was in prison for fifteen years for a murder he did not commit. Your Mr. Sinclair, when he was still teaching over at Berkeley, found the evidence that eventually set him free. I knew when they charged him with the murder of that woman that they had done it again: arrested another innocent man. There's no justice, is there, Mr. Antonelli—only in the life to come. Where he is now, he's better off; there's a special place in heaven for ones like him. You can be sure of it, Mr. Antonelli. I know it's true."

For his part, Albert Craven was not sure of anything, except that life was not fair.

"There's something peaceful, even comforting, about a funeral," he said in a voice filled with sorrow and fatigue, "when it's a funeral for someone my age or older. But this? A funeral for someone this young and gifted? It runs against the order of the universe; it breaks the great chain of Being. This is what happens when fathers bury sons, instead of the other way around. This isn't peaceful, this isn't comforting: it's obscene. It's a death without meaning, a senseless killing, a murder. Nothing in the world can make this right."

There was nothing that could be said against the stark finality of that judgment. Julian's life was over, he was dead and buried, and no power on earth could bring him back; but there was still the question of whether he was going to be remembered as a killer who had died in prison, or an innocent man wrongly convicted. Sitting in the dark at home, watching out the window the golden yellow lights blinking along the black periphery of the bay, I knew that in the great scheme of things none of that mattered; that it was a false dilemma, the empty echo of human vanity and pride. Six people had attended his funeral, only six; and one of them had never met him and two others had scarcely ever exchanged a word with him outside of class. Who would remember, who would care, if his name were cleared of murder?

No one would remember; but then, the same thing could be said of all of us, the only difference how long before the world forgot. What was important was not that anyone remembered Julian Sinclair, or knew that he had died the victim of another man's crime; what was important was that the last account be settled, so that the book that is written about each of us could be closed and put away. I had to finish what I started. I went on television, the first night of the new show and, as advertised, revealed the name of the man who had tried to kill me and who had now, to all intents and purposes, killed another man as well. I opened with the two words we had chosen for the name of the show, the title I had shamelessly stolen from Zola's famous indictment, "I Accuse."

"I accuse Robert McMillan of murder, not once or twice, but three times! I accuse him of murdering his second wife. He drove her car off a cliff and made it look like an accident. I accuse him of murdering his third wife, Daphne—slaughtering her with a knife. And I accuse him of murdering Julian Sinclair, by letting him go to prison for the murder he committed where Julian died. I accuse Robert McMillan of attempting to murder me. I was thrown clear before the car fell onto the rocks in the ocean, or someone else would be standing here tonight, accusing him not of three murders, but four. I accuse him of the attempted rape of Rachel Burke, a young woman he attacked in Sydney, Australia, several years ago. I accuse Robert McMillan of cowardice for refusing this network's invitation to appear on camera and call me a liar to my face.

"There was a trial when Daphne McMillan was murdered and Julian Sinclair was wrongly convicted. Tonight, for the next hour, we're going to try to set the record straight. We're not going to retry the case; we're not going to engage in some make-believe court proceeding. We're going to reenact the crime itself. We're going to show you what happened that night, beginning when Daphne McMillan first arrived at the home of Julian Sinclair—what she said to him, what he said to her. This isn't something staged on a movie set somewhere: the house you're going to see is the one where it all happened, Julian Sinclair's house in the Berkeley hills. The words that pass between them, the feelings they express, the plans they made—all of it has been taken from the notes that were taken during the long hours of conversation I had with Julian Sinclair during the months between the murder and the trial.

"We're going to show you the two of them, Julian Sinclair and Daphne McMillan, saying good night to one another; and while they're doing that, we're going to show you Robert McMillan, waiting outside for his chance."

I paused, hesitated; for a moment I stared down at my hands resting on the table in front of me. I looked back into the eye of the camera.

"I made a mistake when I defended Julian Sinclair. I did not real-ize the extent to which television had made a fair trial all but impos-sible. Whether I could have done anything about it is another question. Television convicted Julian Sinclair, and for that we all bear some responsibility. It is too late to do anything to save him, but per-haps television can now help clear his name and he can be remem-bered for the decent and honorable and remarkable person he was."

The network claimed that the volume of calls and letters received over the next several days exceeded anything in its experience. There were of course those laced with the usual obscenities, insisting that Julian Sinclair was a murderer who deserved to die in prison, but the great majority, after what we had shown them, took the other side; some insisting that they had known Julian was innocent all along, others expressing outrage that the real killer had been allowed to get away.

"We may have created a lynch mob of our own," I remarked with a bitter laugh as I showed Albert Craven one of the angrier letters written.

He glanced at the full-page letter full of bad grammar and mis-spelled words. His fine gray eyebrows went higher the further he read.

"Are there a lot like this?" he asked as he handed it back.

"Enough," I replied. "Enough to make you wonder whether there is any sanity left in the world. I thought I could make people see things a certain way, the way it really happened the night Daphne McMillan was killed. It's what I do in court; what I do in every trial: show the jury what happened by turning it into a story. I've been do-ing this for years, telling it so they can see it in their minds, the way it happened. But now, instead of a jury, I show it to millions of people as a dramatic reenactment—pictures, moving pictures—so they can see it happening, not in their minds, but right in front of their eyes; and instead of a debate, a discussion—what a jury does, or is supposed to do, in deliberations—they just decide that McMillan is more guilty than Julian ever was and all they want to do is hang him!"

"Well, that's a prospect I wouldn't lose much sleep over," replied Albert with a weary smile.

He was right of course: there was not any point worrying about something that was not going to happen, and that would not bother me very much if it did. No one was going to kill Robert McMillan out of a desire to do justice for the dead; though I admit I found myself on occasion wondering what kind of defense might be put on for someone who did. I remembered what Julian had asked me, that last time I saw him, about the old trial by ordeal and trial by challenge. Were we really all that much more civilized than our violent, God-fearing English ancestors? McMillan had tried to kill me and had failed by the slimmest of margins, and the only retaliation I could think of was to repeat on television the same accusations that had yet to have any effect. I should have shown up on his doorstep and done what Harry Godwin would have done: beaten him half to death with my fists or been beaten in the attempt. What did I do instead? Challenge him? Yes, well sort of—to a duel with law books in any courtroom of his choice. Imagine my astonishment when, finally, he picked the gauntlet up.

The day after the show, according to the reports, two-thirds of those who saw it thought Julian Sinclair had been innocent and that McMillan was the murderer; most of the rest were undecided. A day later, after all the coverage of that first reaction, the percentage of those, whether they had actually watched the show or not, who were certain that McMillan was the killer had reached the low eighties and might climb higher still. It was the kind of public opinion that was irresistible, and Robert McMillan was smart enough to know it.

It must have been some media consultant, some overpaid publicist that convinced McMillan that he should start a legal action against his accuser by doing it on camera. The show had aired on Monday evening. Three days later, Thursday at 4:45, just in time for the local news, Robert McMillan, followed by two lawyers, a process server and camera crews from every station in town, barged into my office to denounce me for the liar I was. I leaned back in my chair and smiled.

"My lawyers are going to sue you for every dime you have!" he cried, his eyes rigid with excitement.

Right on cue, the process server, a small, balding, inconspicuous man, stepped forward, handed me a rolled-up summons and then, as if he had never existed, vanished back inside the crowd. The cameras moved closer, jostling for the better view. McMillan and his lawyers waited with stern impatience while I opened the papers naming me as the defendant in the suit they had filed.

"And here I was just wondering what I could do on next week's show," I said in a kind of aside, as I reached forward and pushed a button on the intercom. "Would you mind bringing our guests some coffee?" I requested, looking up to see who might want some. "Doesn't seem like anyone wants any; but bring some anyway, in case someone changes his mind."

I began to read the first page of the complaint; but then, with a quick, apologetic smile, motioned toward the two empty chairs in front. "Would anyone . . . ?" McMillan and the two lawyers glared at me, impatient for a scene. Glancing at each lawyer in turn, I gestured again. "You both get paid by the hour. Sit down. This may take some time. You do want me to read it, don't you? I assume you want me to say something about it—why else are the cameras here? But no good lawyer would want someone to comment on something he hadn't read—or do you disagree with that?"

The façade of righteous indignation; the appearance of a man ill used and unfairly treated; the attitude of injured innocence was becoming more difficult for McMillan to maintain. The muscles along his jawline tightened. His eyes went cold, harsh, full of malice.

". . . In and for the city and county of San Francisco," I read with a slow, appraising glance. I looked at the lawyers in their tailored three-piece suits. "It certainly appears that you have the jurisdiction right; although, I suppose—theoretically, at least—with a broadcast that went everywhere, you wouldn't necessarily have to file it here. On the other hand . . ."

Several of the handheld cameras were lowered to give their holders' arms a rest; some of the cameramen, and a few of the reporters, began to lean against the wall.

"I'm suing you for libel . . . !" cried McMillan in an angry, choke-filled voice.

I held up my hand, shook my head and sat forward. "You're suing me for slander," I corrected him. "Libel is when a defamatory remark is written. The truthful things I said about you, I said on television. Now, as your lawyers can also tell you, there is a separate count for each time a defamatory remark is repeated. So, because I want to be as fair as possible, let me assure everyone in this room and everyone who watches this later on television that there was no mistake, no misunderstanding; that I meant everything I said about you three days ago; that I would not dream of taking back a single word; and that I'll say it again, right here, right now, to your face: You murdered your second wife, and you murdered Daphne McMillan; you lied in court, under oath, about what happened; and you sent an innocent man, Julian Sinclair, to his death in prison. Earlier this summer you tried to murder me."

Rising from my chair, I pointed my arm straight at him. "I accuse you, Robert McMillan, of being a murderer and a liar. And with respect to this lawsuit," I said with a defiant grin as I waved the summons in his face, "I could not be more delighted. I've been waiting a long time to get you back in court!"

If his lawyers had not restrained him, I think he might have tried to attack me there and then.

"You're a liar, Antonelli!" he shouted, struggling to get free. "I never tried to kill you! I didn't have anything to do with it!"

He regained his composure. With a glance at each lawyer, they let go. All the cameras on him, he looked at me and insisted he was innocent.

"I never killed anyone," he said in a calm, quiet voice. "I did not kill my second wife; I did not kill Daphne; and I certainly did not try to kill you. I swear on my mother's grave that's true. I can understand how you might feel. A client of yours—a man you defended, a man you believe to have been innocent—sent to prison; but I don't understand how you can try to do to me the very thing you say was done to him: convict me of something I didn't do by trying me on television. You may be able to defend doing that—I'm afraid I can't. I'm sorry that it's come to this, that I have to bring a lawsuit to defend my name; but you really haven't left me any choice."

He said this with such anguish, such sorrow—his voice broke before he could quite finish—that I almost wondered if I might have made a mistake.

He started to turn away, to look into the watching cameras and plead innocence with his eyes. It was there just an instant: the shining glimmer of triumph, the utter certainty that he could make anyone believe anything. He was guilty, guilty of everything I had said and probably a good deal more besides. Proving it, however, was not going to be as easy as I had hoped. Julian had been right about him: Robert McMillan was far too intelligent to make a mistake, much less stumble into a confession. For the first time I had to confront the possibility that in the lawsuit in which I was now the defendant, the plaintiff, Robert McMillan, might very well win.

"What was all that commotion?" asked Albert Craven after the last camera and reporter had left the premises. He bent down and picked up a jagged scrap of paper, part of the debris left scattered on the carpet.

"McMillan actually came here himself? You've done it, then; you've got him going. Only someone desperate would try a stunt like that." He spied the summons lying folded on my desk. "That it? The complaint. Who do we get to represent you? Or do you represent yourself? Let's do it together!"

Beaming at his own suggestion, he slid onto the chair and rolled his hip to the side. His easy, confident manner broke the beginnings of my depression. It reminded me how long we had waited and what we had waited for; that it was our one last chance to make McMillan pay for his crimes and rescue Julian's name from a false and cruel oblivion.

"First thing we have to do is reach Harry Godwin. I need Rachel Burke."

"For the trial, of course," replied Albert. He bent forward, an expression of the utmost seriousness in his eyes.

"Eventually, perhaps; but right now I need her for the show."

"It's Thursday evening—that's Friday afternoon in Sydney. That doesn't leave much time. Wouldn't you be better off waiting a week or so; let everyone know what you're going to do; remind them what you've said before: that you have a witness to McMillan's violence, a woman he tried to rape?"

He was right as usual. It would be much more effective to take my time, build slowly to a conclusion, instead of rushing forward with the best witness, and the only evidence, I had. I had to be careful; I could not let myself be carried away by the emotion of the moment. I could not afford—not when I was finally this close—to make a stupid mistake.

"Why don't you call Harry and let him know what's happened?

Tell him that I'm going to need Rachel Burke on the show sometime in the next few weeks. Then ask him, if you would, whether I should ask her directly, or whether it would be better coming from him."

During the weekend, while I prepared for the show on Monday, the second broadcast of "I Accuse," I tried not to let my thoughts run too far ahead. A civil action, a lawsuit brought for defamation, could go on for years. Lawyers made fortunes from delay.

I tried not to think that far ahead, because each time I did, it made me wonder how long I could keep it up before the public's attention turned, as it always did, to something new. It was better not to think about what might happen; better to concentrate on what I could do now: keep applying pressure in the hope that before the world lost interest, McMillan would make the one mistake that would prove him for the murderer he was. I tried not to think too far ahead, because my real fear, the one that came to me in the night when I could not sleep, was that before I could stop him, Robert McMillan would kill again.

Early Sunday evening, I finished preparation for Monday's show and got ready to go out. I was meeting an old friend for dinner. I was almost out the door when the telephone rang. I thought it might be her, telling me she was running a little late, and I hurried back inside.

"This is Erskine . . . Erskine Rhodes."

His voice was strangely formal, hesitant, as if he was still uncertain what he was going to say.

"Yes, Erskine; what can I do for you? I'm just on my way out. Is it about tomorrow's show?"

There was a dead silence.

"Erskine? Are you still there?"

"Yes, sorry," he said. "Yes, it's about tomorrow's show." He lapsed again into a silence, but recovered more quickly than before. "I'm sorry to ask this on such short notice, but it's really quite important.

Can you get down here—to the station—right away? Something has happened, and we have to make some changes. Harry Godwin thinks this is the best way to handle the situation. He said to tell you that."

"What changes?" I asked as he paused. "What situation?"

"We're not going to do your show tomorrow; we might not be doing it for some time. We need you to take over—Mr. Godwin thinks it will work—for Bryan Allen. We want you to start doing the show every night."

"Why? What's happened? What situation are you talking about?"

Erskine Rhodes cleared his throat. I could see him, his elbows resting on his meticulously clean desk, staring straight ahead in that small, square room filled with clutter.

"Bryan was arrested—late this afternoon."

"Arrested? For what?" I asked, relieved that it was not something serious. I tried not to laugh at the vision of Bryan Allen being pulled off the road for having too much to drink.

"For murder."

I did not believe it; I could not have heard right. It was a mistake.

"Murder? Who is Bryan Allen supposed to have killed?"

"The police arrested him for the murder of Robert McMillan."

Chapter Twenty

I WAS NOT certain what I felt about the murder of Robert McMillan. I did not feel sorry that he was dead, that he was the victim of a homicide; if anything, I had a sense of relief that I no longer had to worry about whom he might kill next. I did not feel sorry for Robert McMillan—he had gotten what he deserved—I felt sorry for myself. I had been cheated out of my revenge, left with nothing. But then it began to occur to me that what had happened might be better than revenge. It brought about a conclusion, a final scene, that no one would have appreciated more than Julian himself: McMillan murdered and Bryan Allen accused! It seemed so fitting, so perfectly appropriate, that the leader of that electronic lynch mob that had cheated Julian of a fair trial and sent him to his death in prison, should now be charged with murder.

Robert McMillan had been murdered and the police had arrested Bryan Allen for the crime. I knew from the moment I walked into the television station Monday evening and witnessed the frantic, hushed whispers, and the tense anticipation, that what had happened to Julian Sinclair was now ancient history. The only name anyone remembered was Bryan Allen and the only thing anyone wanted to hear about was what he had done.

I had spent hours with Erskine Rhodes the night before, reviewing everything the network thought we had to do. Treat Bryan Allen like anyone else arrested and charged with a murder, had been the pious injunction of the network executives in New York. But what did that mean when the accused was one of the best known names in America and the treatment they were talking about was going to be done on the show he had made famous? After a brief pause someone on the conference call said what was in all their minds: "It's going to be great television!" I felt an obligation to remind everyone that no one yet knew anything about what had happened; that all we knew was that Allen had been found at the scene of the murder—McMillan's house on Russian Hill—and that he had been arrested. There was a momentary pause, as if everyone was waiting to see who would speak first; and then, with what felt like relief from a temporary embarrassment, we took up the more urgent question of what to do about the name of the show.

"Think we should refer to it as 'the recent tragedy,' or 'last night's murder'?" asked Erskine Rhodes, his pencil poised above a clean sheet of white paper.

We had less than ten minutes until airtime; he was still working on the lead. I was standing with my back against the door, my arms folded across my chest. With growing irritation, I tapped my foot on the hard gray linoleum floor.

"I was supposed to do one show a week; now I'm supposed to do five?"

Rhodes had made his own decision. He moved his hand across the sheet of paper, making the last-minute correction.

"Don't worry about it," he remarked, a slight grin on his mouth marking satisfaction at the change he had made. "You'll be terrific.

It's the same thing you were going to do, only now you get to do it more often."

He glanced over what he had written. He nodded once, picked up the sheet of paper and, as I followed behind him, headed toward the studio.

"It's your show. You're not filling in anymore. Don't worry about it. You'll be terrific."

Just before we reached the set, Rhodes pulled me aside.

"Look, I don't have any idea what happened; but you can take it from me that a woman was involved. Bryan was always making arrangements to meet a woman somewhere. Remember the first time you filled in for him, when he was off on assignment? It was some woman he had met. He was always doing that. He didn't care if they were single or not. You never heard it from me, though—okay? But I'll bet you anything that's what happened."

"The woman McMillan was engaged to?"

Rhodes shrugged his shoulders. "Wouldn't know."

"But if he was fooling around with the woman McMillan was going to marry," I replied, becoming more confused, "McMillan might want to murder him, but why would he . . . ?"

We started toward the set, stepping over the thick black cables twisting across the cold cement floor.

"It's the same thing, though—isn't it?"

"Sorry," replied Rhodes with a puzzled glance.

"Same motive they said Sinclair had, or almost. In both cases, someone gets murdered because of a woman who supposedly belonged to Robert McMillan."

I settled into my place at the end of the table and exchanged a brief greeting with each of the guests. They had all come on short notice. Paula Constable, dressed in one of her various shades of red, straightened her straight-shouldered jacket and moistened her lips. The young and attractive deputy district attorney from Los Angeles arched her neck and raised her chin, a look of intense concentration in her brown, soulful eyes. The remaining guest was not a lawyer at all, but a media consultant, there to give his opinion on the likely effect of a murder accusation on Bryan Allen's career. We were there not to praise Caesar, but to bury him. The network had every confidence that the ratings would far exceed the largest audience that had ever watched "The Bryan Allen Show" before.

"Good evening," I began as the camera moved in tighter, "and welcome to 'The Bryan Allen Show.' I'm Joseph Antonelli, host of 'I Accuse.' The reason I'm here tonight is because, as all of you must know, Bryan Allen has been arrested and charged with the murder of Robert McMillan. We are here tonight to discuss the tragic events of the last twenty-four hours and what they mean. Among the questions we intend to take up is whether someone who has appeared on television as often as Bryan Allen can get a fair trial, or whether, precisely because of his celebrity, he has been given an advantage over other people. Has justice come to mean one thing for the rich and privileged few, and something else for the great majority of us who have never been on television?"

It was not what Erskine Rhodes had wanted me to say, but by now I was not in the mood to read what he or anyone else had written. I did not care what some faceless New York executive thought would be a great show for television. I was going to say exactly what I thought and do exactly what I wanted. Now that McMillan was dead, there was nothing for me to do but watch events unfold, taking a certain cruel pleasure in the way the arrogance of famous people so often brought them down. Because if the arrest of Bryan Allen taught anything, it was the age-old lesson of how fast the famous fall.

Paula Constable reported that though the police and prosecution were keeping as tight a lid on things as she had ever seen, she had confirmed through her own sources that the case against Allen was airtight. The motive, she explained with a look of practiced impartiality, was exactly what she had suspected.

"Right away, I knew it had to involve a woman. Don't misunderstand me. What people do in their private lives—as far as I'm concerned, that's their business, not mine—but Bryan was a little too flagrant about some of the things he did; a little too willing to take chances—if you know what I mean. Single women, married women—what can I say? Bryan liked them all."

"Let's be clear about this," I interjected the moment she paused for a breath; "you're saying that the police think Bryan Allen murdered Robert McMillan because of a woman?"

Her long black lashes blinked in rapid succession, like a metronome keeping time to the calculations going on in her mind.

"Yes. Susan Lind, the woman engaged to McMillan. She and Bryan Allen were having an affair," she went on, her eyes shiny, triumphant. "Everyone knew about it," she added with the shrewd instinct of a woman who understands that you cannot sway the crowd until the crowd exists. "The whole city knew," she continued, making me and everyone who did not move in the circles in which the affairs of celebrities were common knowledge feel left out. "It's a wonder something did not happen before this. That's why he did it," she insisted with a fierce, determined stare. "McMillan found out, and something happened."

Something happened? That was all she was going to say?

"What happened?" I asked, leaning toward her, a skeptical smile on my mouth. "Bryan Allen was arrested at the scene of the murder. But if he had been having an affair with the woman McMillan was going to marry and McMillan found out about it, why would Allen go to his house?"

"Maybe McMillan demanded he come over and explain what was going on," said the L.A. deputy district attorney, Ellen Robinson, anxious to join in. Her voice was soft, but insistent. I turned to her immediately, and so did the camera.

"If McMillan was upset, that might explain why he might try to kill Allen; but why would Allen kill him?"

"Because she was going to break it off with him; because she had decided to go ahead and marry McMillan!" insisted Constable, her eyes blazing as she pounded her small sharp-boned fist on the table. She had the answer, whatever the question, and she would not stop until you listened.

"That is what you said about Julian Sinclair before he was arrested—that he was having an affair with McMillan's wife. And now you're telling us that another man was having an affair with another woman to whom McMillan was either married or engaged? What exactly was it about the women in McMillan's life that they all got involved with someone else and ended up dead?"

She started to reply, but with a tight, angry smile, I cut her off.

"You were wrong—dead wrong—about Julian Sinclair; so you'll have to forgive me, Ms. Constable, if I'm not all that eager to believe this new rumor you claim you've heard."

I turned to my other guest, the media consultant; but Constable was not about to be denied the last word.

"Wrong about Julian Sinclair? Wrong about his affair with McMillan's wife? As I remember, I wasn't wrong about anything. Julian Sinclair was found guilty of murder and sent to San Quentin. Yes, yes, I know," she said, talking over my objection. "You've always insisted that he was innocent, that he didn't kill the woman with whom he was—or was not—having an affair and that McMillan killed her instead. But you were never able to prove that—were you? And now McMillan is dead and I guess you never will. Trust me on this one,

Antonelli," she cried with flashing, belligerent eyes. "Allen killed McMillan, and the motive was that woman—Susan Lind—just the way I said."

"Trust you on this one? You were wrong about Julian Sinclair! You're wrong now! Bryan Allen did not kill Robert McMillan. Why? Because it doesn't make any sense; and because—as I kept trying to insist the last time this happened—we have to think he's innocent, because if we don't, we're just another mob, dressed up in better clothes. Wait for the trial; let a jury decide. Isn't that what a lawyer is sworn to do?"

Her mouth hung open, enraged; but before she could answer, I looked across to the media consultant.

"But assume that Bryan Allen were to be found guilty of murder. What does that do to the credibility of shows like this? Will the public start turning off their sets?"

"No, I don't think so," he began. "It's probably the other way around. It may add to their credibility. It's what Allen always said, isn't it? 'The police know what they're doing.'"

The ratings were even better than expected; better than anyone had dared hope. The next day, the network announced that the Bryan Allen show would now be called "Justice for All, with Joseph Antonelli." I wanted to quit.

"You can't do that," insisted Albert Craven in a sympathetic voice. "You can't do that to Harry. You owe him something for what he did, giving you a show of your own so you could go after Robert McMillan. We both owe him for that. It isn't his fault McMillan got killed; and it certainly isn't his fault that Bryan Allen killed him. Why do you want to quit, anyway? You're a hit!"

Albert Craven gave me a droll smile and settled back into the overstuffed chair behind his ugly, gargantuan desk. With his shiny onyx cuff links and his soft shiny shoes, he had the enviable look of a man who had everything, including the knowledge of how little any of it meant. Craven had lived too long to think there was any point in trying to change things, to try to correct the madness of the world. That was the lying illusion of ignorance and the noble illusion of youth, the belief that the efforts of anyone could make any real difference in what had been building for longer than anyone could remember. Let young men like Julian, if there were any more like him, make the world over in a new, more tolerable image; Albert could only wish them well. He would watch it all with the calm detachment of a man who had learned the lesson that the only changes a man can make are the changes he makes in himself.

"I'm a fraud," I replied, and in a strange way, I was rather proud of it.

"Yes," agreed Albert, the smile on his face shrewd, cunning and ultimately enigmatic. "But a fraud on purpose, which makes the difference; and which explains why you've become so good at it; and why, even if you did not owe it to Harry to continue, you would."

"Does it?" I asked, certain he was right, now that I had heard it, but reluctant to admit it too quickly.

"Yes, it does. It's the curiosity, don't you think? The need to see just where, just how far, something goes. You have to stay with it—for a while. Through the Bryan Allen trial, I imagine. That's a fair run; enough to let you see the way the whole thing unravels. The trial, because it will reveal as much as we are ever going to learn about Robert McMillan, including perhaps whether he left behind any evidence about the murder of his wife—still that chance to do something for Julian Sinclair. And then, beyond the trial itself, the chance to see inside how television now shapes the way we see things and the way we think. You have to stay there through this." Albert raised his eyebrows and threw me a serious, searching glance. "It's the only chance you'll ever have to make sure that this once at least it's done right."

After that conversation I was clear about several things. I would stay with Harry Godwin and his network until the end of the trial for the murder of Robert McMillan and then I would quit. I would become again a lawyer who only tried cases; and I would try, as best I could, to come to terms with all the ways in which I had failed Julian Sinclair.

Though I had talked only with Albert Craven about quitting, Paula Constable expressed a mild, and somewhat mocking, surprise that I was still hosting the show.

"It has my name on it," I reminded her gently as we sat together on the set a few days later, just minutes before the show. She wore the same shade of red lipstick, but the red jacket was a shade or two lighter than the one she had had on before. I wondered what it was like, walking into her closet: was it was like falling into a shower of red roses or a pool of blood?

"Yes, and I meant to tell you how great I think that is. You're going to be just terrific, better than Allen ever was. No, what I meant was," she went on, eyeing me with a kind of friendly suspicion, "that I was almost certain you'd be the first person he'd ask to become his lawyer. Hasn't he called?"

"Bryan Allen?" I asked, stalling for time.

He had called, twice; but I could not forget that he had, as much as any witness for the prosecution, convicted Julian Sinclair. The terrible truth was that I hoped he was guilty of the murder of Robert McMillan and that he would be sent to prison, just like Julian, for his crime.

"Yes, Bryan Allen—who else? Did he call you? I heard he was going to ask."

"I'm not taking any cases. I have the show, and I can't do both. Even if it wasn't a conflict, there isn't time."

She took a deep breath, and then, with a brief, perfunctory smile, changed the subject to some famous friend of hers she had run into the other day and how much she had raved about the show. I wondered what that breath and smile meant; why it seemed like a sigh of relief. I began to smile myself when, as soon as the show started, she began to reverse herself, insisting now that she was beginning to have doubts that the police had in fact arrested the right man, that she had earlier been misinformed and now had better sources of information. It was too early to say exactly what had happened the night Robert McMillan was murdered, but she had "reliable information" that the reason the police refused to release anything to the media was that, at this point, the case against Allen was "purely circumstantial."

It was a marvel to behold. Paula Constable could start to argue one position and in the middle of the first sentence begin to argue the other side. I think she could have changed direction in the middle of a fall. Her opinions were as changeable as the wind; her principles good for only one season. She came back on the show the next week. And without a word of warning to anyone—without so much as a hint to me of what she planned to do—announced that the lawyer who had first been hired had been replaced, and that from now on the defense of Bryan Allen would be handled by her. With a quick, no-nonsense smile, Constable assured us—and through us, the world—that Bryan Allen was innocent and that she could not wait for the chance to prove it at trial.

"And then, when the trial is over," she said, arching an eyebrow in my direction, "Bryan will invite us all back on his show and we can explain—or some of us can—why we were so certain that he was guilty!"

Chapter Twenty-one

For someone who had made a career on television, Paula Constable turned into a mean opponent of the First Amendment and the public's right to know. Within days of becoming Bryan Allen's lawyer, she requested a gag order to stop anyone with knowledge of the investigation from talking about the case. The district attorney joined in the motion and the court approved it. There was a total blackout; no one knew anything beyond the fact that Robert McMillan had been murdered and that Bryan Allen was going to be put on trial.

McMillan had died of stab wounds. It was naturally assumed that this meant the murder weapon had been a knife, but the public report avoided the use of the word. If a knife had been used, why was the phrase "a sharp-pointed instrument" used instead? It was a mark of how desperate people were to have something to say that so much speculation was devoted to what, in all probability, was nothing more than another example of the way the civil service—in this case the police bureaucracy—can mangle the English language.

Paula Constable refused to appear on the show and she refused to talk to the press. She was under a court order not to discuss the case, but the order had been issued at her request. The Allen case was the case she had always wanted; the case that would make her one of the most famous lawyers in America. After all those years of waiting, she finally had her chance; everything now depended on what she did in court.

I was looking forward to the trial, no longer just because of what I was hoping it might reveal about Robert McMillan and the things he had done, but to see how well she performed. Then, a week before the trial started, Paula Constable called.

It was a little after nine in the evening. She said she was calling from her office; she wondered if we could get together somewhere for a drink. There was something she had to talk to me about, something important. She suggested a place in North Beach—a "tourist joint," as she put it—where there was a better chance we would not be recognized. She said she could be there in half an hour.

She was waiting for me in a wooden booth in the corner past the crowded, noisy bar. She was not wearing lipstick, and she was not dressed in red. There were circles around her eyes; her skin was blotched and puffy; her mouth sagged at the corners. She looked like she had not slept in days. She had already ordered a drink.

"Thanks for coming," she said in a raspy whisper as I slipped into the booth and signaled to the waiter. She looked a wreck, and I smiled my sympathy.

"Nothing quite like getting ready for a murder trial, is there? Long days, sleepless nights; always more questions, never enough answers. You hate every minute of it; but then, when it's over, you remember that you never felt more alive."

She stared at me with blank incomprehension. She was too preoccupied, too involved in the case, to grasp the fact that it would soon be over, much less that she would look back on it with nostalgia.

"I need to talk to you—off the record; something just between you and me. Except that later, after the trial, after the verdict—then you can use it, what I tell you, agreed?"

I felt an obligation to remind her that the gag order, the one she had requested, meant that she could not talk at all until the trial was over. Her eyes flashed with something of their old defiance.

"If I don't tell you now, you won't believe me later. But you can't use it; you can't say anything about this to anyone—not until it's over. Bryan Allen insists on taking the stand in his own defense."

I waited for what she was going to say next. She looked at me as if she had said everything she had to and could not understand why I did not grasp its significance.

"I've told him he should not. That's what I want you to know: that I advised him against it; that I advised him not to testify. Now do you understand?" she asked.

She moved her drink a little bit one way on the table, then a little bit the other. She kept biting on her upper lip, curling it down over her teeth. She could not stop blinking her eyes.

"I told him that if he testifies, there won't be anything I can do for him; I told him that if he takes the stand, he'll be convicted. You're my witness that I told him that. You can say that you learned it from a source close to the defense. But promise me that, that you'll tell what happened; that it was his decision, and that, I was against it."

Allen did not have a criminal record; he was not some felon with a long history of adjudicated violence that could be used to impeach him if he took the stand; there was no lawless behavior that would make a jury believe that because he had done it before he must have done it again. If Allen had ever been arrested for a traffic ticket, no one knew anything about it. Then why was his lawyer trying to make certain that she had someone who could later support her assertion that she had opposed his decision to become a witness, sworn to tell the truth? I could think of only one reason.

"You have to withdraw; you can't represent him. Advise the court that you have an ethical conflict; the judge has to grant the motion."

Constable threw me a puzzled, impatient glance. "What are you talking about? What ethical conflict?"

"The defendant has the right to testify in his own behalf," I began, amazed that I had to remind her of something this basic. "You can't stop him if he decides he wants to testify; but neither can you put a witness on the stand you know is going to lie. If he told you that he did it, that he's guilty of the crime, and still insists on his right to testify, you have a conflict and you have to withdraw."

She looked at me with jaded eyes, amused at my forgivable ignorance. I was giving her textbook advice for a situation that had no example in the rules.

"If I knew he was going to lie, I wouldn't be so worried," she remarked with a rueful glance. "Perjury isn't the problem: the problem is he wants to tell the truth. Which might be all right, if it wasn't for the fact that a lie—any lie—would be more believable."

"Why?" I asked, immensely interested. "What happened with McMillan? Allen didn't kill him?"

Paula Constable raised the glass to her lips, watching me as if there was a question she wanted to ask, but was not sure she should.

"I've already told you more than I'm supposed to," she said with a guarded expression. "He pled not guilty; we're going to trial. He's going to take the stand; he's going to tell a story like nothing you've ever heard before; and the only question will be whether the jury waits to get to the jury room before they convict him."

"You're just going through what I always go through before a trial: You think there isn't any way you can win, but then, a few days later, you're convinced that no jury in their right mind would ever convict the defendant."

She smiled, leaned forward and placed her small hand on my wrist. "I wish I could tell you the story he told me, the story he's going to tell in court; because if I could, your own reaction would prove my point."

She finished her drink and shoved aside the empty glass. She fixed me with a narrow stare of intense calculation. Then she shook her head as if she had decided that there was no point to what she had been thinking, that it made no sense, and even the mention of it would show her to a disadvantage.

"What?" I asked, curious at what I could only suspect had something more to do with me than some question about the trial.

"Julian Sinclair."

That was all she said, and there was nothing in her expression to tell me what she meant.

"Have you found something? Evidence that connects McMillan with Daphne's murder?"

There was no reaction, no response; just that same blank stare.

"It was tragic what happened to him, wasn't it?"

She was not asking how I felt, what his death had meant; she was establishing a fact, a premise from which other things would follow.

"Dying like that in a fire in prison. Then you had to bury him. That must have been hard. I know you were close to him, that he wasn't just another client. You've never doubted he was innocent. Everything from the end of that trial until now was because of that, wasn't it?"

I did not know what she was after, why she kept searching my eyes.

"If he hadn't died—if he was still alive—do you think you would have gone after McMillan as hard as you did? You forced him into it, you know."

"Forced whom? McMillan? What did I force him into?"

She began to subject me to a scrutiny that became uncomfortable.

"I forced McMillan to file a lawsuit; I forced him to go after me face-to-face in public; but I'm not sure I could have forced him into the kind of mistake that would have saved Julian."

"Saved Julian?"

"Saved his reputation," I replied, irritated with this relentless demand for explanations to questions she refused to ask. "What is it you want? Is there something you think I know about Julian that would help your case?"

She looked at me with a strange immediacy, as if we had reached the decisive point in a dialogue that I could not pretend to understand. "Is there? Is there something about Julian Sinclair you think I should know?"

"He was convicted of a crime he didn't commit and he died in prison; beyond that, I'm afraid I can't help you. Why? What is there about Julian Sinclair that could possibly help the defense?"

"You're covering the trial, aren't you?" she asked with a smile that only heightened my profound sense of unease. "You'll see."

We said goodbye on the corner outside. Before she left she made me promise that I would not forget what she had told me about how strongly she had argued against Allen's decision to testify at his trial.

"Every murder trial is about the dead," she remarked, her gaze intense. "This one perhaps more than any other." As I started up the street, she called out, "Do you believe in ghosts, Antonelli? Allen does."

Ghosts? What was she talking about? What had Allen seen, or, perhaps more to the point, thought he had seen? Because after all the months he had spent in jail waiting trial, it would not be any great surprise if he had become just a little demented. Cut off from the world; deprived of normal, intelligent conversation; surrounded by drug-crazed addicts and rattle-eyed predators talking strange rumors and stranger conspiracies—God knows what strange things he had come to believe. I did not have time to worry about it. Allen was her problem, not mine. I still had ghosts of my own.

Though it was more a hope than an expectation, I was intensely interested in what might come out at trial that would help clear Julian Sinclair of the murder of Daphne McMillan. It was, I know, in one sense useless; but while I was resigned to the world's need to move forward, I was stubborn enough to think that even a small measure of justice was worth having, no matter how late it came. And so the week before the Allen trial started, I went on television and reminded everyone of what had happened to Julian Sinclair and the lamentable sequence of events that had led to this, the trial of a man accused of murdering the person I was convinced had murdered several others and had tried to murder me. I promised that each evening while the trial lasted I would give a blunt and candid assessment of what I thought the strengths and weaknesses of both the prosecution and the defense; and then, because I could not help myself, and because I thought I owed it to Harry Godwin to do what I could to help the ratings, I used what Paula Constable had told me to promise at least one revelation.

"Every defendant has the right against self-incrimination. No one can force a defendant to testify. Only the defendant can decide if he wants to take the stand and tell his version of what happened. Bryan Allen is not going to hide behind his right against self-incrimination. He is going to testify, and his testimony is going to include some of the most astonishing claims ever made by a defendant in a trial for murder."

Though he had been locked up for months, shut off from the world, when the trial opened, Bryan Allen did not look changed at all. The real difference had more to do with attitude and disposition than his appearance. His eyes stayed focused now for longer lengths of time, watching as Constable and the prosecution took turns examining prospective jurors. The quick change of expression had been replaced with a kind of steady, controlled impatience. It was the chastened eagerness of a man who has learned to wait, and who, more important, has been taught concentration.

Voir dire did not take anything like as long as I had expected. The questions were brief, perfunctory, as if both sides had decided that it was a waste of time; that one jury would do as well as another, and the only thing that counted was their own ability to put on a case. Harrison Mills, the prosecutor, seemed so anxious to finish that at one point he dispensed with questions altogether. Three jurors in a row were greeted with the glassy-eyed smile of a ticket-taker and waved through; each one, in the routine language of jury selection, "passed for cause." His opening statement was equally terse.

Harrison Mills was a prosecutor of the old school. Slouching, slender, with unruly hair and disorderly clothes: a shirt worn so often during a trial that it led to the suspicion that it was a captive's calendar, measuring the days by each new shade of gray; shoes unpolished, with laces close to tatters; socks with holes mended until the threads had begun to unravel; pants that, if they were close to the same color as the coat, he considered the second half of a suit. He had the nervous, preoccupied look of a man who often fell asleep at night in his chair with a book he had opened and then forgotten, dangling in his hand. Harrison Mills believed that criminals should be prosecuted for their crimes, and he believed in it with a kind of righteous fervor. He would not have gone into private practice for all the money in the world. It would have been for him the ultimate embarrassment, his life a failure, a disgrace, to find himself even once on the other side, arguing leniency for someone who had broken the law. He lived in a world of moral absolutes and was honest to a fault. He was utterly incorruptible, and had he ever run for district attorney, I would have voted for him in a minute.

Mills put on the case for the prosecution without, as far as I could tell, a single unnecessary question. Stern, implacable, moving from one witness to the next, he bent forward, alert, attentive, while Constable engaged in cross-examination. Whatever he was thinking on those occasions, he never gave it away. He had as much expression as a hangman, and his expression never, or almost never, changed. The only sign of surprise I ever saw happened not on cross-examination, but at the beginning of his own examination of the prosecution's last witness.

When Susan Lind walked into court, every eye turned toward her. Blond and beautiful, she held her chin in that classic and irresistible attitude of easy, teasing indifference. After a series of preliminary questions, Mills asked her why, engaged to one man, she had started seeing another.

It was the smile, the soft, sweet, seductive smile she could not quite hide, that gave her away. The answer underlined what that silent smile had already said.

"Because I wanted to."

It stopped poor Harrison Mills in his tracks. Whether he was married, whether he lived alone, he had no knowledge of a woman like this. And for all my reckless wandering, it was still stunning, almost shocking, how selfish she was, and how little she tried to disguise it. It was all there, written in her cold, bright eyes: how little it mattered to her whether the man she was with shared any of the pleasure she insisted on taking for herself. She was the kind of woman who would have preferred to make love with a man who spoke some language she did not understand; anything, if only she could be left alone with what she felt. She would have made any man crazy, and someone like Robert McMillan most of all. She did not seem to have any doubt that she had had the same effect on Bryan Allen, too.

"Because you wanted to?" Mills repeated, still confused.

"Yes, I wanted to. Bryan was famous; Robert was rich. And in that sense, they were both attractive."

Mills shut her out, pushed aside everything extraneous and drove back to the only important point.

"You began an affair with Mr. Allen while you were engaged to Mr. McMillan. You decided to end the affair. Mr. Allen was upset. Is that what happened?"

"I saw Bryan Allen; that's true," she said without emotion. "I saw him while I was engaged to Robert; that's also true. I told Bryan I could not see him anymore; and yes, he did not take it very well. But whether that had anything to do with what happened that Sunday, the day Robert died, I really could not say."

"To your knowledge, did Mr. McMillan ever find out that you were seeing Mr. Allen?"

"Yes, he knew. I told him that I had been seeing Bryan; that I wanted to be sure how I felt before I went through with the marriage; and that now I was."

On cross, Constable surprised me. She had abandoned her red flashy clothes for something simple, more sedate: a gray skirt and jacket and a pair of dark shoes. She rose from her place at the counsel table, but did not move a step.

"Before his death, there were accusations that Robert McMillan had murdered two of his three wives. Isn't that the reason why you started seeing the defendant, Bryan Allen? Because you weren't sure it was safe, that what had happened to those other women, might happen to you?"

"No, that's not—"

"Are you denying that you told Bryan Allen that you were worried, that Robert McMillan had a violent temper, that he had tried to attack you once, but that you had managed to get away?"

"No, that isn't right," replied Susan Lind, though without the same confidence in her voice. "That's an exaggeration. I was talking about something that had happened one night when Robert had been drinking too much. He wanted me, but in his condition I didn't want him. I wasn't in any danger."

Constable glared at the witness. "You're under oath. Are you going to testify that you never felt threatened, never thought yourself in danger, from the deceased, Robert McMillan?"

If there was one thing Susan Lind had learned in a long life of conquest, it was never to back down. The only thing worse than telling a lie was admitting that you had.

"I never felt in danger," she said, carefully choosing her words.

"But you thought you might?"

"I did not say that."

"I'll repeat the question: Did you think you might at some point find yourself threatened with violence by Robert McMillan?"

"No. Why would I think that?"

Constable shrugged. "I don't know. But if you didn't think he was violent; if you didn't think there was anything to the accusations that had been made against him; if you believed that he had been slandered the way he insisted in that lawsuit he filed, then perhaps you can explain why three days before he was murdered, just weeks before you were going to be married, you bought a gun?"

Chapter Twenty-two

Piece by piece, like a master craftsman methodically at work, Harrison Mills built a case that, unless the defense was able to produce some stunning new revelation, left no room for doubt. The coroner testified that the death of Robert McMillan had been caused by a single stab wound to the throat.

"And was the stab wound caused by a knife?"

It seemed a strange question to ask. The answer was stranger still.

"No, not in the usual sense."

Harrison Mills directed the clerk to hand the witness a long thin package. The coroner carefully unwrapped it.

"Could this have caused the stab wound you found on the body of Robert McMillan?" asked Mills over the gasps of the crowd.

My mouth fell open when I saw what the coroner held in his hands. The murder weapon was a fencer's foil. I had the strange feeling that I should have known, that in some sense I had known.

Mills asked the coroner to describe the exact nature of the fatal wound.

"The foil penetrated the front of the throat and was driven through the back of the neck."

"Through the larynx?"

"Yes."

"Could you tell from the angle of penetration, measured from the entry wound at the front to the exit wound at the back, what position the victim must have been in at the time the wound was inflicted?"

The coroner, balding and heavyset, nodded briefly.

"The thrust was in a slightly downward direction. The victim was found in a chair. Given the length of the foil, the killer must have been standing a few feet in front of him."

Mills started to turn away, and then, as if he had just remembered, stopped.

"One thing more, Dr. Thompson. Other than that stab wound to the throat, were there any other wounds on the victim's body?"

"Yes, his right hand."

"His right hand?"

"The inside of it was burned and blistered."

"And could you determine what had caused that to happen?"

"I can't be absolutely certain, but from the shape of the burn, the pattern of the blisters, it appeared that Mr. McMillan had held an oblong piece of red-hot metal in his hand."

"Could it have been some kind of accident? Something that happened perhaps earlier that same day—he had not realized the stove was on and picked up a kettle—something like that?"

"No, this was no accident. The burns went too deep. He held something in his hand, held it tight, held it for a long time. He had to have been forced to do it. The pain would have been excruciating."

After the coroner, Mills called the lead detective, who testified that the foil belonged to Robert McMillan and that the killer had apparently taken it from above the fireplace mantel where it was normally kept. There were two sets of prints on the handle. One of them belonged to McMillan; the other belonged to Bryan Allen.

"When you arrived—tell us what you saw."

"The victim, Robert McMillan, was in a chair in the living room. That sword," he said, pointing toward the foil, "was shoved through his throat."

"Through his throat?"

"Yes, all the way through, driven into the chair behind him. It was done with tremendous force."

Mills asked him about McMillan's hand and whether he had been able to determine the cause of the burns.

"A piece of iron, four inches by two inches and about a quarter-inch thick. It was lying on the floor, next to the chair."

The detective identified the object, marked as an exhibit.

"It had been heated in a fire. It was still hot when we got there."

"What else did you find when you got there?"

"We found him," he said, pointing toward the counsel table, "the defendant, Bryan Allen."

The moment Harrison Mills was through, Paula Constable was on her feet, smiling broadly.

"You certainly weren't surprised to find Bryan Allen there, were you, Detective Lawrence?"

"I don't know what you mean."

She tossed her head, the smile now a shrewd, knowing grin.

"You don't know what I mean? He was the reason you were there! He was the reason you found the body! Bryan Allen called the police. Isn't that true, Detective Lawrence?"

"He called 911."

"He called the police and he waited until you got there. Correct?"

"Yes."

"Waited until you got there and then told you who the killer was, didn't he?"

Lawrence made a dismissive gesture with his hand. "He told us something that wasn't possible, that's what he told us."

"He told you someone else killed Robert McMillan. He told you he was innocent!" she insisted.

THERE WAS NOTHING Paula Constable could do. After the prosecution had finished its case, she had to put Bryan Allen on the stand and, whatever she thought about his story, let him tell it.

Paula Constable's hands were shaking when she called the defendant's name. Her voice began to crack when she asked him to state his name for the record. Her mouth tightened at the corners and she bent her head; her rigid thick black lashes covered her eyes. Angry with herself, she stamped her foot and with perfect timing threw a revelatory glance at the jury.

"Talk about great beginnings!"

She cleared her throat, rapped her knuckles on the corner of the counsel table and with a purposeful swagger moved a few steps away until she was standing directly in front of the witness stand.

"Now tell us—tell the jury," she said in a firm, confident voice, "tell everyone what happened that Sunday afternoon that Robert McMillan was killed. Tell us first," she added quickly, "why you went there. Was it your idea?"

"No, McMillan called me."

Allen bent forward, his fingers intertwined. He looked past Constable to the courtroom crowd.

"He said he wanted to see me. He said he wanted to confess."

You could feel it, the sense of keen anticipation. I leaned forward, trying to get a closer look; to see whether that look of intense concentration in Allen's eyes did not carry with it at least a trace of retribution. Now, finally, after months of silent waiting, he could tell the world what had really happened.

Constable turned toward the jury, a meaningful look in her eyes. "Confess?"

"He called me. He said he wanted to tell the truth about the murder of his wife, Daphne McMillan—and that he wanted to tell it to me. And not just her murder, but the murder of his second wife and the attempted murder of the lawyer, Joseph Antonelli. He said he had written it all out, and that he would give it to me: his signed confession. But he said I had to come at once, that if I didn't, he would give the story to someone else."

"And that is the reason you went there that afternoon?"

"I was a reporter; I had a television show. A story like that? Of course I went!"

"Tell the jury what happened when you got there—from the time you knocked on the door."

"I knocked on the door. There was no answer, but I heard noises, like some kind of struggle. Then a moment later I heard McMillan scream for help. I tried the door. It was not locked. I pushed it open. I heard the sounds of footsteps, someone running out the back. Then I saw McMillan, sitting in that chair in the living room with that sword in his throat, covered in blood."

"Was he dead?"

"No, not quite. He thought I could save him. He made this gurgling sound and tried to raise his hands. He wanted me to take that thing out of his throat. I reached for it, had my hand on the handle— that's why my fingerprints were on it—but then I decided I had better not, that it would only make it worse. I called 911, told them to get there right away, that a man was dying."

"So the reason you went there was because he called you and told you he wanted to confess to murder?"

Filled with nervous excitement, Allen's eyes darted all around the courtroom.

"He wanted to confess to everything, just like I said: the murder of Daphne McMillan, the murder of his second wife, the attempt to murder Antonelli."

Constable gave him a searching look.

"Didn't you think it a little strange that he would suddenly call you up and tell you a story like that? Did you think that perhaps he was just telling you that to get you over there because he wanted to do something to you because you had been sleeping with the woman he was going to marry?"

"I might have, if I hadn't heard his voice."

"His voice?"

"It was different, full of fear. I thought it must be because of what he had decided to tell me, the strain of making that confession. It was only when I got there that I understood that he had been afraid for his life, that he had called because someone had that sword pressed up against his throat and that if he didn't he would die."

"Do you know who it was? Who made him call you? Who killed him with that sword?"

"He told me who killed him just before he died. He could barely make a sound, just that awful, gurgling noise. I had to bend down next to him to hear."

"Who? Who killed him? What name did Robert McMillan give you?"

"Julian Sinclair!"

It was as if everyone in the courtroom had been struck dumb. There was not a sound from anywhere.

"Julian Sinclair," repeated Allen, a look of grim defiance in his eyes. "I didn't believe it, either."

"You didn't believe it?"

"Sinclair died in prison. It had to have been someone else. McMillan was trying to tell me that someone else had decided to get revenge for what McMillan had done to Sinclair. That's the only thing that makes sense. McMillan was dying, and he knew it. How he got out even those two words, I'll never know."

Constable turned toward the jury.

"Someone else killed Robert McMillan? You didn't go there, torture him with a piece of red-hot iron and then run him through the throat with a fencer's foil?"

Allen had been on the stand long enough to feel comfortable. The jury and the courtroom crowd had become just another audience. He took her question the way he had taken a thousand idiotic remarks he had listened to on his show. He shrugged, turned up his hands, cocked his head, pressed his lips together and half-closed his eyes. It was his trademark, the gesture that had made him famous; the surefire answer to every lie anyone had ever tried to tell him; the look that told everyone watching that he was standing up for them against all the crooks and killers and the crooked lawyers paid to defend them.

"Come on! You think I'd do something like that? With a sword? Do I look like a guy who would use a sword—or whatever you call that thing? It has my fingerprints on it—of course it does! I told you how that happened. I tried to save his life! I called 911!"

Her head bent low, Constable dragged her hand along the jury box railing as she moved slowly forward.

"And he told you, or tried to tell you, who killed him?"

"Yes, but all he could say was 'Julian Sinclair.'"

Paula Constable went back to her place at the counsel table and stared without expression straight ahead. Bryan Allen looked all around, searching, as it seemed, for a friendly face, or at least some sign that someone believed what he had said. Several members of the jury looked down at their hands; several others shifted quietly in their chairs. With a kind of fatal inevitability, Harrison Mills rose slowly from his chair. Standing in front of the counsel table, the fingers of his right hand resting on the edge of it, he studied the witness with a cold, penetrating stare.

"You went there because Mr. McMillan called and told you he wanted to confess. Is that your testimony?" he asked in an efficient voice.

"Yes."

"To confess not to one murder, but to two?"

"Yes."

"And not just two murders, but an attempted murder on top of that?"

"That's what I said; that's what he told me."

"You admit you were having an affair with the woman engaged to be his wife?"

"Yeah, I admitted that."

"But that was not the reason you went there?"

"No. Why would I do that?"

"Because she was breaking off the affair; because you couldn't stand the thought that she was going back to him."

"I wasn't in love with her; I didn't care what she did."

"She seems to think you did."

Allen started to turn up his hands in that trademark gesture. Mills cut him off.

"Did it surprise you when McMillan told you he wanted to confess?"

"What do you mean?"

"Did it surprise you? Or had you always thought he killed Daphne McMillan?"

"No, I didn't—"

"Had you ever suggested to Ms. Lind that she might be in danger if she did not leave Mr. McMillan?"

"I may have mentioned some of the things I had heard."

"Did Ms. Lind tell you that she felt herself to be in danger? Did she ever tell you that Mr. McMillan had a violent temper, that he had even tried to attack her?"

"Yes, she did."

"So then, you were not surprised that he wanted to confess?"

"Of course I was surprised that he wanted to confess."

"But you were not surprised about what his confession was about: that he had killed his third wife, Daphne McMillan, and murdered his second wife as well?"

"No, I guess I wasn't."

"So all those things you said about Julian Sinclair during his trial for murder . . . What was that? Just something you did for ratings?"

"Objection!" shouted Constable.

"Never mind. Let's stay with Mr. McMillan's confession. Where is it?"

Allen shrugged. "Where is what?"

"The confession. You testified—would you like me to have the court reporter read it back?—that he told you on the telephone that he had written out his confession, that he had signed it, and that he would give it to you when you got there. Where is it, Mr. Allen? Where is the confession that Robert McMillan signed just for you?"

"It wasn't there. The killer must have taken it."

"The killer? Yes, the person who wanted to revenge what happened to Julian Sinclair. He took the confession with him, instead of leaving it for the police? He took the confession that according to your testimony he must have forced McMillan to write? And just how would that serve the purpose of clearing Julian Sinclair's name?"

"It's the truth, that's all I know."

Mills had not moved. He stayed in that same position, one hand resting on the table, the other one clutching the lapel of his jacket, his shoulder bent forward, measuring Allen's slightest reaction with the grasping singularity of an eye determined and relentless. Now, for the first time, Mills dropped his gaze. Nodding slowly to himself, he moved with an air of distraction across the front of the courtroom until he was within an arm's length of the jury box.

"But that isn't what you told the police, is it?" he asked, raising his head as he turned toward the witness. "You did not tell the police anything about Robert McMillan's supposed confession. You never told anyone that he had admitted that he murdered his wife and sent an innocent man to prison. You did not tell the police, you did not tell anyone, about this written confession you were going there to get. You did not tell the police, you did not tell anyone, that when you got there, it was missing. Why is that, Mr. Allen? Why did you wait until now—your trial for murder—to tell this story? Why didn't you tell the police when they first arrived? Could it be that you had not thought of it then? Could it be that you only thought of it when you decided that your only chance was to make up a story that a jury might think was true because no one could make up something as bizarre, as outrageous, as ludicrous as this?"

There was nothing Paula Constable could do; nothing anyone could do. Mills was right: the story was bizarre, outrageous; everything he had called it and more. Allen had not told it to anyone before because no one would believe it, and he only told it now because he was desperate. When Allen reached the counsel table, he shot a frightened, pleading glance in my direction. He wanted me to believe him, and the strange part was that I did. I believed every word he had said; not because I trusted him, but because, knowing what I did about what had happened to Julian Sinclair, it seemed too fitting, too appropriate that it should have an ending like this. It was as if the ghost of Julian Sinclair had orchestrated everything from the start.

Perhaps there were ghosts after all, the kind that haunt the conscience. Perhaps during those long months of close confinement, Bryan Allen had begun to think about what had happened to Julian Sinclair and to think that some of it was his fault. It would have played on his mind, all those days and nights in a cell, until it became so real that when he came to court and told it, he believed every word. That was one explanation; there was another: It had happened just the way he said it had, that someone had decided to take revenge on Robert McMillan in a way that only Julian might have approved. But who would have done a thing like that?

No one else believed Bryan Allen, certainly no one on the jury. It was not quite as bad as Paula Constable had predicted, but it was bad enough. The jurors did not render a verdict before they left the jury box; they made it to the jury room and, though not very long for a murder case, deliberated the better part of a day.

Allen looked nervous and confused while he waited for the judge to examine the verdict form before the jury foreman made the announcement. I had the feeling that he was not wondering so much about the verdict, as how any of this had happened; and that the verdict that pronounced him guilty of murder did not bother him nearly so much as his inability to understand, even now, why he had been set up and who had done it.

Chapter Twenty-three

B RYAN ALLEN was sentenced to life without possibility of parole. He did not have the kind of reflective intelligence that would have made him wonder what Julian Sinclair must have felt when he was on the way to San Quentin when he was going there himself. He did not think about Julian, and after he had been sent away I did not think much about him. I did not think about much of anything except trying to get back to my old routine and the life I used to know.

I left the network, quit the show and told myself without quite believing it that I had done my best, that I had tried every way I knew how to make up for my failure to save first the life, then the memory, of Julian Sinclair. Robert McMillan was dead, and there was at least some justice in that. There was also a certain justice in the conviction of Bryan Allen as his killer, though whether for a murder he committed or an innocent man he helped send to prison was a question that required a finer moral sensibility than my own. I went back to the law and, as I had done for most of my life, forgot everything but the next case, the next trial and what I had to do to win.

Another season passed, and another one after that; trying cases, taking life as it came. Sometimes, when I looked across the bay and saw the lights in the Berkeley hills I would find myself wondering what Julian might have become, the great things he might have done. Sometimes I thought about Julian on purpose in the belief that as long as anyone still remembered him, there was some part of who he had been that would not perish. It seemed an easy, decent thing to do.

It was the first week of October, one of those burnt autumn days when the air is dry and hot and you feel the warmth of the dying sun on your face, that the call came from Frank Sutton. It was not a day to spend inside and I was anxious to leave the office while some of the day was still left.

"I don't know anyone named Frank Sutton. Tell the operator we won't accept the call," I told my secretary, wondering why I had to. A moment later, she buzzed me back.

"He said Julian Sinclair told him to call."

"Mr. Sutton, this is Joseph Antonelli. What can I do for you? Julian Sinclair told you to call?"

It was hard to tell from Sutton's voice how old he was, but he was not young. He spoke slowly, pausing after every few words as if to make certain that I understood why he had called and why it was important. He said that he had known Julian and that Julian had asked him to give something to me. He would not say what it was, nor would he tell me why he had waited this long after Julian's death to get in touch with me. If I wanted to visit him in San Quentin, he would be glad to see me, but he would not talk about any of this on the telephone. He made it quite clear that if he had not thought so highly of Julian, he would not have called at all.

Two days later, I drove up the long narrow street that ran right next to the bay, gave my name to the guard at the gate to the prison and parked the car in the visitors' lot. Inmates in light green khaki pants and shirts were raking leaves in the flower beds outside the walls. After I signed the register, a bulky guard checked my driver's license, marked the back of my hand with something that could be seen only under a violet light, and let me through a double set of iron bars. The door shut behind me and I was in the courtyard where the fountain, filled with water, did not work, and a tall palm tree, bent with age, made it look like a dry oasis. The library, where I had found Julian the last time I had come here, was straight ahead on the other side.

Turning left around the corner, I found Frank Sutton, sitting on a wooden bench against a cell block wall, one skinny leg crossed over the other, squinting peacefully into the midday sun. Another inmate also dressed in blue sat next to him at what appeared to be a respectful distance, talking quietly. When they saw me, the other man got to his feet, but did not move away until Sutton told him that it was all right, they could talk later.

"Sit down," said Sutton, his arms still folded. He made no effort to stand up and he did not extend his hand. I had known when he called that he was not young, but I had not expected him to be quite as old as this, in his late seventies, and perhaps, because everything slows down in prison, even older than that.

"I've heard about you," he said. "Even before what Julian told me."

Sutton laced his hands together behind his head. He leaned back, a distant, thoughtful expression on his wizened face.

"This is where we lived," he remarked with a casual nod toward his left, where, a hundred feet away, a steel door led to a concrete building six or seven stories high. "North Block. Julian lived on the fifth tier; I lived on the floor above that."

"I thought there were only five tiers in the block, and that Julian's cell was on the top."

"You don't miss much, do you?" said Sutton with a shrewd glance. "You're right: North Block has five tiers. You ever been inside? No?

Well, let me give you a little history. If you go through that door right there, you'll see another door. It looks like one of those bulging hatches you see in a submarine. It leads to the gas chamber. In the old days, before the death penalty got so popular, and before they started delaying things sometimes fifteen, twenty years with appeals, death row was on the top floor of the building; the floor above the ceiling for those five tiers. Follow? Sixty-six cells wasn't enough. So they moved death row. But the thing was, those were the best cells in the place—windows that opened, views out over the bay. Sort of like the Nob Hill of the prison, if you know what I mean. Like old money, too," he went on, enjoying the analogy to life outside. "We don't let in the nouveau riche—have to have at least twenty years before you get considered for admission."

The smile on Frank Sutton's face was shrewd and cunning, but his eyes betrayed something more serious and, strangely enough, more friendly.

"You knew Julian. You think you knew him better than I did?" Before I could answer, he shook his graying head abruptly and withdrew the question. "That was stupid. We both knew him; maybe in different ways. He loved you, by the way. He never said that. Why would he? But you could tell the way he talked about you that you were someone for whom he had nothing but respect. He never talked that way about anyone else."

Sutton sat up and then bent forward over his knobby knees. With a harsh, disparaging glance, he tossed his head toward a well-guarded crowd of mostly young men, mainly black and Hispanic. They were being split apart to form groups on each side of a shed-like area with a metal roof and open at the sides. All of them were dressed in orange.

"New arrivals; transferred from another prison so they could fight each other here. They think they're tough, that no one is going to push them around. They'll learn."

Sutton motioned toward a middle-aged black man with a short thick neck and grim cold eyes. He whispered something in his ear.

"I'll take care of it, Frank," said the other, his eyes come to life.

"There was something I was supposed to do," explained Sutton. "I did not know for sure what time you'd come." He studied me for a moment before he asked with what appeared to be nothing more than simple curiosity, "Was this the first time it happened to you? It must happen to a lot of lawyers—most of the ones I knew weren't very good—but you're one of the best. Was Julian the first?"

I did not have to ask him what he meant.

"Everybody in here—well, maybe not everybody; but a lot of them claim they were set up; that they didn't do it; that the police made a mistake, or planted evidence; that a witness lied; that their lawyer didn't know what he was doing. They're all innocent, and they're all guilty as hell. Julian never once said he was innocent, and everyone—and I mean everyone: the guards, the warden, that woman works as the librarian—knew he didn't do it. Let me tell you something: if what happened, hadn't happened—he would have ended up running this place."

Sutton caught the question that had stayed in my eyes. His scarecrow shoulders shuddered as he laughed.

"Yes, including me. I'm guilty as hell, just like all the rest. Murder, that's what they charged me with; life without possibility of parole is what they gave me. As I say, I was guilty—according to what I would call a strict interpretation of the law." His head turned from one side to the other. "In fairness to myself, I'd have to say that there were what a lawyer of your skill and experience would have called 'extenuating circumstances.'"

Caught in his mood, I interjected, "Not 'mitigating circumstances'?"

He frowned, bit on his lip and shrugged. "To murder as most

people think they know it; but not murder as it was charged. I didn't kill anyone; someone else did."

"In the commission of . . ."

"Right; a felony, and not just any felony, a bank robbery." There was a steely glint in his aging eyes, a kind of cheerful defiance about what he had done. "And not just any bank robbery. It was the . . ."

Frank Sutton. Now I remembered the name. He was right; it was not just any bank robbery: it was one of the biggest bank robberies in American history. I was barely out of law school when it happened.

"You got away with millions!"

He looked at me the way an artist might look at someone who was only interested in how much his most famous painting might bring at auction. What difference did it make how much he had stolen? It was the degree of difficulty that made the thief. He had done something that was supposed to have been impossible—entered a time-locked vault built to withstand everything short of a nuclear blast—and had done it in a way that had left all the experts scratching their heads. Whether the vault had contained half the currency then in circulation, or had not held a dime, had nothing to do with the achievement. Which was not to say that Sutton did not understand the popular mind. When the judge who sentenced him asked how much he had stolen and what he had done with the money, Sutton had made his famous reply, "I didn't have time to count. All I can tell you is that when I buried it I had to dig three holes."

"'Three-hole Sutton,'" I said out loud, remembering the name the papers gave him. "There were people who spent years looking for all that buried money."

"Some of them still are. I get letters all the time asking me to tell them, or at least give them a hint. Even when I tell them the truth: that I just made that story up, that the money was never buried, they don't believe me; they think I'm just trying to throw them off."

Sutton paused. With his fingernail, he picked his teeth.

"Four and a half million. That's how much we got. Know what I did with it? I bought U.S. saving bonds; not all in one place—different banks, different towns. Four and a half million in bonds, after twenty-five years, at full maturity—it's a lot more than that. Bonds, not stocks: I never believed in risky investments. That's the trouble with people: always trying to get something for nothing; always in too much of a hurry.

"'Three-hole Sutton,'" he said, shaking his head at the myth he had created. "All because of that one bank job, the best one I ever did, everything planned down to the second; and then this idiot ruins it by shooting a guard. We would have gotten away with it; no one would ever have caught us. It would have been the greatest bank robbery of all time, and this kid I barely knew, a last-minute replacement, who was only supposed to stand there and make sure none of the people out front did anything stupid, gets nervous. I never shot anyone in my life. They caught all four of us, but they never got the money. I made sure of that. Those bonds are worth close to ten million. I know I can trust Julian to spend it well."

"Julian? He's dead."

Frank Sutton stroked his chin while he studied me with cunning eyes. "Died in a fire in his cell," he said, repeating the formal record as he slowly got to his feet.

I followed him over to the cyclone fence that ran from the end of the library. Down below, the baseball field and the running track stretched out in the distance, and beyond that, the shop buildings and the maintenance sheds. A wooden guard tower, lonely and dilapidated, stood at the edge of the small spit of land that jutted out into the bay.

"See those buildings way out there at the edge, the other side of the fence. That's what they call the ranch annex. That's where you get to live when you're at the end of your sentence, if you never tried to escape and you don't have a record of violence. They do the gardening and the landscape work. They also put out fires."

Sutton held onto the wire screen with both hands. An enigmatic smile curled across his desiccated mouth.

"It's right over there, San Quentin's very own fire department; every member of it an inmate from level one—the ones who could walk away, but don't, because their sentence is almost over. The chief isn't an inmate—he's hired from the outside—but the others . . . It was years before I realized what that meant, before I put it all together." Sutton turned his head just far enough to catch my eye. "Everything is always simple at the end. You must have noticed that: how all the complications come at the beginning, that the farther you go, the fewer problems there are. And this was really just a problem of reverse engineering: you break into banks; you break out of prison."

He gestured one last time toward the edge of the prison and the freedom that lay out there, waiting, on the other side. And then, smiling to himself, he walked back to the bench.

"I had it all figured out, the way it could be done, how I could get out of here. Not just escape, mind you; but do it in a way that no one would ever know. That's the perfect part, the reason why it had so much appeal. It's the perfect crime, only better. It isn't the crime that someone gets away with; it's the crime no one knows was committed. Well, as I say, I finally had it all worked out. It gave me something to do, kept me occupied," he remarked, leaning back against the cement wall, his hands wrapped around his upraised knee. "And then Julian came, and I started thinking about my age."

"Are you trying to tell me that Julian isn't dead? That he didn't die in that fire? That he escaped?"

Sutton nodded in a way that suggested that he had heard the question, but that the question was not relevant: there was something more interesting than whether someone was alive or dead.

"I never met anyone like him. Did you?" he asked, certain that Julian must have had the same effect on me. "He was different than all the rest. He had something to offer. You know what I mean?" he went on, his glance suddenly shy. "He was what I would have liked to have been if I had known at the beginning what I learned at the end. I'm not educated enough to describe it; but you knew he knew—that there is something in the universe, some force, some power—I don't know—that makes it all make sense. You knew he understood that the only thing really important was living within yourself, being who you are born to be—not what someone else makes you think you ought to become. And you knew that about him the first time you looked into his eyes. There was a kind of comfort in that."

The burning intensity in Sutton's eyes that had made everything he said seem so vivid and real, began to fade away. He looked across at the open shed where the mob of new inmates had been lined up and, one by one, patted down for weapons.

"The eyes of most people here are dead. They did not die in here; they died before they ever lived. Except, mainly, the religious ones; though most of them are just plain crazy. But Julian! There was something you don't see—not just in here, but on the outside."

Sutton paused. He thought hard for a moment. A light came on in his eyes.

"He was what you would have liked to have been, but you had never known it, until you met him, and then you knew. That's it, don't you think? When you met him, when you saw that look in his eyes: then you knew what it must be like to know what it's really like to be alive. That make sense?"

With a modest shrug, Sutton let me know that that was as far as he could go, as close as he could come. He knew I understood exactly what he meant, and that, because I had known Julian, I agreed.

"That's when I decided," he remarked, as he slumped against the concrete wall.

"Decided?"

"That it was better that he got out instead of me. Don't get me wrong," he added in the way of men who do not want to be thought noble or kindhearted. "If I had been younger I would have gone in a minute. But I'm eighty years old—next spring; been here since I was just a boy of fifty-two," he said with a gruff smile. "What was I going to do outside? Make a fool of myself chasing younger women, trying to get laid? It isn't so bad being here. The food is decent; I sleep good at night; get plenty of exercise; have a nice view of the bay. I do what any guy my age likes to do: I watch the Giants in the spring and summer, and the 49ers in the fall. And I get to do what any old man likes to do in the twilight of his life: I get to bask in the knowledge of my own good deeds, all the better for the fact that there are so few people who know what they are. Julian is one of those who know, and now so are you. Shall I tell you how we did it, how we got him out of here, and did it in a way that no one would ever know he escaped?"

I had been listening with growing excitement and, more than that, an indescribable sense of relief. I felt like one of those lost souls on death row, waiting through the endless days for his own execution, suddenly told that he had been exonerated and within a few hours would be released. Julian was alive. He had not died in that fire.

"We buried him; we had a funeral," I started to complain.

"The librarian told me it was a nice service," said Sutton, dazzled by his own success. He had engineered the perfect escape, the one no one would ever know about, the one that ended at a graveside with the people who cared about Julian mourning his death. The final tribute, the confirmation of his triumph, was the flash of anger he saw in my eyes at the way I had been not just deceived, but used.

"The main problem was we needed two bodies. The problem was not that we needed two of them, but who the other one would be. That's what made it interesting. The guy who shared the cell was dying. He was old, almost as old as me. Chronic smoker, coughing all the time. Cigarettes will kill you. You don't smoke, do you? Good. When he died, that was the day we had to do it. But, you see, when it was all over, there had to be two bodies found in the cell, both of them dead and burned beyond recognition. And one of them had to be about the same age as Julian and pretty much the same size."

"You killed someone to . . . ?"

Sutton pulled one foot up onto the bench and stretched out his hand for support. His face wrinkled all over as he thought about the best way to explain.

"You might say the guy killed himself. You know how there are some people you just don't want to be around? Outside, you just don't invite them over; inside, you have to get a little more inventive. Look, the guy was a rapist, a guy who liked young kids. He didn't think we knew, but we did.

"The fire started in Julian's cell. Nothing but smoke, but it set off the alarms. The fire department—look over there, it's only a couple hundred yards away—comes rushing over, all these guys wearing their firemen uniforms: the big brimmed hats that cover most of their heads, the bulky rubber coats, the big boots—in those outfits they all look alike. First thing when a fire starts is the guards—they have only a couple in the block—have to get all the inmates out. In all that smoke and commotion, it was not that difficult. A couple of the firemen brought extra stuff—another coat, another pair of pants, boots, a helmet—the whole outfit. Julian put it on, the second body was left on the floor, and instead of putting the fire out, the guys who got there first brought a little something to make a real fire, a hot one. Burned the guy's face off, and burned his hands so there wouldn't be any prints. Then they put it out. And then . . ."

"The firemen went back to the firehouse," I said, taking up the story as if I had heard it through to the finish once before and could tell it now myself. "And Julian with them; and then from there to the ranch annex where they live; and then he just walked away, across the open fields, to the highway."

Sutton knew what I was thinking about: the risk that had been run by everyone involved, the ones who, if they had been caught, would have spent years more back inside the walls of the prison, rather than the few short months left on their sentence.

"He helped everyone; he did not care what they had done, why they were here. He treated everyone with the same kind of respect. And he never once asked anyone for anything in return. We all knew he was different; that he was not just smarter, but better. Everyone had that sense about him: that he was the best we had ever known. You should have seen the look in their eyes, the ones who helped pull it off, the day after he was gone. It's the look you see on the face of new fathers that tells you that things now have a meaning, that you have a future to look forward to, that there is now a reason to hope. Not bad for a bunch of guys who weren't supposed to know how to do anything right."

I had more questions than I could count, but only one I thought he could answer.

"It's been more than a year. Why now? Why did you decide to wait until now to tell me that Julian did not die?"

Frank Sutton got to his feet and shoved his hands into his pockets. His gaze wandered aimlessly around the bleak wire fences of the only home he had.

"I don't know the answer to that. All I know is that Julian asked me to tell you and that he would tell me when. He said he would write to me and let me know. They open all the mail. He had a code. I got it the day I called you."

Sutton reached inside his denim jacket and pulled out a postcard.

"Must be a pretty place," he said as he looked at the picture on the front before handing it to me. It was a photograph of the French countryside. I read the few words printed carefully on the back and started to smile.

"'Uncle Frank'? 'Your nephew J'?"

Sutton nodded. "The postcard meant I was to contact you right away and tell you what happened. I didn't understand what he said about where he had been or where he was going; maybe that part is for you."

I looked at it again and then gave it back.

"Saw the Château d'If," it read. "Now heading home. I'm expecting an old friend."

Chapter Twenty-four

I COULD SEE the lights from a quarter mile away as I drove through the Berkeley hills. The first leaves of autumn had begun to fall and the driveway had not been swept. A warm wind, summer's ghost, moved breath-like through the trees. In the distance, far across the bay, the Golden Gate loomed dark, romantic and mysterious in the scarlet purple night. The soft, seductive sound of a jazz piano floated from behind the door left far enough open to let me know I should come inside.

Nothing had changed; every piece of furniture was exactly where it had been before. The walls had long ago been repainted, the carpet replaced; nothing tangible left of Daphne McMillan's last terrified moments, nothing left of death. In the middle of the dining room table was a vase full of flowers; a bowl of fruit sat on the kitchen counter. There was the comfortable smell left over after the oven has finished baking and the stove has been turned off, that peaceful, do-mestic aroma of quiet everyday life. The music, something Dave Brubeck had done, was coming from a radio on a bookshelf in the liv-ing room. Through the window I could see across the bay to the nighttime city, dressed up in gold and silver, across to Russian Hill, where Daphne McMillan used to look back over here. It seemed such a long time ago, a lifetime in which so many things had changed.

Now that I knew what had happened, I was not surprised that he had been staying here, or that he had never left. The postcard was French, but the stamp was American and it had been mailed from here. He had been here all along, living in the anonymous safety of someone thought dead, the same reclusive, self-sufficient life he had led before. He was not wanted by the police, and he had been forgotten by nearly everyone else. Who would notice him—who notices anything they don't expect to see? He had been here the whole time, from the night he walked away from San Quentin. Where else would he go? He had always lived alone, surrounded by his books, talking with himself in that endless dialogue that went on inside his mind.

I sat down in the cushioned easy chair, put my feet on the ottoman, switched on the floor lamp and tried to imagine what it had been like, sitting here in the evenings, watching the television coverage of Bryan Allen's trial. I could almost sense what he must have felt watching the way the same story was told a second time, Allen as clearly guilty of McMillan's murder as he was supposed to have been guilty of the murder of McMillan's wife. The laughter seemed to echo in the room. But was it—or had it been—the grim, gallows humor of one who knew and regretted the bitter truth; or had it been the distant laughter of one who sees and understands the way in which everyone responsible would suffer, each of them, the fair measure of revenge? And then I wondered what he had thought of the part I had played, and whether it had met all his expectations.

There was a reason he had led me here, and a reason why he had not wanted me to come before. There was one thing left to do, one last chapter before the book he had written could be closed forever and put away for good. In some vague fashion, I had known it from the moment Frank Sutton first told me that Julian was not dead. I got up from the chair and walked into the book-lined room that had been his study. A small package with my name on it sat next to the shiny steel blade of a fencer's foil.

IT WAS SURPRISING how little emotion Albert Craven showed when I told him the next morning what I had learned. But then Albert was of a generation that, even more than my own, had been raised in the belief that there are few things as important as always keeping oneself under control.

"Julian's alive! How extraordinary!" was about all he said before I played for him the videotape I had spent half the night watching over and over again.

Everything Bryan Allen had said at his trial had been true. What Allen did not know was that it had all been captured on film. Julian had the whole thing on tape: McMillan, with a sword at his throat, calling Allen on the telephone; the spoken confession about the murders he had committed and the murder he had tried to commit. The written confession, signed in McMillan's own hand, had been enclosed in the package, along with the tape. After he had seen everything, Albert had the same question I had asked Frank Sutton.

"Why now? Why did he wait?"

"I did a little calculation," I replied. "As of yesterday, Bryan Allen has been in San Quentin exactly the same number of days as Julian spent in prison."

Albert leaned back in his oversize chair, turning toward the window and the sun outside. He had the look of a man who had lived long enough to know that things seldom end as well as they should and that it is something of a triumph when they do. He leaned farther back, a smile growing wider on his small, cherubic mouth.

"With the tape and the written confession, there won't be any question that Bryan Allen is innocent, that he told the truth. We could, I suppose, be good citizens and turn this new evidence over to the authorities. On the other hand," he went on as he slowly bent back around until he was leaning forward over the desk, "we could do what, under the circumstances, strikes me as rather more appropriate. Why don't I call Harry and see if he doesn't think I'm right? I'll call this afternoon, when it is morning down there."

It was nearly five when Albert walked into my office with a gleeful, droll expression in his eyes.

"You can guess what Harry thought!"

"That it will be 'great television.'"

"And he's right. They're going with it three days from tonight."

"Three days? Don't they understand Allen is still in prison?"

Albert shrugged. "They need time for promotion."

"Did you tell him how we got it? Did you tell him that Julian isn't dead?"

"No. Harry always keeps his word, but a secret like that . . . No, the story is too big, too much of a temptation. All Harry knows is that the tape came to us anonymously."

We agreed to go out to dinner the night of the broadcast and then watch it together. We talked awhile longer, about what Bryan Allen would be like if he went back on television: whether he would be as quick in his judgments as he had been before, or whether he might come out a completely different person, the subject of a religious conversion or a fanatical advocate of reform. You never knew what an experience like the one he had had—sent to prison when he should have been free, then let out when he had no hope of ever being free again—would do to someone. Albert and I talked about a lot of things, but especially what might happen to Julian and whether, now that it was finished, we might ever see him again.

"He'd be a fugitive if they ever found out he was alive. Strange business, isn't it?" remarked Albert as he rose to leave. "Innocent of the murder of Daphne McMillan and now the world will know it; but guilty of escape, a felony, if the world finds out he isn't dead."

"And guilty of the murder of Robert McMillan," I reminded him. "No matter how much he deserved to die. Blistered hand or not, whatever God's decision, I'm afraid trial by ordeal went out a thousand years ago."

"Then I hope we never see him again," said Albert. "I hope he is somewhere where he will never be found, somewhere no one will ever think to look for him. He deserves a life."

Albert turned and headed for the door. Suddenly, he stopped, and with an embarrassed look asked a favor.

"I forgot," he said, checking his watch. "It's almost quarter to six, and I have a dinner engagement. It's the business with the law librarian. I talked to you about it last week. The one we had for years—strange old woman—retired, and we have to find a replacement. I've interviewed four or five already, and there's another one waiting. At least I think they're still waiting. They were supposed to come at five. Would you mind? I just can't."

I put on my coat and grabbed my briefcase filled with the work I had for later that night. There was no point coming back to my office for it after the few short minutes I imagined the interview would take. I walked into the law library and found the latest applicant at the far end of the large table, hunched over a book. He certainly had the look of a male librarian, frazzled grayish brown hair, rather heavy gray eyebrows and a gray mustache. His eyeglasses were of an astonishing thickness. He was one of those quiet men with stoop shoulders and tired eyes, the kind you see on crowded trains, reading their papers on the long way home from work, the faces you see every day and can never quite remember.

"I'm sorry, but Mr. Craven had to leave for a meeting. My name is Joseph Antonelli. I'm afraid no one told me yours."

He was on the other side of the table, twenty feet away. His eyes did not move from the page. I wondered if beyond his bad eyesight, he was a little deaf.

"What are you reading?" I asked as I moved closer.

"Maitland's *Constitutional History of England*," I remarked as he closed the cover of the book and I caught the title. "You have an interest in old law books? There are probably more librarians than lawyers who have read that one," I said, trying to put him at ease.

He fumbled with his glasses, struggling to get them folded, then put away in his pocket. Everything about him was awkward, clumsy, abrupt.

"I'm interested in the old law," he said in a voice so low I could barely hear him. "I have a particular interest in what they used to call an appeal to heaven, or trial by ordeal."

I looked at him more sharply, confused by the strange way he had started to look at me.

"I'm Joseph Antonelli," I said, watching the way his eyes seemed to become more alive. He took my hand, his grasp firmer, stronger, than I had expected. His shoulders seemed to straighten and his chin lifted up.

"I know it has been a while," he said in a voice I had never forgotten. "But I was hoping there might still be a place for me in the firm."